# WALTER WANGERIN, JR.

# The CRYING for a VISION

SIMON & SCHUSTER BOOKS FOR YOUNG READERS
Published by Simon & Schuster
New York   London   Toronto   Sydney   Tokyo   Singapore

SIMON & SCHUSTER BOOKS FOR YOUNG READERS
1230 Avenue of the Americas
New York, New York 10020
Published in association with the literary agency of
Alive Communications, P. O. Box 49068,
Colorado Springs, CO 80949.
SIMON & SCHUSTER BOOKS FOR YOUNG READERS
is a trademark of Simon & Schuster.
Book design by David Neuhaus.
Manufactured in the United States of America

10  9  8  7  6  5  4  3  2  1

Library of Congress Cataloging-in-Publication Data
Wangerin, Walter.
The crying for a vision / Walter Wangerin, Jr.
    p.  cm.
Summary: *Waskin Mani,* "Moves Walking," the son of a Lakota
woman and one of the stars in the sky, is torn between his devotion
to the mystical world and his destiny of confronting the powerful
one-eyed warrior Fire Thunder.
    1. Dakota Indians—Juvenile fiction. [1. Dakota Indians—Fiction.
2. Indians of North America—Great Plains—Fiction. 3. Fantasy.]
I. Title.
PZ7.W1814Cr 1994 [Fic]—dc20 93-48589 CIP AC
ISBN: 0-671-79911-8

"It is coming back, I feel it in my bones. Not the old Ghost Dance, not the rolling-up—but a new-old spirit, not only among Indians but among whites and blacks, too, especially among young people. It is like raindrops making a tiny brook, many brooks making a stream, many streams making one big river bursting all dams. Us making this book, talking like this—these are some of the raindrops."

—John (Fire) Lame Deer to Richard Erdoes
in *Lame Deer: Seeker of Visions*,
published by Simon & Schuster, 1972

# A Dedication and Thanksgiving to the Lakota People

A Lakota may refer to himself as *icke wichasha*, "a man, a human, the basic two-legged thing—a plain person." Or else, speaking of his whole nation, he might say *oyate icke*, meaning "the *real* people," that first, wild, native race which stands between sky and earth, linking the two: the Indians!

In consequence all other races are *oyate unma*, "the other-people," grouped by the single fact that they are not Lakota. So there is pride in the title. *Oyate icke*: the Lakota are *ankatu*. Distinct. Superior. Representing the purest of humankind.

But by a paradox there is also a universal commonality here. For if they are "the people," the thing itself, then fundamental humanity is represented in them as well, and in them therefore may *any* people see itself.

*In them.* In the clean, uncomplicated knowledge which the Lakota achieved concerning themselves and their relationship to the whole created world.

*In them*: not only in their culture, which through many generations learned the plains and loved the buffalo and lived in union with nature, red and blue; not only in their history, which sent them west before there were ponies, then gave them ponies and therewith swiftness and distance and glory; not only in their external behavior: codes, relationships, modesty, morals, courage and virtue—

—but also in their vision.

In their spirit, their stories, their legends may an "other-people" find itself reflected.

In the rituals with which they give external expression to an inner awareness. In the ceremonies by which the Lakota have passed wisdom from generation to generation.

This people has named and known itself. A shining self-awareness. A public give-away. For in them knowledge becomes a song and songs are sung and anyone can listen and someone might learn.

By a gracious invitation I experienced several Sun Dances near Rosebud, South Dakota. There was peace in that place and genuine friendship: *wolakota*.

The welcome with which non-Indians were received is largely due to a man named Elmer Running. He is the *wichasha wakan* who leads this Sun Dance. Years ago he saw in a vision all races and all peoples dancing in the same Sacred Circle. With great courage he acted upon his vision. The private conviction became a public gift, and thus the *oyate icke* have invited *oyate unma* into relationship. It has not been easy. Such changes are never easy. But Elmer Running is a brave man and a prophet.

To him and to his people my story is dedicated.

But that which is *to* them is also *of* them.

For, although it is a fiction, I've woven Indian legends into my tale, sometimes whole, sometimes just the threads, taking the tone and the vision of a legend but making the narrative new.

For I spent many years studying this culture at its strongest, proudest period—when it was still untroubled by the intrusions of the *wasichus*—and have sought to commemorate that glory by reproducing its history and tradition as accurately as possible.

For my story presents the Lakota as *oyate icke* indeed, that common people in whom all peoples might see themselves. Therefore, good and evil mix in them just as virtue and vice exist together in any one family or nation on earth.

For I have found in the Lakota vision a rich analogue for the relationship *any* people of genuine faith experiences with creation and the Creator. It was my fortune, then—and my artistic choice—to use their world as the controlling metaphor of this novel.

Reader, *wachin ksapa yo!* Look not at the tale but through it for the truth.

Finally, I must speak a personal word of thanks to Marlene Whiterabbit Helgemo, who made my time on the Rosebud both possible and bountiful.

*Pila miya!*

Walter Wangerin, Jr.

# BEFORE THE STORY
# A Waniyetu Iyawapi of Slow Buffalo's Band

On the skin of a buffalo the painter has painted a picture for each year of Slow Buffalo's band. These pictures are a Winter Count. They tell the long story of this band of Lakota.

Look carefully: over the years the lives of the people changed twice, violently, once for glory and once for sorrow.

First, for many years, the times were calm and very good. There was peace. The band was small but it was not hungry. See, the painter has painted buffalo for these years in order to signify that there was food enough and contentment as well and friendship with the four-leggeds. All was well. These were the red and blue days, truly.

But then the painter begins to add numbers to the band, both of people and of ponies and of tipis, because the band grew suddenly in size. And in glory. Here is a face painted black. Here are the jagged lines of lightning on a man's leg. This one band now led many, many warriors into battles greater than anyone could remember. Even the painter of their Winter History does not know how to signify the enormity of this war. He draws a sun with bites taken out of it as if the daytime sun, like the nighttime moon, could be eaten.

Finally the painter must draw famine. Immediately after the war comes hunger. This is the Year of the Scaffolds, because so many people died, so many were buried. Do you see that the ponies and the dogs are all painted as bones here? That is because the people ate them. And there are no buffalos in these pictures. There are no four-leggeds at all, nor winged creatures either. This is the Year of Great Loneliness when all the animals went away and the people were so sad that they ceased to sing.

The last picture on the Winter Count shows a boy with black hair and black eyes. There is a man standing on the boy's chest and raising an ax to kill him. But the painter has painted this boy as big as a mountain.

# Part One

# 1

# Moves Walking

Now, then, the story starts here, with a small question: why was a five-year-old child sitting in the tipi of the chief, a little boy cross-legged and scowling as fierce as the rabbit? What could have been the reason for the boy's elevation?

Well, if he were one filled with ability this was an honor.

If he'd been bad, of course, this was discipline.

But the boy showed nothing remarkably good or bad about himself: skinny body, long glossy hair, the shoulder-bones popping through his skin, kneecaps like cracked firewood. He was staring at the chief and trying hard to frown as gravely as that old man—who himself sat cross-legged toward the doorway. The chief owned a heavy hanging face, an enormous nose, a great drum of a belly. The boy kept scowling, puffing his cheeks and sticking out his bottom lip. It wasn't working. He might have been able to scribble a little wrath onto his brow but not into his black eyes.

Bright, rising suns were the black eyes of this child, eyes that followed all he saw as persistently as the mosquito, probing the motion of his elders. Hungry eyes. But it must be said on his behalf that he scarcely noticed how angry his gaze could make his elders.

*Moves Walking*, they would shout at him, *stop that! Don't stare like that! Honor those older than you. Stop that! Stop that, you wablenica, or I will hit you with this stick!*

No, with eyes as large as lakes the child could not look grim.

Nor could he make his belly big.

Why, then, on this particular day in the Moon of the Grass Appearing (April) did Moves Walking—a boy but five years old whose Lakota name was *Waskn Mani*—occupy a position of some importance within the band, sitting in Slow Buffalo's personal tipi on the left side of the doorway so that he was almost opposite the great *itancan* himself?

Not for honor. Not for punishment either. But because his grandmother was also there, sitting on the other side of the door. There were three in the tipi. She was the third, a tiny woman as small and dark and wrinkled as an old potato, reaching forward to rub her feet and shaking her head. The *itancan* too was shaking his head because they were in the middle of a conversation about youth. These two people were very old with many memories between them and only one friend fully trustworthy, only one friend fully understanding, and that friend for each was the other.

Moves Walking was in the chief's tipi because he had no choice. He had to stay by his grandmother and she was here because the old man had asked her to come and he had asked because on this particular day the rest of the village was crazy with celebration and the chief was not pleased. He wanted company in his gloom.

Outside the tipi people were running and screaming and laughing. Inside the tipi a small boy felt neglected. The sticking out of his bottom lip was a genuine effort at pouting. He didn't want to look grim *like* the chief; he wanted to look grimly *at* the chief.

Outside the tipi little children were squealing so loudly they frightened themselves. Young men were whipping up their ponies and thundering down the village rows, wheeling their mounts into dangerous turns, showing off. Women of every age were making the tremolo of encouragement as if the men were engaged in battles and winning.

But the *itancan* sat in his tipi and gazed at the wrinkled old woman and heaved a heavy sigh.

So did the small boy sigh. No one noticed.

*Waskn Mani* was required to stay by his grandmother because she was, so far as anyone could tell, his only living relative. From the beginning no one knew who his father was; his mother had never named a man; and then while the boy was still in a cradleboard she too had disappeared; so the people of the village began to call him *wablenica,* "orphan."

Little boy, little grandmother. She sat on the right side of the doorway, her legs straight out in front of her, seeming as small as he who sat on the left. But there were differences: the boy's eyes were huge and his skin was smooth; her eyes were tiny and bright and pressed into a badlands of a face. Little grandmother: for her the years had been torrents and terrible droughts creating deep gullies across her face—but her eyes were clean. Her eyes were hazel-bright and clean.

Shrewdly now she watched Slow Buffalo heave his sigh. She said, "*Tatanka Hunkeshne,* what is the matter with you?"

All at once the village fell quiet. The silence outside was like a pressure, people holding their breath and waiting. Inside, the boy's black eyes were nearly popping from his head because he knew who was coming; he knew the hero was almost here and he couldn't stand it.

Then someone shouted, "Hi-ye-he!"

*Waskn Mani* clapped a hand over his mouth.

Then a hundred people were shouting greetings and bellowing praises: "HI-YE-HE! HI-YE-HE!" The whole village exploded in a sustained thunder.

The boy put two hands over his mouth. Poor *Waskn Mani* felt yells in his throat too. The hunter was home! At this very moment the warrior of glory was riding toward their tipis.

*Waskn Mani's* eyebrows rose in speechless appeal. His nostrils flared, his small chest panted, but no one was paying attention and he didn't yell. Oh! Oh, listen! There were the hoofbeats of one walking pony! Even beneath the roar of the people the boy could feel those hoofbeats in the earth.

Fire Thunder! That mighty hunter, that dreadful warrior, was right now passing outside the skins of the chief's tipi.

How could a boy *not* yell?

How could a boy not die?

Then many, many ponies were passing by and both of the ancient people with him bowed their heads. The *itancan* closed his eyes in a seeming weariness but the old woman was counting.

Two and five and ten and twenty—and by the sound of their step they were loaded down with buffalo meat: forty ponies. Fifty ponies!

*"Tatanka Hunkeshne,"* the old woman said the name of her friend. "Did you count what just came home? Fifty. The first hunt of the season and the first pony raid, both—and this young fellow all by himself brings back enough food to satisfy three villages. Aren't you glad? Doesn't this cause some pride in the heart of an *itancan?"*

Already the sounds outside were subsiding from roars to the rhythms of work. Meat-drying racks were dragged into place; great strips of buffalo meat were being cut to hang there, later to be pounded with whole cherries and bone tallow into a good nutritious food called *wasna*. The sounds of a village at work now grew soft and continuous like the ticking of ten thousand ants: people were lashing willow frames together upon which they would stretch new buffalo hides. They were sharpening fleshing tools for scraping the skins clean. They were building high fires and filling buffalo paunches with water, the fires to heat stones which they would drop in the water to make it boil, to render fat from the bones for *wasna*: Hi-ye-he! Happy day! Good and happy work! A winter of hunger was ended. Richness had returned.

But Slow Buffalo the chief kept his great head bowed, his old eyes closed.

"*Tatanka Hunkeshne,*" the old woman said, "what is the matter with you?"

He made a deep sound in the cave of his nose: "Hmmm."

She said, "Listen, *wicahchala:* critical people might think that an old hunter is jealous of a young one, yes? I am not such a person myself, of course, but gossips might say an old warrior begrudges a young one his glory."

Slow Buffalo's big belly began to jump upward: "Hm! Hm!" *Waskn Mani* thought these were spasms but then the man's shoulders started to shake and a rumbling rolled from his nose. He was laughing. He raised his head and said, "Old woman, I broke a tooth on some *wasna* today." He grinned. Lo, there was a whole new gap in his smile. "You and your feet, me and my teeth. Woman, woman, we are coming to pieces, ho-ho-ho!"

*Waskn Mani's* grandmother also began to giggle. It was clear that these two were enjoying a joke together, though the boy had no idea what was funny about crumbling teeth and crooked feet. He stuck out his bottom lip so far he could see it. Here was the chief of the entire band displaying his gums while the rest of the people were busy working.

Why should a child have to sit for this?

His grandmother said, "So then, that is your trouble? You won't be able to feast on new meat tonight? Hee-hee-hee!"

"Ho-ho!"

At that very instant there came a scratching on the doorflap. Someone was asking to come in—a giant, according to the tremendous shadow he cast on the yellow buffalo skins. Immediately the mood inside the tipi changed.

Laughter died on the chief's lips. His face fell, his eyes snapped upward and the old woman squinted at her friend: "So this is your trouble?" she whispered.

"Not his success," Slow Buffalo said, "but his manner. There is something here that scares me concerning our future." All at once he raised his voice and shouted, "*Hau!*"

The mood of the boy, too, had changed. No bottom lip, no pouting now! His face flamed with anticipation. He had covered his mouth with both hands again because happiness was booming in his chest.

"*Hau!*" shouted the chief. "Come!"

So the flap was drawn back. So sunlight flooded the tipi blinding the boy—and into that sunlight, bowed low by his entering, stepped a man.

Fire Thunder.

Oh, what a man now unfolded beside small *Waskn Mani:* as for height more glorious than the thundercloud, a man like a single cottonwood standing alone midfield, tall and tough; as for strength muscled and mighty and shining, his head ascending to the smoke hole, his shoulders a shelf of the heavens. Behold how his frame filled the tipi, cords of power down his arms, a brace of muscle at the forearm. *Waskn Mani* could reach and touch the back of the huge left hand but he didn't dare. He wasn't even breathing. Here was a warrior, oh! Here was a hunter in nought but a loincloth, a knife at his hip, braids on his broad back, and—slanting down his forehead and cheek in order to cover the left eye forever—an otterskin headband.

Whoever had seen beneath that slash of a headband? Who knew what was hidden there? The right eye flashed like black obsidian; the left remained as mysterious as God. And the jaw of Fire Thunder was so absolute that young men whispered, *Inyan:* stone. This jaw was of stone and perhaps the left eye was an eagle's beak!

*He fights in silence,* the young men said. *He fights in solitude. He never cries out and even when he is done he does not utter stories. Others must sing his glories for him—*

In his right hand, now, the warrior–hunter carried a parfleche bag. Fire Thunder had come to the chief's tipi in order to observe a ritual, bringing first meats as a gift.

Slow Buffalo said nothing.

*Waskn Mani* squirmed in discomfort. Someone should speak to such a hero, welcome him, acknowledge him.

of this one, though he gave them no encouragement and seldom even spoke to them. Emotionless, cold, solitary even in a crowd, Fire Thunder lived at the edges of circles.

Now he lay by the council tipi picking grass.

The little boy moved toward this giant in stages, a few hops at a time. It required much boldness—more, surely, than this afternoon when he blurted his words without thinking, because to think first causes nervousness. So he sat a while on the far side of the fires, thinking. Then he crept round near the storytellers and squatted there and listened to them, thinking, thinking.

The storytellers said, "We saw it with our own eyes. We promise, it is true!"

All of the people near *Waskn Mani* strained to see with the eyes of their hearts. On account of the mightiness of Fire Thunder no one had questioned whether it was true: they believed the story even before it was told. They only wished to *see* it.

The storytellers crouched in front of the flames. "We saw him ride his pony into a herd of stampeding buffalo," they whispered, "straight to the middle of the herd, shooting and shooting *Tatanka* down and he never cried *Yuhoo!*" they whispered.

"Now listen! Here is the story we have to tell.

"One bull at the head of the herd knew where the hunter was behind him. Suddenly that bull drove his hooves into the earth and wheeled around and bellowed and split the stampede into two by standing still, scraping the ground. He was *Tatanka,* very big and very mad. Then he lowered his horns and he charged back through the herd right for the hunter, and many buffalo began to turn and run with him until it was like a flood rushing in upon itself!

"But Fire Thunder never swerved! Fire Thunder only whipped his pony the harder, galloping, galloping toward the buffalo bull, notching an arrow, taking aim with two arms and shooting *Tatanka* in the neck just below his hump, but that old bull was so mad that nothing could slow him. He kept coming and Fire Thunder kept coming and when they came together the buffalo drove his right horn into the pony's chest and ripped it open so that all the ribs were split and stuck out. The pony pulled up with his eyes wide open and then he went down in dust but the hunter did not! No! Listen!" shouted the storytellers. "Listen! Fire Thunder sprang from the back of the dying pony to the back of a passing buffalo! Hee-hee! He landed facing the tail! He grabbed that tail and twisted it and made his buffalo go wherever he wanted to go. Hee-hee! Well, Fire Thunder followed the bull that had come back looking for him and he caught up to him and he ran beside him a while going backward and then he shot *Tatanka* so hard that the arrow passed through his heart and out the other side and we saw this story from the beginning to the end and it is true. Yuhoo! Yuhoo!"

The whole village cried out, "Yuhoo! Yuhoo!" Such pride in their voices, such joy in their eyes.

*Waskn Mani*, too, felt his face grinning because of this story and he squealed "Yuhoo" with all the Lakota. But then he forced himself to hush. He had a plan. He had a question to ask. On hands and knees he crept past the legs of those now rising to dance, past the drum and the drummers who sang with their heads thrown back to the black skies and their mouths wide open. Great flames made even the tipis seem to dance.

There was Fire Thunder. Over there, lying on his left side and leaning his head on the flat of his hand. He seemed not to have heard his own story. He was gazing at the tip of his knife now balanced on his right forefinger. He was chewing something. As he chewed the muscle in his jaw clenched and hardened.

The five-year-old boy gathered his last piece of courage and crawled toward the top of the head of the reclining giant. It felt to him as if they were in a bubble together. No one else. No sound else. His heart bucked with its question because for the first time he believed there was the real chance of an answer. This was the thing the boy thought about more than any other thing, *Where had his mother gone?*

She had loved him. She had said so.

She had wept over him and made him promise to obey his grand-mother. He still remembered his mother's exact words and the sound of her voice. And he had promised and then she had turned and run west into the night and had never come back again.

So the boy whispered, now, *"Ate?"*

His voice was very soft. Perhaps the drumming and the singing drowned it out. Perhaps the giant hadn't heard.

"Father?"

Did the hunter stiffen then? Did his good eye squint and fix on some point past his knife? *Waskn Mani* could not be sure. He raised his voice and said, "Father, did you see my mother in the west?" He went up on his knees and said, "Do you know where she is? Can you teach me how to get there?"

The boy was looking down upon the tremendous head of the war-rior like a puppy preparing to lick its master's ear.

*"Father?"*

Fire Thunder seemed not even to breathe. His eyelid drooped as if with sleep but the muscle in his jaw was pulsing with a steady power.

*Waskn Mani* reached his pointer finger to that motion and said, "Her name is Rattling Hail Woman, *Wsu Sna Win*—"

In the instant he uttered her name his finger touched Fire Thunder's jaw and the giant erupted. He roared. He rose from the ground with so horrible a roar that the drumbeat froze on the air and the dancing stopped and the whole village turned to see what had happened.

This is what they saw: they saw the warrior standing at full height above a boy who was bent down in a crouch as if praying. In the war-rior's right hand was a knife raised on high. The warrior's left hand was stiff at his side, one eye blazing, one eye covered—but all this lasted only an instant before Fire Thunder turned and strode out into the night.

The boy was not praying. He was bleeding. The left side of his head glistened in the firelight. His cheek and neck were laced with a running blood. Blood ran down his arm into the grass. When the people drew back his hair they saw that his left ear had been cut off, cleanly and completely cut.

But the boy continued crouched and quiet, staring at the ground. It was a frightening silence in one so young. Even as the adults knelt down beside him he did not shift his eyes. He did not cry. He did not speak.

The people said, "Who is this child?"

"Moves Walking," they said. "His name is *Waskn Mani.*"

"Well, where is his mother? Why doesn't she come to help him? Where is his father?"

"He doesn't have parents."

"No parents? A *wablenica?* Ah, the poor child."

"Poor indeed! He must have done something very bad to cause such wrath in Fire Thunder."

# Part Two

# 3
# Weeping Star

The swallows dropped from a high evening sky and swooped lake-
water then soared again on the twitch of their wings. They flew for
pure pleasure, circling and circling as if there were laughter in the
motion. Also, they were feeding. When they shot straight down for
insects their wingfeathers made a vibrating sound like a bowstring
twanging: *Brrrrrrrup!*

*Waskn Mani* liked the swallows, messengers of the West Wind,
friends when there were so few of them.

He stood alone on the northern shore of a little lake. It was a regular trick of his to lift his hand and invite a dragonfly to hover just
over the palm as if tethered by a spider's string; suddenly a swallow
would shoot from nowhere and the dragonfly would climb a quick
ladder, so the bird had come for nothing and would rise to the wide
skies again, laughing.

A swallow is called *pshica* because of the way he jumps.

By now *Waskn Mani* was nine years old.

Once or twice in the last four years the great Fire Thunder had spoken ill of this particular child. No more than two times surely— but even one word from the hunter was enough. Moves Walking, as they called him, stood alone. He gave his large-eyed attention to the four-leggeds and the wingeds.

He was a lithe one now, his spine a row of big bumps, his ribs apparent, his arms both long and loose. He was a good climber, lean-legged with toes that gripped. He climbed cottonwood trees faster than squirrels.

This boy, unlike any other, neither cut nor braided his hair. It hung like a black veil below his shoulders. It concealed the hole in the side of his head and the puckered pink flesh around it—the scar where his left ear had been.

*Waskn Mani* was chiefly silent. He seldom smiled. Mostly he was ashamed.

Some distance south of the lake there rose up an enormous mountain so high and so holy that it was a consolation to the heart of a child. An unchanging presence. The boy could feel its strength as a pressure upon his face and his chest. Ever and ever this mountain's head seemed tipped toward heaven, as tipis gaze to the sky to pray.

*Brrrrrrup!* The swallows dropped for insects in the dusk, seriously feeding now. They looked like black twigs, since the sky had deepened to a rare green color, cloudless, and all things turned to shadow in such a sky. The swallows knew that the lake holds warmth longer than the ground does and that insects like to fly on a rising warm air. *Brrrrrrup!*

On the northern face of the mountain was a wide black scar, the result of a forest fire which (the Lakota said) had been caused by lightning some seven years ago. That fire must have been intense because it killed every living thing both above and under the earth, nor had a single green blade come back since then. Very black.

The mountain itself had been named for the strange shape of that burned place. Like a black painting on a tipi, here was clearly the picture of a human, arms upraised as if in anguished supplication, the braids whipped wildly around the head, the hands to the high stones, feet on the greensward below. It looked exactly like a woman. Therefore the name of the place was *Scorched Mountain Woman.*

*Waskn Mani* came often to the lake to gaze upon the mountain with its picture of sorrow. "Someone is praying," he would say to the dragonflies that hung in bright colors beside him. "Someone is sad like me."

And on this particular night in the ninth year of his life it seemed that the boy had actually spoken the truth—and then his heart began to knock against the bones of his chest: a miracle was happening! What should he do? Whom should he tell? Hi ho, he should run to his grandmother and tell her right away! Right now! Go!

What happened was this: in the purple night as stars began to sprinkle the sky a swallow shouted, *Look!*

So *Waskn Mani* looked south to the mountain and there, as if caught on the peak of it, was one star larger and more luminous than all the others.

It was waving to him.

It was such a beautiful star, but by the soft beckoning motion the boy understood that this star was sad, so terribly sad, probably sadder than him.

She was crying.

Well, his heart twisted because of the miracle, to be sure, but his heart also was suffering serious sorrow with the beautiful stranger before him.

"Star!" he whispered, "what is the matter? Why are you crying?"

Then suddenly he saw that her great brightness was shining here, too, on the surface of the lake, as if she had come down to be close to him, rocking in a little boat; and that alone—the descent of this star to him especially, to *Waskn Mani,* little boy—made him love her immediately and completely.

"What is the matter?" he whispered. "Please, please, what can I do for you?"

But the light on the lake was only a reflection. No, she was not near to him. She was as far away as the peak of the mountain, waving and pleading but he could not hear her answer.

Suddenly the boy cried out at the top of his lungs, "Star! I know what you want! Yes, this people will welcome you here. Yes, yes, Slow Buffalo's band will honor you and love you. Come! Come down and we will give you a place among us!"

For a full two breaths the star held still. She was listening to him. Oh, his poor heart bucked so painfully!

"I'll go get them!" he shouted.

He turned and raced back to the village.

But when he tore into his grandmother's tipi and grabbed her hand he couldn't speak for a while. He was gulping and sobbing. "*Unchi,*" he said, the tears streaming down his cheeks. "*Unchi,* there is a star who wants to come down to us. Maybe she wants to tell me something about my mother. We have to go welcome her. *Unchi, Unchi,* she is so sad. Like me. All of the people must go out to welcome her."

# 4

# A New Wound

Under instruction from his grandmother *Waskn Mani* did not go back to the lake that night.

She said, "Perhaps this star is sad. Perhaps it is only the heart of a boy that is sad. Either way a boy must go slower and think longer. There is no hurry. True things last."

*Waskn Mani* said, "Sad things should not last!"

But his grandmother didn't answer the argument. She put her finger to his lips and frowned a thousand-wrinkle frown.

So he lay wakeful and restless all night long.

Once he heard the stiff vibration of feathers outside the tipi, *Brrrrrrup!*—and he thought a swallow had said, *Gone,* and that caused panic in his breast. But then he wasn't sure whether the swallow had come by at all. Messengers of the West Wind.

Then immediately at sunrise the boy began to act with amazing boldness. He who had no standing among the people, who was young and orphaned and scorned by the foremost warrior of the Lakota, now ran among the tipis telling everyone to gather at the small lake west of the village, to gather exactly at dusk in order to welcome a star as a guest within the band.

"What? What?" they said. "*Gather* says this boy to us? And *must?* The big-eyed boy says *must* to us?"

"Moves Walking," they said, "who do you think you are?"

"And what sort of fools do you think *we* are," they said, "that we should welcome a star? Go away, *wablenica!* Climb a tree. Leave us alone. Go far, far away."

When the boy would not go away nor cease his pleading, when he came to a group of warriors, the tears now standing in his eyes because of his efforts to persuade the people, mighty Fire Thunder turned and uttered two words regarding the boy. He did not say *wablenica*. In a measured murmur he said, "*Atkuku wanice.*" It means "no father on hand."

It means "Bastard."

From that day forward the people had a new phrase by which to refer to the boy Moves Walking. They said *Atkuku wanice*.

And there was another word which they also began to apply to Moves Walking, less vicious than Fire Thunder's word but no more kind than his. They shook their heads and raised their hands and repeated, "*Witko, witko.*"

Crazy, crazy.

So *Waskn Mani* stopped begging the people to come out and welcome the sad star. He tried a different plan. He went to the tipi of the Village Crier and bit his lip in order not to tremble, then scratched on the closed flap and called that skinny old man by name. "*Hehlokecha Najin,*" he said. "Standing Hollow Horn, may I please come in?"

"No!"

"Please. It is going badly today."

"Go away."

"Well but you are a good man, Standing Hollow Horn, and my grandmother speaks well of you and you are the crier and so therefore now you have a job to do—"

"A what? I have a what? There is a boy here who thinks he can tell me my duties—*hoc hoc hoc!*"

The poor Crier had bad lungs. When he got excited he coughed so much that he couldn't talk any more. And seeing that he was more skinny and crooked than chokecherry branches all dried up, the man was often excited.

*Waskn Mani* chewed hard upon his lip. He felt he was going to cry and crying can only make things worse.

"I," he said. "We . . . well, everyone, you know, ah, the whole village, I think. O *Hehlokecha Najin,* you must call all the people to the little western lake tonight because a star is stuck on *Scorched Mountain Woman* right at the peak and she needs a welcome in order to come down to us—"

"STUCK! A STAR IS—" The entire tipi began to shake. And a certain sound went forth from the tipi throughout Slow Buffalo's band. A choking sound. It was either coughing or laughing or wrath, who could tell?—though everyone could hear it because this Crier could waken the plains when he wanted to and this Crier likewise was noted for the fury with which he stated his strongest opinions, so everyone heard the choking sound get louder and louder until it produced a truly thrilling word, and everyone heard that word, too:

"*Tachesli,* boy! *Tachesli!*" A very dirty word.

The entire village burst into laughter. People slapped their knees and fell on the ground and howled, genuinely enjoying the joke.

*Waskn Mani* went off by himself. He had failed. He felt very sorry for the weeping star.

He climbed a tall cottonwood tree and lay down on a high branch and this time he did not stop them but he let the tears fall from his eyes as easily as summer rain. It was common for the boy to climb *waga chun,* the rustling tree.

But soon he was not alone. There came below him a big-bellied old man whose nose poked out in front of his face as huge as a squash. This man did not look up. He stopped by the treetrunk and stared straight ahead and said, "This is how I know that you are up there, *Waskn Mani,* by the water falling down on me."

It was Slow Buffalo, *itancan* of the band. "Excuse me," the chief said, "but do you plan to come down and welcome this marvelous star yourself tonight?"

*Waskn Mani* shrugged. He said nothing.

The chief, still not raising his eyes, said, "Excuse me, but here is a piece of advice which, if to you it means go, then go. If it means a fool should forget his folly then stay and do not go."

The boy nodded.

Slow Buffalo said, "*Wachin ksapa yo.* That is my advice." Now he did look up, directly into the young boy's eyes. He said, "Be attentive, boy. Pay attention to every living thing because anything might be carrying the news of heaven down to you. Anything. Do you hear me?"

Solemnly *Waskn Mani* nodded.

"So then," said the chief, and he lifted up his knees and walked away.

*Wachin ksapa yo.* Be attentive. Even an ant can tell the truth, but who would know this if first he does not listen to the ant?


That evening the black-eyed child went to the lake alone. He stood on the north side because that is where the path came out of the woods and he faced south toward the mountain. He began to wait for the evening.

The westward sun lit the mountaintop with crimson fire.

The swallows said, *Brrrrrrup!* and ate insects.

A small fat girl came out of the woods and stood somewhat behind the boy saying nothing. She had slant eyes. She never spoke to anyone. Then a woman came out too and said, "Red Day Woman, what are you doing here?" But these two were not related and the woman neither pulled the girl away nor left herself. She just stood there. And then another woman came. And another. And soon it was the whole village gathering behind the boy on the north side of the lake.

But the first woman reached out and pinched the boy on his upper arm. "Don't think we came because we believe you, boy," she said. "Don't grow proud of yourself. Proud children are like thorns on bushes. We came for a little entertainment."

Even the Crier had come by now.

*Waskn Mani* felt very nervous. He had wanted the village to come but not like this, to test his truth and maybe to laugh at him. He felt the fire of embarrassment in his face.

The sun was gone now. The mountain looked cold.

Suddenly the woman pinched him again, hard. "Do something with your hair," she said. "Your hair is a shame."

Many others said, "Hee hee," so even though the boy had never turned to look at her the woman pinched him again. "Have you started to look at the *wichinchalas* yet, boy? Maybe if you looked at pretty girls on earth you'd forget about stars in the sky—"

"Hee hee! Hee hee!" said many women.

But then the skinny Crier muttered, "A woman who is *ishnati*, if she spits on a rattlesnake that snake will die."

So then many men roared, "Ho ho ho!" And the woman quit pinching the arm of Moves Walking.

The swallows swooped all around the people and over the lake: *Brrrrrrup!* That was a comfort to *Waskn Mani.* Somebody here was not laughing at him. He stared up at the mountain. Oh, the white snow was like a ghost against the green evening, huge and heavy and holy! Everything seemed holy to this child, everything laid the great weight of holiness upon his soul.

He felt frightened and alone.

Then all at once, even before the sky had sunk into its perfect blackness, there she was again—there was the beautiful bright star caught on the peak of the mountain and waving to him, to him, to the little boy alone: *Hello!*

And yes she was weeping. Ah, the sorrow within her was almost unbearable. The poor boy drew a sharp breath of air. The people behind him fell suddenly silent, all of them, male and female, young and old.

Without a thought *Waskn Mani* began to wave back. His whole body tingled with sadness and delight. This was not courage in him because he had no choice. He had to do these things.

He cried out, "Star! O Star you came back! I love you, I love you, and I wish you would be with us here. Welcome!" he shouted. "Welcome! Welcome!" Then he thought of the most powerful and lovely word in the language, proof of his goodwill and of his welcome, and he sprang high into the air and yelled this word in a piercing voice to the star at the peak of the mountain:

"*Wolakota!*" he cried: "Peace. The deepest of friendship. I love you! Come!"

Lo: in that moment in the dark purple of the evening the star departed her place at the mountain and began to fly down and downward toward the valley of the village and the lake.

People behind the boy began to whisper.

*Waskn Mani* could scarcely believe his good fortune. He grinned so hard his cheeks hurt and his heart swelled to bursting.

Then it became apparent that the star was not alone. Behind her there trailed a long cloud of twinkling dust, countless lesser stars, a host of small stars flying hither.

Except for *Waskn Mani* only one other person had raised her hand to wave a greeting. The fat slant-eyed child called Red Day Woman was drooling and grinning but the rest of the people were wailing, "No, no!"—terrified by a sky that had cracked and now was falling down on them.

A nine-year-old boy was dancing on the lakeshore and waving his arms and crying in glorious joy, "Come down! Come here, ten thousand stars! You are all welcome, welcome—"

But the whole village behind him was dropping to the ground and trying to hide. People bit their thumbs in order to keep quiet.

Suddenly an enormous form emerged from the forest and in perfect silence seized Red Day Woman and stilled that child by lifting her and tucking her bodily beneath his left arm. In two steps the same dark figure approached *Waskn Mani* and murmured, "*Atkuku wanice.*"

The boy turned and was straightway struck across the face. He fell backward. Immediately the knee of a giant came down upon his chest and upon his mouth a huge right hand. It was Fire Thunder the one-eyed, saying nothing but by his full weight pinning the boy to the ground and silencing him.

So then, everyone was still. An entire band of Lakota had become mere shadows on the ground.

The star flew low and lower. She sailed slowly over the valley and the lake and the forest, and behind her flew the host of little stars.

But no one was talking now. No one said, *Yes, come, stay,* or *welcome.* No one uttered a sound. So the beautiful sad star began again to ascend and all the little stars followed her. Up and up they went and farther away until the night was black and the only stars visible were those so distant that they could not trouble the people.

The weeping star was gone.

The night was cold and empty.

The Lakota rose up and without a word returned to their tipis.

Fire Thunder left *Waskn Mani* lying on his back and carried Red Day Woman away like a sack of turnips.

The boy felt so ashamed of his people. He felt so sorry for the star. He was bleeding from his lower lip where the mighty hunter had struck him. He felt so lonely.

# 5

# "Black Eyes, J Love You"

All the next night the star did not return to the mountain. *Waskn Mani* waited on the shore of the lake till dawn began to streak the skies. No star.

Then he put his head down and walked back to the village.

Nor did she come the night after that.

Nor the next.

In sorrow and shame the boy kept watch for five nights and six and seven. No star.

On the evening of the tenth night he heard noises in the woods, soft crunchings and moss-steps. It might have been a wolverine beginning his night's hunt—but then his old grandmother came hobbling from the trees and down the north bank slowly on bad feet. She leaned her weight on the boy's shoulder and sat down beside him. Her face was as wrinkled as a walnut, the high curves touched by dusk light, the seams as deep as ditches.

She sat catching her breath a while and then she placed some things in her grandson's lap: two pairs of new moccasins, a bag of *wasna,* a knife. She sighed and leaned forward to her crooked feet and began to rub them.

*Waskn Mani,* nine years old, was taller than his grandmother now. She had a perpetual crouch in her back and a caven chest. Her grey braids fell forward. This tiny two-person family sat side by side, gazing south as that grand presence, the mountain, sank to darkness in the sky. The swallows swooped and twittered.

*Waskn Mani* touched the moccasins and said, "Do you think I will be going away?"

"I don't know," his grandmother said. "Maybe."

"Why?"

"I don't know," she said. She watched the mountain. Yes, it was the blacker shadow bulking upward in the sky. "Listen, *hokshila,*" she said, "there is a kind of gopher who shoots bits of porcupine quill into your body, or else sharp blades of grass, and then you get boils. Watch out for that clever little gopher, will you?"

"So then, I *will* be going away."

"Boy, do you promise to watch out for that dangerous four-legged?"

"Yes."

"Good. Thank you. I feel better."

"*Unchi?*"

"What?"

But the boy said nothing then. Instead he reached for the braid at her bosom and ran his hand the length of it then brought that grey rope to his face. He closed his eyes and sniffed it. As a buffalo snuffles the grass *Waskn Mani* snuffled his grandmother's grey hair and then he laid it against his cheek.

"*Hokshila,* why do you do that?" she said.

His bottom lip was trembling.

"Because I love you, *Unchi,*" he said. He bent down and placed the braid across his eyes. "And because the smell of your hair reminds me of my mother. I miss my mother."

Then with his head still lowered he began to cry.

His grandmother patted his back for a very long time. Then she said, "*Waskn Mani,* look up."

He lifted his eyes. Suddenly the boy was rubbing the tears from his vision and slapping his face. He jumped to his feet. "Oh, star!" he cried, clasping his hands together. "Beautiful star, you came back!"

There she was, touching the mountain with one white beam. Oh!—she was more radiant than ever and at the same time more mournful, merely watching the child now, not even waving, expressing nothing.

"Wait!" shouted *Waskn Mani.* "Don't go away again. I'm coming, I promise. Wait till I get there. Dear star, please!"

Somebody tapped his shoulder. It was his grandmother handing him again the two pairs of moccasins and *wasna* and the knife. She said, "Watch out for that gopher."

"*Unchi, Unchi,* I will!" he cried. "*Pila miya:* thank you."

And so he was gone, running southward after all, his hair streaming back with speed and wind and willingness, his face awash in moonlight.

The boy was strong for his size. A good climber. And desire gave him endurance.

All night he traveled the valleys and the cutbanks between the lake and *Scorched Mountain Woman.* He leaped the foothills as though his feet were deer's feet.

By dawn he was scrambling difficult rock, breaking the skin of his knuckles and knees. Then he entered high forests, the skirts of the mountain, and ran in dappled light. He was a young cougar. He smelled the trails of the animals and ran in them.

When he was thirsty he drank from the streams. When he was hungry he chewed some *wasna.* Or picked berries. But he never thought of shooting a creature with arrows. What he was doing was holy. He knew this by instinct. It would be a transgression to kill anything on such a mission as this.

That afternoon he came to the scorched earth, that vast tract of char and blackened rock—the place of the lightning-fire which had given the mountain her name. The air was rank with soot, stinking and bitter. He felt sick. His eyes stung. And when he stepped forward his foot clattered dry bones and he looked and saw a great rubble of bones, thousands and thousands of bones burned black and white. Oh, what a congregation of creatures had perished here! As he climbed them he begged their forgiveness. More than that, a dreadful sense of grief rose up from the ground as if the earth itself were groaning. *Waskn Mani* hastened his climb. This was such a tragic region, so sorrowful that he could scarcely breathe. Death.

By evening the boy was above the timberline, tired and cold and stiff and bleeding but clinging to the brow of the mountain. He glanced below himself and for the first time in his life he was looking down upon the spotted eagle, wheeling in the golden air below. The sun was setting. The boy breathed in awe, *"Wanbli Galeshka,* greetings!" The eagle dipped and sank and vanished.

Above himself the boy saw snow, the snow-caves in which water melts and the streams of the earth begin.

Then it was dark. Then *Waskn Mani* was trudging those ancient snows upon the skull of the mountain, the summit. He was numb to his calves and sore in every muscle and very slow. He blew puffs of white breath. All around him was the vast night, the round sky, but no stars near enough for introductions. The weeping star was nowhere in sight.

He thought he would sit to wait for her.

But when he laid his body down, straightway he fell asleep.

And soon he was dreaming.

A voice said, "O Black Eyes, I knew you would come!"

In fact, *Waskn Mani* felt the voice as if it were a tingling on his neck. It said, "I heard your borning cry, Black Eyes. Yes, and I knew you would sacrifice yourself to come. And the Great Spirit promised that if one would sacrifice himself we might go home again. All we need is a form for the earth, a body the earth can abide."

Another younger voice whispered, "How can he choose a form for us if he doesn't know us? Couldn't he wake up and see us?"

The beautiful voice said, "Yes." That marvelous murmuring deep voice said, "Yes. This one deserves to know our secrets." And something feathery began to brush his cheek.

Then there were many, many voices calling: "Wake up, child! Little boy, wake up and see us!"

Some were laughing with glee. Others announced, "We've known you nine years. It's time you knew us too."

And the beautiful voice spoke lower and closer than them all. "Black Eyes," she said, "I love you—"

# 6
# Starmaiden

So *Waskn Mani*, the Lakota boy lying at the top of the world, opened his eyes, and lo: there, so close to him that the back of her hand caressed his face, was the loveliest maiden he had ever seen, young and dark and smooth, dressed in white buckskin, smiling sadly, but smiling directly into his gaze. He started to stand up. Fixed on her forehead was a fire-white star. Behind her, bobbing up and down in order each to see him, were a hundred children also smiling. All with lesser stars on their foreheads, a floating host of starchildren.

*Waskn Mani* rose up with surprising ease. Then he realized it was the hand of the starmaiden that had lifted him, holding his elbow lightly but with absolute strength, and he saw that he wasn't standing on the snow at all but on the air. And his body was warm. He grinned back at everyone—nine years old and happy.

"Am I," he whispered, "the one you call Black Eyes?"

The starmaiden murmured, "Yes."

"Does that mean—" The boy lost his grin. "Does that mean you love *me*?"

"Yes." She put forth a finger to his chin and on the point of it raised him yet higher till their eyes were even. "Child, I have loved you nine years long." The starchildren enclosed them in a bright circle and the starmaiden shined on the boy. It was a moment of perfect light, but her smile was not happy.

"Black Eyes," she said, "we caught your mother the morning she bore you. We honored her courage; but her baby we loved—"

The boy gasped. "*Mihun?*" he fairly squeaked. "My mother? You met my mother?" He grabbed his face in both hands and began to pant and chatter at once. "Where is she? How is she? Where can I find her? Can you take me there? Star! Beautiful Star—"

Suddenly he jerked backward and cried, "Oh, no!" The motion made him sink earthward. "Oh, no! You're sad because something happened to my mother! What—"

But the dark starmaiden put her arms around the boy and held him tightly, whispering, "Hush, hush, Black Eyes. Be still—"

His eyes were wide and hot and filled with the tears of yearning but he struggled to be still. He pressed his face into the buckskin of her shoulder and held her too and found that she was sky-cool and infinitely soft.

The starmaiden was saying, "We met her only once, just once. Hi ho, but she was a valiant woman! We could never forget her, and maybe it was two years later when we thought we heard her voice again as if she were pleading. She seemed to say, *Have you seen my son? Have you taken his measure? Haven't I done well in him?*"

All the starchildren floated near and patted the boy on his back and arms, agreeing that this is exactly what they had heard.

*Waskn Mani* said, "She loved me, then, just as she said. Oh, Star, I miss my mother so much."

"This is something we understand well," said the starmaiden. She took his hands in hers and went back from him a space.

When he looked into her face again he saw that she was sad, yes, terribly sad. Her eyes held new water and she nodded and he recognized the very same motion he'd seen from the lake: when she nodded the star on her forehead waved and beckoned in sorrow.

"We understand missings and lonesomenesses," she said, and all the children nodded and all the small stars cried.

The young boy softly whispered, "What is the matter then?"

She said, "We want to come home."

*Waskn Mani's* face flushed. "That's exactly what I thought!" he cried. "Oh, forgive my people for not welcoming you—"

"Hush. Listen," she said. "Welcoming is not enough. We can't come home unless we find a form the earth will take. Black Eyes, we died a long time ago. We are each a *wanagi*, a ghost, and ghosts can't live below. We need bodies again."

It was very quiet now in the dark at the top of the world. The starchildren silently and solemnly watched the living boy.

"Ghosts," he whispered.

"Aye," the starmaiden said, "and are you frightened now too, like the other Lakota?"

It seemed to *Waskn Mani* that the tips of her fingers were white ice. Her hair was parted precisely in the center. Her eyebrows tilted upward. Her mouth was partly open. Her ears curved like white shells. Oh, if the maiden were ice it was such beautiful ice! And sad, sad. This was confusing.

She said, "Long ago we were the children of a village in which someone committed a terrible sin. But no one would confess that he had done it so the entire village was condemned to die, even the innocent.

"Black Eyes, this is why we understand the missing of good things: in one day all the people died. All. Even the children. And I was the child of the chief.

"But we loved our mother the earth so much that we refused to walk the *wanagi tacanku* south, the ghost road that crosses the sky to the old woman who judges the dead. We begged the Great Spirit for mercy, and so we became the starchildren ever near the earth but never on her, yearning downward but unable to return till someone should sacrifice for us.

"You, Black Eyes. That was you.

"And now will you help us one more time?"

*Waskn Mani* said, "Is it permitted that maybe a ghost would be able to hug a boy again?"

So the starmaiden drew near, cool and soft and radiant, and she embraced the boy and kissed his cheek and *Waskn Mani* said, "No. I am not afraid. No, there are so many reasons why I love you, beautiful star." A wind began to blow around them now. It lifted his long hair. He said, "What must I do for you?"

She said, "Think up bodies for us. Tell us what form we might take on earth. But hurry or we'll have to leave you."

The wind became insistent, whistling at his right ear and numbing his flesh as if the whole world were turning ice.

Bodies. Not the beautiful two-leggeds any more? The boy could hardly make that change in his mind. He loved her the way he saw her. What other thing could she be and still be herself?

"Hurry! Hurry!" the starmaiden cried. "Before we set you back on earth, hurry! Teach us new forms!"

And *Eeeeeeeeeeee!* the wind was screaming now, tearing the boy's hair. He glanced down and suddenly saw that the mountain was gone. They were flying! He and the maiden were streaking ahead of a stream of lesser stars, all descending toward the dark forest. The eastern sky was growing grey. Morning was breaking!

"We want to come home," the starmaiden cried. "We want to be with you. But how shall we come to stay?"

Poor *Waskn Mani* yelled, "I don't know! I don't know! Can't we slow down a little?" It was all happening so fast. Already he could see dots of orange light ahead of them, the night fires of his village. "Let's go back to the mountain and start over."

"No, we're dimming in the dawnlight!"

"But you'll be back tomorrow? I'll climb the mountain again—"

"There's just one sacrifice, Black Eyes. You have already made it. Everything has begun. We must finish it now."

He saw the small lake below them, circling. They were sinking down now.

The maiden beseeched him, "Some mortal form, child! Dear mortal boy, what shall we be?"

"I don't know! I don't know! Don't put me down! Don't go away! Please don't leave me alone again!"

"We have no choice."

Light grew stronger in the sky. All the stars grew weaker. The boy tried to clutch the maiden with his own hands but they passed through her.

"I'll lay you on the lakeshore grass," she said. Even her voice was vanishing into shadow. "Black Eyes, we do not blame you," she whispered. At last she said, "We love you," and she dropped him.

He scrambled to his feet just as the bare light of their forehead stars made final swoops above the lake. The boy was about to give voice to his great sorrow—but then he noticed the star–reflections all bobbing on the surface of the water and suddenly he was yelling such silly words as "Yow!" and "Hi ho!" and "Yuhoo!" Happy words. He was jumping up and down and shrieking for sheer joy and grinning like the swallow's wings.

"Starmaiden! Starmaiden! Yow, Starmaiden!" he screamed. "I know what form you should take on earth. Oh, I have such wonderful bodies for you all!"

# 7
# Water Lilies

When the sun rose over the village that morning and shined on the little lake west, it also shined on a carpet of green and purple leaves floating on the surface of the water.

Among these leaves sat one hundred and one flowers, pure white and as bright as the stars in heaven.

Water lilies.

One refulgent lily, unfolding exactly in the center of the lake, was so abundant she seemed to be waving. She nodded and danced with unsullied joy and her petals were hands upraised in praise.

A young Lakota boy was paddling over the same lake in a boat of buffalo hide, letting the green vines hiss along the sides. Dragonflies hovered above his hands, iridescent and devout in the daylight. Swallows swooped his shoulders. But the boy spent most of his time leaning toward that largest lily, his hair hanging to the water, listening and laughing softly to himself.

*Witko.*

*So what do you think happened to that boy, Moves Walking? For years he used to stare in sadness. Now suddenly he grins crazy. He and the frogs must have a secret. Maybe they know where these big white flowers have come from. And those pads the frogs sit on—*

# 8

# Standing Hollow Horn

"Moves Walking!"

Someone was calling but the boy's eyes were closed. All sound had turned to murmurings around him now. Insect buzzings. A sleepy wind blew over his skin. He was smiling: "Mmm–mmm." The little round boat rocked in the midst of lily leaves.

"Moves Walking! Moves Walking! Boy! Idiot! Disease! You bloody nose! You runny bowel, *answer me!*"

This was the Moon When the Cherries Are Ripe (July), the deep bright warm days when even the deerflies are slow and fat. The boy's fingers floated in the water. He felt small bumps of fish-snouts asking, *Are you food?*—and then small nips and suckings.

"MOVES WALKING! MOVES WALKING! MOVES WALK-ING!"

Well, here was an amazing thing: someone was calling his own name.

The boy sat up and peered toward shore through a blinding sunlight and there he saw a skinny old man stomping his foot, shaking both fists, jumping around like a chicken in a rainstorm.

*Waskn Mani* raised his hand and waved. "Standing Hollow Horn," he said. It was the Crier of the village. Perhaps he had a message for the boy. *"Hau!"*

But that greeting seemed to offend the old man worse than no greeting at all. He whirled his arms around and screamed in the high whining voice that Criers use: "MOVES WALKING, THIS IS NOT A VERY GOOD BEGINNING!" All over the lake frogs went plopping into the water.

*Beginning for what?*

*Waskn Mani* lowered his hand and tried to think if he had forgotten something.

Well, but then lowering one's hand must be the worst offense of all because Standing Hollow Horn started to spin in full circles ashore shrieking, "WHAT DO YOU THINK IT MEANS WHEN SOMEBODY CALLS YOU?"

The boy didn't know what to say. He might offend the Crier again.

"IT MEANS COME—hoc, hoc! IT MEANS—hack, hoc, hem, harf—COME—hoc, hoc, hatcher—*HERE,* YOU HANGNAIL!"

Poor old man.

In fact, *Waskn Mani* had no idea what the fellow was trying to say; but this coughing was twisting his spine into impossible positions and his face was turning purple. So the boy began to paddle in, calling, "Wait!"

When he got to him the Crier was doubled down and squeaking pitifully, sticking his head out like a crane. Right away *Waskn Mani* began to beat the poor man on his back.

That seemed to work. The Crier turned white. Then red. Then black. He took an enormous breath then pulled back the hair from the boy's right ear and roared so loud that birds flew up and prairie dogs went down their holes, "DON'T HIT YOUR GRANDFATHER, YOU INGROWN HAIR!"

*Waskn Mani* stopped and stared at the old man who was now adjusting various parts of his insulted self. Skinny legs, narrow hips, no butt at all: when he coughed he was in perpetual danger of losing his loincloth. Even now he was tying it tighter and muttering, *"Wan! Wan!"*—a pretty good curse word. This old fellow had a foul mouth and no reason not to use it. No family. No great hunger for reputation, although age gave him some small advantage. No desire for praise from anyone since everyone was, in his estimation, a fool, male and female, young and old, warriors, hunters, and chiefs. Standing Hollow Horn was indiscriminate in his despisings: if the creature had two legs, it was likely to have less sense than a fish, however fierce the face on it.

At the same time he had (in spite of himself) sympathy for runts, lesser creatures troubled by the fools who thought too highly of themselves.

*Waskn Mani,* whom the Lakota called "Moves Walking," clearly was a runt.

That wide-eyed staring idiot even now stood blinking like a calf newborn and whispering, "Are you my grandfather?"

The word he used was *tunkashila:* "Are you my *tunkashila*?"

"It's a damn-fool idea. But I thought of it. Therefore, *ohan,* yes, yes—I will be your grandfather. Someone has to teach you how to be a *wichasha,* a man."

The child gasped. His face darkened with an unspeakable emotion and his eyebrows went up and down like butterflies' wings.

"Stop that!" said the old man.

*Waskn Mani* was grinning like a coyote pup. Someone had just adopted him!

"Stop that, stop that! Don't smile, don't be glad, don't disobey, work hard—and do not hit me any more. STOP THAT!"

So the boy started to frown. But his mouth kept grinning. And his enormous eyes shined for the thing now happening to him. He turned and whispered to the water lilies, "Did you see that? I have a *tunkashila.*"

"I DON'T APPROVE OF WEIRDNESS," shouted the old man. But all at once he put forth a long finger and touched the lower lip of the child and *Waskn Mani's* smile went away. Standing Hollow Horn picked at a scab in that place. "I know who did that," he said.

"Now this is what I will teach you, boy—to fight for yourself, do you hear me? It doesn't matter how famous the enemy is. Two legs make a fool. And strong legs make a strong fool. You have to fight fools and the stronger the fool the harder the fight. Do you hear me?"

*Waskn Mani* whispered, "So you are going to be my *tunkashila*," and he did in fact split his face with grinning. Blood ran from the scab to the corners of his lips. Standing Hollow Horn put some spiders webs on the wound together with a bit of sage.

So that was the beginning. If it was not a very good one, well, it was not a very bad one either.

# 9
# Itomni: Happy

"Aim for that bush," said Standing Hollow Horn. "Aim for that black-bird's nest."

Barely visible in summer foliage was a rude structure of sticks and reeds two feet from the ground.

"Aim," said the old man, pointing past the boy's face, "for that feather sticking out."

*Waskn Mani* said, "But what if somebody's living in there?"

The old man knocked him on top of his head. "Idiot! It's an empty lodge. When a feather is cocked like that—"

But the boy had let his arrow fly. It whistled and arced and hit the nest exactly at the feather, driving it through.

Standing Hollow Horn bent forward and gaped. "Moves Walking, Moves Walking, how did you—? Boy, do that again!"

*Waskn Mani* was using a small bow painted red and red arrows with knobs on the ends instead of points. His grandfather had made them for him, saying that the red was to signify his own, Standing

Hollow Horn's, wounds received in serious battle. He expected his grandson likewise to distinguish himself.

"Do that again," the old man said with a suspicious frown.

But the boy had already notched another arrow and was ready and, yes, did again precisely what he had done before, thrusting the first shaft through with the force of the second.

Standing Hollow Horn began to hiccup and couldn't quit.

Again and again *Waskn Mani* shot, every arrow true. He seemed incapable of missing and now he was grinning for pleasing his grandfather too. In fact, the child giggled because, though the Crier still glowered like thunder when he went to gather arrows, he always came back in skinny-legged dancing, crying, "Yip! Yip!"—all with a furious frowning face.

Lo, how an angry man and a solitary child could be *itomni* after all, very happy.

All summer long the old man taught the young one. Both were astonished by the progress and the repeated revelations of skill.

On Standing Hollow Horn's own pony *Waskn Mani* learned to ride with his knees alone, dropping the bridle to free both hands for shooting buffalo. The day when he would actually ride in the dust of a running herd—that day would come. For now, he also learned to hang low on the pony's side from one leg and one arm to shield himself from the arrows of an enemy. And even at a headlong gallop, whether upright or else slung low and shooting beneath the pony's neck, this boy sent every arrow straight to its mark.

"Grandson!" the Crier screamed at such exhibitions. "Hoc, hoc, hacker, *harf*!" No one, not even *Waskn Mani*'s grandmother, could recall that Standing Hollow Horn had ever admitted that he was having good red and blue days. "Grandson! What you can do!"

*Waskn Mani* only missed the shot (but then he *always* missed that shot) when aiming at some bird, some living thing. His hands shook. Things that had eyes which, when he looked at them, looked back at him distracted him. "Idiot!" the old man roared. "Contrary, wrongheaded, two-legged fool! You did that on purpose!"

*  *  *

In the Moon of the Black Cherries (August), in the breezy dusk of a certain day the Crier came into *Waskn Mani's* tipi and squatted down and laid between them fifty arrows straight and smooth, each as long as a grown man's shin and sinewed with terrible flints. Wide points caused greater bleeding.

"So," he said, "what did my grandson learn today?"

The boy fingered the flints, so thin and sharp that light passed through the edges. Every shaft shined, still moist from the rubbing between grooved stones, and every shaft was fitted with three feathers at the butt. Standing Hollow Horn knew how to make good weapons. Dangerous darts.

*Waskn Mani* said, "Fifty, Grandfather? Fifty arrows?"

"It's a hunter's number," the old man said, glaring into the boy's eyes.

"You told me a hunter took twenty—"

"A buffalo hunter, toenail! Don't argue. Accept the gift. Use it. Now, what did you learn today?"

The boy grew quiet and lowered his huge eyes. "I learned," he murmured, "that blackbirds and ponies are good friends."

"What? What does that mean?"

"Well," said the boy, sticking the tip of his finger in the notches of these magnificent arrows, "when ponies trot through tall grass they stir up grasshoppers. So blackbirds fly down and catch them."

"What? What?" The skinny Crier was gathering black clouds in his brow. "What is the grandson upon whom I am spending my attention telling me?"

"Well, that's why blackbirds sit on ponies' shoulders," said the boy. "That's why they chat about life together."

"*Life?* Idiot, what you're telling me has nothing to do with—hoc, hoc—with hunting and war and—hack, hacker—manhood! HARF!"

"But you asked what I learned today. That's what I learned. Grandfather, look: these arrows are longer than my arms. Maybe I'm not ready for such points yet—"

"Contrary, wrong-headed, two-legged—hocah! Harf! Ponies and

blackbirds, is it? Friends, is it? It's laziness and idiocy! You will use these arrows—hoc!—to make—hoc! hoc!—meat. STOP HITTING YOUR GRANDFATHER!"

Well, but then during the Moon When the Plums Are Scarlet (September) Standing Hollow Horn himself acted like an idiot. Perhaps he was losing control in his own age, for he bound his fate to the boy by declaring publicly that Moves Walking was superior even (ah!) to Fire Thunder.

*Witko, witko,* crazy! Old folk should not involve themselves in the troubles of others. Things get too complicated too late in life.

Nevertheless, as the man and the boy returned their pony to the corral one evening, four men stopped talking and watched them. Three of these were the boastful sort who sought Great Fire Thunder's approval. The fourth was Fire Thunder.

Now, the boy was not exactly sitting on the pony. He had drawn his legs up and was crouching on its haunch like a wolf cub on a hill, tilting his face to the sky. Swallows were circling him, dropping for the insects the pony kicked up. The child was altogether absorbed in the birds' flight. He floated on that pony like a cloud, unconsciously confident.

Standing Hollow Horn had grown used to such behavior. He scarcely noticed it any more.

Then just as they neared the corral the boy rose up on his feet. While the pony was walking he stood full height and reached his hands yet higher and in a clear voice called, *"Pshica!"*—and a swallow swooped to his hand and landed. The entire gesture was swift and graceful. The boy and the bird made a single silhouette.

But suddenly one of the men recognized the child and cried, "Oh, it's *Atkuku wanice,* the bastard!" *Waskn Mani* glanced over and lost his balance and tumbled down to the ground.

"Ha ha ha!" roared the warrior. "The lover of little stars falls faster than he climbs and shows his split end to the sky!"

All at once the Crier was screaming. No plan, no decision, sheer idiocy, old age maybe. But he meant it: "Bull's pizzles! Buffalo chips!" he yelled. "This boy is the best of you all! My grandson at nine years old shoots better than warriors sick for glory—"

There. He had declared his adoption of the runt whom people mocked. And he had done so in the face of Fire Thunder. There.

The three warriors burst into laughter and pointed at the skinny screaming Crier, his kneecaps larger than river-rocks, his head gone purple, thrust forward like a crane.

Fire Thunder said nothing. His expression under the slash of his headband was impassive. That goaded Standing Hollow Horn into yet greater boastfulness.

"My grandson," he screamed, "can outride and outshoot each one of you buffalo farts. He misses nothing. He brings down beasts at an early age. FIRE THUNDER, YOU CAN'T HIT CHILDREN ANY MORE! YOU SHOULD NOT HIT CHILDREN! AND THE DAY IS COMING WHEN YOU WILL FEAR THIS BOY—hoc, hoc, hoka—WHEN YOU WILL FEAR EVEN TO—hoc! Hack! Harf—"

Well, and that was the end of Standing Hollow Horn's threat. Fire Thunder, his jaw *inyan*, had simply walked away, three warriors following. Moreover, the Crier had, to his own exquisite fury, lost his talk in coughing. He went down on his knees with the coughing. Oh, he wanted to kill these bubble-headed warriors, but all he could do was cough, cough!

Moves Walking came close to the man and began to pat his back quietly. There was the flash of water in the boy's eyes.

Standing Hollow Horn did not acknowledge the tears. When he got his breath again he knocked the boy away and cried, "Hunt!" He jabbed a finger into the boy's chest. "Hunt something. Kill something. Bring me meat. Prove me right, boy. Do you hear me? Don't make a fool of Standing Hollow Horn. Don't kiss that sparrow, kill her! AND STOP BEATING YOUR GRANDFATHER ON HIS BACK!"

# 10
# A Pair of Warm Moccasins

Slow Buffalo's band made several moves in the next two months, first to follow the buffalo herds for autumn's last hunts and finally to find a protected place for the winter.

The parfleche bags were full to bursting. There were many hunters in this band because great numbers of young men were coming here to seek glory with mighty Fire Thunder. But because so many hunters were also so young and hungry the *akicita okolakicye*, the soldier society, also had to grow larger and fiercer, using whips to restrain the hot-bloods from breaking forth and stampeding a herd before the band could make a properly planned assault. One hunter too eager and too selfish could spoil the hunt for everyone.

Slow Buffalo and his advisors appointed only the most trusted warriors to the soldier society; that is, he selected none but those who had been raised within his sight. This caused resentment in the hearts of newer men. Moreover, it seemed that there were fewer and fewer men of the old band to discipline more and more arrivals.

The chief did not rejoice, despite his band's abundance.

In fact, after the village had found its wintering place Slow Buffalo began to spend long parts of every day in the sweat lodge singing at the top of his lungs, praying, begging *Wakan Tanka* to have mercy on his people. Who could understand the old chief's behavior?

"Listen to that," the hot-bloods growled together. "We bring prosperity to the old man's village but he acts as if we were some sort of evil. What do you think? Is he insulting us?"

Every day the *itancan's* prayers broke into tears and then great sobs came from the sweat lodge. Throughout the village the people could hear it: "Hownh, hownh, hownh," he wailed.

Well, in order to prove their greatness the young men set difficult tasks for themselves. They played violent games together. They hunted and killed with ever grimmer spirits, and lightheartedness began to pass away from Slow Buffalo's band.

Anyone who did not hunt or kill was called—with no hint of humor—*hokshi cala:* a baby.

This caused *Waskn Mani* much sorrow, not because he himself was called *hokshi cala*—he was used to scorn—but because Standing Hollow Horn was!

Late in the Moon of Falling Leaves (November) the boy carried a pair of warm moccasins to the tipi of his grandfather and scratched on the flap which was closed.

Of course the flap would be closed. The day was cold and grey and the wind was sharp and the sky hung low with snow and the skinny old Crier shivered much these days. So he kept the flap closed.

But why didn't he answer *Waskn Mani's* request to come in?

He scratched again.

He had made these moccasins himself.

So he called the name of his grandfather in gentle Lakota and he scratched a third time. "*Hehlokecha Najin?* May I come in?"

"Who's there?"

"Well, it's me."

"Why?"

"I'm sorry Grandfather, but what do you mean?"

"Why are you there?"

"Oh. Well, because I feel sad—"

Suddenly the wind blew the boy's hair up so that the scar was uncovered, whiter than ever beside a cheek gone dark with strong emotions.

There was silence in the tipi. But *Waskn Mani* said, "Did you say something, *Hehlokecha Najin*?"

"No!"

"Oh. Well, maybe it was the wind. I have brought you a present."

He bowed his head as if to smell the leather of new moccasins. The wind shrieked and snaggled his black hair again.

He said, "*Hehlokecha Najin*, did you say something that time?"

"No! No! What is the matter with you?"

"Well, but may I come in?"

The man inside yelled, "How long have I been teaching you? Tell me that!"

"Well, since the Moon of Making Fat—"

"Yes, and now it is autumn. The pony grew a beard of frost today. Six months is a long time. Have you thought about that?"

"No, Grandfather."

"Think about it. Think if I should be proud of you now."

*Waskn Mani* kept his head down, blinking, trying hard to think, and then he said, "Grandfather, are your feet cold?"

A choking sound came out of the tipi. "Ack! Ack! Why do you talk about my feet?"

"Well, because I have a present for you."

"Ah-ha! The wrong-head has a present for me. Let me guess. Is it a hawk?"

The boy said, "No."

"Well, maybe it is a badger. If you didn't hit a hawk perhaps you hit a badger today. Is it a badger?"

The boy stared down at the ground. "No," he said.

"No! Of course not. But maybe you hit a deer?"

*Waskn Mani* whispered, "I missed the deer."

"A very big deer, boy!" roared Standing Hollow Horn—and though he was hidden inside his tipi one could imagine the color of his face. "That deer stood still and looked at you. That deer did not run away until you decided to have a talk about the weather!"

"Well, but I saw that your toenails were blue—"

"What? What did you say? Blue *what*?"

"Blue toenails, Grandfather—"

"ACK! ACK! DID THE BOY SAY BLUE *TOENAILS*?"

"So I made some moccasins for you which I lined with fur for the warmth—"

The tipi began to shake. "Hoc! Hoc! Harf!" Then the flap flew back and out jumped Standing Hollow Horn, his face bright red, his neck stretched out like the crane's.

"WHERE—hoc, hocah—IS MY PRESENT? LET ME SEE IT!"

*Waskn Mani* held the moccasins out to the old man who raised his hand and struck them down to the ground.

"THERE! THERE! WHAT DO YOU THINK ABOUT THAT?"

"Well," the boy whispered, "well, but they are good and warm."

"Good and warm? Good and warm? BRING ME WARM AND BLOODY, BOY! BRING ME A CARCASS AND *THAT* WILL BE A PRESENT! Now," spluttered the old man, waving his hand in front of his face, "go away. Go hunt—hoc, hoc. Kill anything. Kill—hack, hartch!—kill the humble rabbit. Go!" Standing Hollow Horn turned back into his tipi and yanked the flap closed behind him. "Go away!"

So then except for the wind, the world was quiet again.

But *Waskn Mani* scratched on the doorway one more time.

"Grandfather?" he whispered. "*Tunkashila*, should I leave the moccasins here for you?"

Like sudden thunder, like the crack of a lightning storm contained inside a tipi, Standing Hollow Horn boomed: "BOYS WHO

BELONG TO NO ONE SHOULD NOT CALL ANYONE GRANDFATHER!"

Some snowflakes came out of the sky and cut ground-level with the cold wind. *Waskn Mani* waited for a little while and then picked up the moccasins and went away.

# 11

# "Weep, Weep"

All that night it snowed. By morning the plains were covered with white—a sifting, hissing slope of blowing snow as far as the eyes could see—and the air was filled with the snowfall.

A boy trudged westward. He bent his head against the wind and pushed through drifts as deep as his knees. He wore leggings and a buffalo robe under which he carried a bow and a quiver of arrows. Fifty arrows. His expression was solemn. An old man in a boy's body.

One small person walked the plains alone.

By afternoon the wind turned, stinging the right side of his face and sending the swift snakes down drifts to the left. Behind him his tracks filled with snow so that he left no evidence of his passage. The snow remembers nothing.

The boy was surrounded by whiteness, the sky indecipherably white. Nevertheless he walked westward, always west.

Then a grey line marked the close horizon ahead of him, a woods of naked trees and evergreens. In the pine boughs the wind made a whistling and among the strong limbs a low moan: *Ooooooo*.

The boy lifted his eyes long enough to find an entrance then bowed again until he had gone into the woods and the wind lost force. Within the trees the snow fell gently down. The wind pulled at the high branches swaying them; but near the ground the air was still.

The boy threw back his robe. His mouth made a straight line. His huge black eyes were hard. He was hunting.

So he followed the whiter paths among the trees, the winding trails of animals, stepping with the entire flat of his foot in order to keep a cautious silence, hunting. His eye twitched left and right. Grey light makes no shadows; it treats all things with equity.

Suddenly the young boy froze staring at a treetrunk stripped of bark and branches, rotten at the core of it. Just at the snowline, lurking in a hollow, was the glint of a living eye.

That was what the boy saw: a round eye.

He let the robe slide from his back. His quiver swung free. The bow came forth in his left hand.

With infinite patience he crept in a wide arc to the back of the treetrunk then he leaned his right shoulder against it, softly, softly—

Now! The small boy drove the old trunk forward. Now! A dead-crunching sound broke at the roots and the whole column swayed then toppled down, *Whump!*—exploding snow on both sides.

All at once four rabbits blew out of the hole, their eyes bright with terror, landing in the deep snow and kicking as if to run. But there was a moment when the motion was futile. The hunter was swift and accurate. He notched a long arrow and shot. It caught a rabbit at the heart. He shot a second time and a third, killing two more rabbits faster than thought. They died shocked, their ears straight up, their eyes wide open.

Well, then the boy notched a fourth arrow and aimed and released it—but he felt a tiny tremble and he missed the heart. The arrow stopped transfixed in the neck of the last rabbit and the poor creature began to bleat an endless series of screams: *"Creee, creee, creee!"*—piercing and rapid and painful. Even with the arrow in her neck she tried to run but couldn't. It dipped and caught snow. She kept thrusting her tongue out with the ineffectual scream: "*Creeeee!*"

Then the sound was drowned in a tiny gargle and red blood spouted from her mouth spotting the snow.

The boy went down on his knees. He bit his lip.

Suddenly the rabbit ceased screaming and began to groom herself, gravely licking her paws and washing her face with them. But she licked blood to her paws. She was matting the fur of her face in bright, abundant blood. She could not cleanse herself. Finally she stopped.

She lowered her head over the long arrow as over a tree branch and stopped breathing. Soon the blood stopped flowing and the forest fell silent and the boy began to cry.

He neither blinked nor wiped the water away. Tears streamed from his eyes to the corners of his lips.

"I'm sorry, I'm sorry, I'm sorry," he said. "I have killed the humblest children of *Wakan Tanka*. I am so sorry."

He crawled toward the rabbits and with his thumb he closed their round eyes. He laid them in a line on the snow. They were as loose as rags in his hands. Their heads dropped back over his fingers. Their fur was warm. They did not resist him. They were dead.

When the boy emerged from the woods a full blizzard was blowing across the plains. Wind lashed his flesh and ripped his robe. He didn't care. There was only a dim light. The stinging snow numbed him through the skullbone. No, he didn't care. He bent his left shoulder toward the north and pushed forward and murmured, *You are right, Standing Hollow Horn. I cannot be your grandson.*

He felt sick with himself.

He thought it would be good to lie down and die in this storm because he didn't deserve to live.

His robe snapped and billowed behind him. He had to hold it with two fists at the neck. He carried no quiver now. No bow. He was naked beneath the buffalo fur.

Well, then he must have walked for hours across the snow-crust above the grasses. It supported the weight of a small boy. Wherever the wind blew violent the crust grew ribbed and strong.

But then his foot hit a hollow place and he sank to his waist in snow and then he stood still trying to think what to do. It felt warmer and warmer just to be standing still. All the world was absolutely black now, the sky and the earth, the forest and plains. There were four somebodies behind him whom he had killed and still he heard the voice of the fourth one. Perhaps he ought to let the snow become his death-blanket too.

"Weep, weep!"

What was that? Such a tiny sound. So small he scarcely heard it underneath the hissing wind. But then it came again: "Weep, weep." Yes, yes, no doubt. Someone was crying in the storm—a little, living misery.

But the boy shook his head. What could he do? Nothing. He folded his arms under the robe and shook his head again.

"Weep, weep."

Suddenly he called, "Where are you?" That was a surprise. He hadn't planned on calling. But immediately the crying stopped and then he felt bad because he might have frightened the poor creature even more, so he hollered, "Don't be afraid! I don't want to hurt you. Where are you?"

"Weep, weep, weep, weep—" Several voices were crying now with shiverings and shakings because they were so cold.

The boy followed that tiny sound. He broke the snow crust at his chest by bringing his elbows down on it. Then just in front of him came again the sorrowful crying, "Weep! Weep!" He put out his hand and touched three living creatures.

They were a family of porcupines all hunched together with their backs turned to the wind, making a little drift on top of the snow but making no warmth for themselves.

"Weep, weep."

"Please don't cry," said the boy. "I'm not going anywhere, you see. I'll stay with you. Can we lie down together?"

So he lowered them into the snow-hole his coming had made, one and two and three, and then he lay on his side, curling his body around the porcupines and pulling his robe over everyone.

The porcupines stopped crying. But he could feel their shivers. He started to shiver too as the feeling came back into him. And then he started silently to cry. The water ran out of his eyes.

So then the oldest porcupine began to lick his eyes, making a soft sound with her rough tongue: *Shh, shh, shh.*

The boy murmured, "*Pila miya,*" which means Thank you.

The porcupine said, "You are welcome, Red Boy."

The boy said, "But it makes me feel worse when you do that, Porcupine, because I don't deserve anybody's kindness any more, you see. No one should be good to me any more."

The porcupine stopped licking his eyes for a moment. "Why not?" she said.

"Because," he said, "today with very sharp arrows I killed four humble creatures of God."

There was a long silence.

Then here came that rough tongue again, *Shh, shh, shh,* licking the tears all down his cheek. So, because of this kindness, the boy burst into loud sobbings. "Hownh! Hownh!" he cried. His whole body shuddered. "Hownh, hownh, hownh."

The porcupine waited a while and then she began to sing a little song:

> "*This Red Boy like a cherry tree*
> *Spreads his branches over me:*
> *A cherry tree still warm in winter,*
> *What a wonder! What a wonder!*"

He whispered, "Please, Porcupine, you should not sing for me. I am a tree that has bad thorns." He said *shica* which means bad. But she sang anyway:

> "*Firewood without a flame*
> *Came walking on the frozen plain*
> *And proved the promise of his name:*

*This boy moves walking in the winter.*
*Waskn Mani. What a wonder!"*

The boy whispered, "You know my name!"

"Yes," said the porcupine. Then she began to lick his neck and this was very comforting. Then she said, "By 'bad thorns' you mean arrows, don't you?"

With unspeakable sorrow the boy nodded.

*Shh, shh, shh,* went her tongue on the soft parts of his throat.

And then she was speaking while the wind hissed far above them. "Have you noticed," she said, "that we are the same, the four-leggeds, the wingeds and the two-leggeds too? Have you noticed this? We all share the grandmother earth. We all get cold. We all cry, though some of us say 'Weep, weep' and some say 'Hownh'—but it's the same. Therefore the little porcupines sleeping against your stomach are your brothers, *Waskn Mani*, and I am your sister."

She pushed her small snout deep beneath his hair. With her tender flesh she found the scar of his left ear and began to lick it. *Shh, shh, shh.* The boy's heart nearly burst with the strong feeling this caused in him. No one had ever been so close or so private. In this moment he loved the porcupine, his sister.

She said, "When a sister dies and when someone feels sorry and cries because she died, what do you call that, *Waskn Mani*?"

The boy said, "Sadness?"

"You call it *Wakan*," she said. "You call it 'Holiness.' We are all one. Each of us is kin to all of us. And when a boy suffers a true sorrow because one humble creature died, then he has suffered too the holiness that holds us all together."

Now the boy and the three porcupines were in a little lodge together, covered by snow from the storm. Here it was warm. Here no wind blew. The smaller brother made moist snorings at his stomach. They were content. The sister at his ear caused such sweetness of feeling that he was grinning in the dark.

She said, "There is a way we name this oneness. We say *Mitakuye oyasin*. All my relations. We are all relatives."

So that was how the boy learned this sacred phrase, from the love of a porcupine who was washing his body as if he had just been born.

She said, "We have arrows too, *Waskn Mani*. Yours kill and so you cry. Ours warn and no one dies. And sometimes when we give our arrows away ours can make poor plain things beautiful."

For the rest of the night she washed the child and he slept very well. And then he went home again with fifty arrows, the hunter's number but not the sort of arrows a hunter uses.

At the beginning of the Moon of the Popping Trees (December) the old Crier looked out of his tipi and found a present waiting for him on the snow. A pair of moccasins lined on the inside with fur, very warm.

Also very beautiful.

For the outside of these moccasins was woven with a tight design of porcupine quills, bright and beautiful quillwork. Here were many animals worked into the leather, none of them shot, none bleeding: the swallow, the dragonfly, the porcupine. Four rabbits. And here was a small boy standing next to his skinny grandfather holding hands, both of them as red as cherries.

The picture meant, *Mitakuye oyasin*.

When Standing Hollow Horn beheld these moccasins he had a coughing fit so hard and long that the water kept running from his eyes.

# 12

# Rattling Hail Woman

All through her childhood Rattling Hail Woman had a grin of such eager glee it looked like a dare to race her. She would stick her chin out and set her white teeth and bunch her cheeks and fix a friend with her flashing black eye: *Race me! Race me!* She grinned like sunlight. She dazzled the people. And in spite of age or dignity they got up and they raced her.

Immediately the child was gone, screaming with delight and serious about winning.

She raced afoot when she was small, on ponies by the time she was four. She raced wild and well even when others were entering womanhood, growing demure. Oh, she burst with pure joy in the contest! So strong was her love for speed, for the challenge and the triumph, that she made high cries in the flight and her opponent simply assumed that such a spirit could not lose. So she didn't.

But then at the finish, when the child broke into wonderful peals of laughter, no opponent felt bad about losing. Everyone won. Absolutely everyone in Slow Buffalo's band, upon hearing the laughter of Rattling Hail Woman, would grin and giggle and finally laugh along.

That was her best gift to the people: her laughter.

"Don't!" the people would cry. "Rattling Hail Woman, don't make me laugh any more!" But they laughed in spite of themselves. And their general laughter would send her into greater gales of exultation and then the whole village would be weeping and gasping and holding its sides and screaming, "Rattling Hail Woman, stop! I can't stand it! You are hurting me!"

Then, "Whew!" the people would say as the roaring subsided. "Whew, that felt so good. Oh, she is a live one, all right. She gets that laugh from her father. No one could laugh like Black Elk—except his daughter, except his daughter."

Black Elk died when the child was five.

Rattling Hail Woman grew up in good days when Slow Buffalo still had all his teeth and the band was small and private glory seemed less important. Men didn't mind losing a contest. Even the young men would rather be friends with Rattling Hail Woman than to be famous. Those were happy red and blue days, to be sure. The Lakota—young and old and male and female—loved the maid because she loved so much so well. She made them glad.

They loved her, truly—yet it never occurred to her friends that they might also marry her.

In time the girl became a woman with womanly longings. But who noticed? Who courts the friend that hunts with him? Or who thinks of marrying the woman that outrides him?

So when Rattling Hail Woman began to wear her braids upon her breast instead of down her back and when her body swelled in the prettiest places, the young men talked with her and laughed with her and loved her mightily but none came courting.

In the sweet spring evenings young men perfumed their ponies and their bodies with sage. They took the best blankets and walked to the tipi of the woman who had caught their eye and there they lined up with the blankets over their heads, waiting to be noticed. If she noticed and if she approved and if her parents did not disapprove then the woman would step beneath the blanket with the man, face to face in that private place. This was the courting of the Lakota.

But as the young men passed the tipi of Rattling Hail Woman they grinned with honest affection and waved and called, "*Hau*, friend! You look good tonight," and walked on by.

She said "*Hau*" too and waved but then she would sigh since no one saw that she had changed her smile. Less eager. Softer.

Her mother said, "*Wsu Sna Win*, perhaps you should not ride ponies so much so wildly. At least not faster than the men."

Rattling Hail Woman said, "Yes, you are right." And while she yet sat sighing in front of her tipi she meant that with all her heart: yes, yes, she must slow down.

Ah, but if in the morning that same young man returned with his pony and mischief in his eye, well, her own black eyes would flash such fire that the two of them would suddenly whip their mounts and tear down a long slope in dead-match together, screaming, yipping and laughing. So then her braids blew backward after all. She could not help it. The hunger in her stomach pleaded speed and her lungs loved laughter. The feeling of a pony's mane all twisted in her fingers, leaning low on his neck, smelling his sweat, hearing the rush of his breath at every shock of the gallop, the jolt of his bones, the roll of his great muscle, the tightening of her own eyes into a headlong wind and the sting of speed on her cheeks—all this bewitched her. In other matters she was changing, yes. But in this one thing, despite her midnight resolutions, she remained the same and many young men loved her.

"*Hau*, friend!" they greeted the girl in front of her tipi.

And "*Hau*," she answered as they walked by. Both grinned, both waved, but inside of the girl the woman was lonely.

And then one day there arrived a new young man in Slow Buffalo's band.

Secretly the women watched him with admiration, both the maids and the marrieds; but the maids grew mute as if stunned by his beauty while the marrieds grew noisy. They called the young man *Tatanka*, meaning the buffalo bull.

They said, "*Tatanka* has come to a small herd, hee hee. Looking for *Pte*, his buffalo cow, hee hee hee."

He was an exceptional man.

He walked with the soft assurance of a mountain cat, with the watchful snap and spring of a four-legged—marvelously muscled, broad-chested, perfectly silent. He opened his mind to no one, neither by speech nor by smiling. He slept at the edge of the village.

"So who will he pick?" the marrieds gossiped, fingers flying as fast as their tongues. "He better hurry or he will kill the crop before he plucks one ear. Already I know five *wikoshkalakas* lying sick with love, too weak to carry water."

Months in fact were passing and every time the marrieds thought they knew whose beauty had taken the young man's heart and every time they bustled over to help her prepare, they were wrong and that maid fell sick with the others.

It was an epidemic. Slow Buffalo considered confronting the silent young man, the striding *tatanka* who seemed oblivious of the effect of his presence. There was, in fact, just one figure that sparked interest in the man's eye. A child. A girl maybe two years old who had attached herself to Slow Buffalo's band during the last gathering of Lakota at the Seven Council Fires. This child had oddly slanted eyes, an enormous thick tongue, a small round fat body and stubby fingers. She never spoke. She was as stubborn as stone. In the beginning no one could make her go back where she had come from, and now she stood to the side of every company with the two middle fingers of her right hand thrust into her mouth, staring. Sometimes the handsome young man paused in front of the peculiar child and gazed at her. Well, all the villagers stroked her now. Everyone fed her. And she was allowed to sleep wherever she lay down because people had begun to think her presence might be *wakan*, sacred.

"See?" the women whispered, "he is begging a name from the

child who cannot speak. The dumb and the dumb are talking together, hee hee hee."

Thus they made jokes. But if the mute girl were some kind of magic among them they hoped it was for good rather than evil. Therefore they called her by a name that represented *washtay*, good fortune, and they spoke of her as though she were already a grown woman in a baby's body. They said, "See? He is begging Red Day Woman for the name of the best *wikoshkalaka* in the band."

The red day is a good day. They called the slant-eyed silent child Red Day Woman.

Then finally came the evening for which every maid and every married had been waiting. The handsome young man entered the village carrying his best blanket and smelling hugely of sage, walking slowly among the tipis. A hundred eyes peered up from under frowning brows: *Who? Where? Which?*

Several women swift afoot crept after him, slipping through shadows tipi to tipi.

Then he stopped before a tipi that none had predicted for him. All over the village women tried not to squawk in surprise.

Most surprised of all was the mother of Rattling Hail Woman. Her eyes grew big as duck eggs. For several moments she could not talk. Then gaping at such monumental handsomeness she shrieked, "*Wsu Sna Win! Wsu Sna Win*, come out! There is a young man come to see you!"

The young man drew his blanket over his head and waited.

Women were jabbing one another in the ribs. It simply had not occurred to them that Rattling Hail Woman was—beautiful.

But look! She was beautiful indeed.

Out of her tipi she came, her black eyes radiant, her dark flesh warm with feeling—and a grin on her lips. A grin too mischievous for her own good. Silently her mother tried to rub it off, wagging her finger and frowning hard. This was not a time for races. This was a time in which to be demure, calm, sweet, steadfast. But the grin stuck on. The black eyes flashed. Rattling Hail Woman, meeting her first suitor, could scarcely contain her delight.

She lifted the edge of his blanket and moved beneath and the two heads formed one lump.

It seemed as if no one else in all the village was courting that night. No one but these two. Women everywhere held their breath wondering whether *Tatanka* had found his *Pte*. And if so what would he say?

Well, what he said shocked them. It sent them into convulsions.

No: *how* he said it caused them to lose control.

For in all these months no one had heard the young man speak. Perhaps they had imagined for him a voice as manly as his appearance.

Well, well: from underneath the blanket, high and sharp and very loud, there arose a strange sound: "Errrrrrrrr." It was like the scream of a prairie chicken.

The women said, "What was that?"

The mother of Rattling Hail Woman immediately got a horrified look on her face. She hissed, "*Wsu Sna Win*, don't you dare!"

Too late. The blanket was already trembling. The girl had commenced to giggle.

The young man in a voice like the shriek of an eagle-bone whistle said, "Rattling Hail Woman, I errrrrrrrrrrrr—"

The women of the village said, "That was him! That was *him*, the beautiful *Tatanka!*"

The mother of Rattling Hail Woman reached over to her daughter's ankle and gave it a severe pinch.

No good. By now the blanket was jumping.

The young man said in the silly whine of a child: "Rattling Hail Woman, my name is Fire Thunderrrrrrrrrrr—"

And that was more than she could take. Rattling Hail Woman, face to face with her first suitor beneath his blanket, began to laugh. And when she laughed so did the people. Laughter broke out all over the village. People roared and fell down and kicked and howled and wept: "Rattling Hail Woman, stop it! I can't stand it! You are hurting me!"

They were blinded by their laughter. They did not notice that Fire

Thunder had rolled up his blanket and was striding away, his jaw set like stone.

So that was the first and the last young man to court Rattling Hail Woman. She was seventeen years old, very old already, a concern to her mother and, in her own deep woman's soul, lonely.

# 13
## "The Spotted Eagle Is Coming to Carry Me Away"

So then the young woman withdrew into her loneliness.

She no longer sat in front of her tipi in the evening. She went inside and lay on her back with her hands behind her head.

She no longer laughed. She gazed all night at the stars that crossed her patch of sky above the smoke hole of the tipi. They did what she could not: they moved in a slow dignity, quiet and radiant and brave, whereas she acted carelessly, compulsively. She wished she were a star. Then she would not love speed too much or laugh at the wrong times.

Night after night as the months passed she stared into the deep sky—and soon she was paying attention to one particular star, a heavenly warrior, it seemed to her, who rode the curve of the universe in grand indifference. Royal.

"I wonder what it would be like," *Wsu Sna Win* whispered out loud, "to love such a star."

When the rest of the village was sleeping she crawled from her tipi to watch his progress westward. He moved in perfect silence with utter confidence. He rose and crossed and set again in smooth unswerving glory. He went high, impossibly high and far away. It made her pant to imagine the regions of his going.

"I wonder," she murmured when the star had descended the western horizon, "what it would be like to marry such a star."

One night she allowed herself to whisper, "Riding Star, I love you." she said *Love*. The word was only a test but the sound of it caused her to gasp and wrap her arms around her bosom. She astonished herself with strong feeling, for in saying it she came to mean it, and the next thing was she called aloud, "How can I come to you?"

And then one morning while she walked alone across the prairie she noticed the spotted eagle circling on wide wings through blue heaven. Without thinking twice she prayed to the eagle, *"Wanbli Galeshka*, you fly highest in the heavens! Oh, carry me to the Riding Star. I love the star. I want to be where he is."

She hadn't expected an answer. Therefore when the bird began to spiral downward she felt afraid. She thought she ought to run away but she stood steadfast, staring up. The eagle sank without a stroke of the wing. He was looking at her. In a sacred manner she saw clearly his fierce yellow eye fixed on her, his feathers splayed by the wind, the soft feathers at his breast flowing in the wind, his talons balled, his beak a lethal hook. She saw all this even at great distances and her heart stopped. Was this vision a sign?

Suddenly the eagle was skimming the ground straight toward her. Then he was beating his wings at her face. She screamed and fell down and he ascended on a mighty stroke. Almost immediately the eagle had soared from sight and the woman was left feeling small and lonely and lost.

She covered her face with her hands. Why had she prayed such a dangerous prayer? *Wsu Sna Win*, her braids on her breast but none on earth to marry her—and the one she loved coursed the midnight sky at impossible heights—foolish, foolish *winyan*.

She wept behind her hands.

Why had the spotted eagle come so near to frighten her?

And then a marvelous thing occurred:

That night while she lay by the fire watching white smoke float up and out the smoke hole a sudden thunder shook the tipi, a crashing of wings, and the entire sky blackened, hiding the stars. *Wanbli Galeshka* had come and covered the tipi and in a sacred manner he was speaking to her.

*Once*, he said, *your prayer may be answered—once by the mercy of God who sends you once where mortals do not go. Step this once in faith into the fire. The spirit of your yearning, woman, may mingle with the spirit of the fire once to rise and leave the earth. Once, before you enter heaven by death. Once.*

The eagle's wings beat the air again and the holy bird arose. But *Come!* he cried. *Fly!* he screamed. *Once!* he swore and he departed.

Rattling Hail Woman was alone.

Not even her mother was in the tipi—no one to consult.

Spontaneously she stood up and walked barefoot into the fire. She was wearing a white buckskin dress. She raised her two arms over her head and twined the fingers together and lifted her face and gazed through the smoke hole to the high-riding beautiful star. Tears began to stream from her eyes.

That same night the mother of Rattling Hail Woman dreamed a dream so vivid that when she woke she wanted to ask her daughter whether it was true but she couldn't. Her daughter was gone.

She dreamed she was standing outside their tipi with a load of firewood on her back. It was night. A pale light shined all around the tipi creating an eerie whiteness. The flap was closed and the woman felt sad because she could not enter.

She said, "*Wsu Sna Win*, are you in there?"

There was no answer. The firewood grew heavier on her back and she bowed down with real fear. "Is something wrong?" she called. No answer. In her dream she heard herself screaming, "Speak to me! Speak to me!"

And then her daughter's voice came out of the tipi singing a haunting song: *"Ina,"* Rattling Hail Woman sang, *"Wanbli Galeshka wana ni he o who e!"*

So then the older woman began to wail and lament because the song said, "Mother, the Spotted Eagle is coming to carry me away," and the woman interpreted these words to mean that her daughter was dying.

She screamed. She threw the firewood from her back. When she looked up she saw that the smoke from the tipi was changing colors, as white as her daughter's teeth, ruddy like her skin, black like her hair, and blacker still like her eyes—then green. Deep green. The green of ineffable mystery, the green of visions, green!

The smoke went straight up windlessly until it disappeared in the night sky.

Then in her dream the mother of Rattling Hail Woman knew that she could enter the tipi if she wished.

But then she woke up.

# 14
# Wicahpi

All night the mortal woman went straight up like an arrow, both solemn and excited because she was thinking of the Riding Star.

For a while the rivers below reflected a flat white moonlight but soon they shrank as thin as sinews and then they disappeared. The pale mountaincaps flattened too and vanished. The earth was swallowed in darkness. And then it was so perfect a midnight that she could not tell how fast she was ascending.

She felt no wind.

Suddenly the sky was alight with a shower of tiny stars like burning bees with the voices of children calling. But just as suddenly she shot into a still more beautiful blackness. So she thought she must be going very fast. Like an arrow.

And so she flew in solitude until the morning.

The dawn frightened her. It broke the sky with more than light. It came like music, the sound of many voices singing *Ahhh* to a hard drum louder and louder. The sun had not yet appeared, but when the woman looked she saw a blue valley full of mist.

And then she put a bare foot down and she was walking in the valley and she felt happy because here was every good and necessary thing a Lokata woman could want.

*Ahhh!* sang the voices of the dawning louder and louder. Then the sun shot flaming arrows from the east and the song grew more frightening: *Hee-ay-hay-ee-ee!* The woman was standing in the region of the daybreak.

And then it seemed that the sun's arrows had ignited a huge fire in the center of the valley, golden, in the shape of a tipi. And then she saw that this *was* a tipi made all of cloud.

The morning light increased and the music swelled until the woman wanted to cover her ears but she didn't for fear of offending someone. Such glorious, roaring music! She became ashamed that all she wore was a buckskin dress, bare arms and bare feet and no adornment.

And then it seemed that the singing soon must kill her by its power and beauty. The drum shook the floor of the valley. The voices roared, *Lo, where he cometh!* She looked up and uttered a mute scream because the sun itself was rushing toward her, its feathers a burst of the first light, its center both heat and whiteness purely. She buckled at the knees and began to fall.

A single voice cried, "*Hetchetu welo!* It is well!"

Immediately the singing ceased. The dawn was done, the day begun and the sun was back where it ought to be. But now there was a man walking down the eastern slope of the valley very far away yet seeming near because his eyes were so large and steadfast and black and lovely, looking directly at her, seeing everything.

In a circle at the back of his head was a sunburst of feathers. Besides that he wore nothing but a loincloth.

The woman was still falling, but going down slowly as if sinking in water.

Now the man was beside her, saying, "Call me *Wicahpi*."

*Wicahpi* means Star!

Here was the Riding Star receiving her, receiving a mortal Lakota into his kingdom of sky and into his tipi!

She sighed and rolled up her eyes and finished falling. But just before she fainted she felt the arms of the Star beneath her back and she heard him say, "*Wsu Sna Win*," and in that instant she loved him completely. For what else does a child require in exchange for her heart than this: that he catch her and call her by name?

So that is how a common Lakota woman came to marry a star.

They had many good days together. Because the moon crossed the earth below their valley, here the weather never varied. For them it was always the same moon. Always. Only day and night changed one for the other with perfect regularity.

In the daylight, then, inside the cloud–tipi the woman would lie beside her star and whisper, "I love you, *Wicahpi*," and his deep eyes would smile, full of knowledge. In the evening he rose and left her, striding eastward and climbing the far slope of the valley until he vanished over the ridge. At night she was alone. But always with the dawn he would return and lie down beside her.

"I love you, *Wicahpi*," she said. He turned his eyes upon her and smiled. She gazed into that fathomless smile. Deep, deep, as deep as the sea or else the midnight sky.

"*Wicahpi*," she said, "do you love me as much as I love you?"

With the palm of his hand he touched her thoughtful brow. "Haven't I given you nearly the whole of heaven?" he said.

"Yes."

Yes, indeed. Two things only he had forbidden her. She could harvest whatever good thing she wished, but for the love of him she must never dig the wild turnip that grew there.

And though she could roam the entire blue valley she must never follow him over the eastern ridge in the evening.

"Do you promise?" he said. Right easily she had promised.

"And so you love me," she said and he smiled his effulgent agreement and so they were content together and the days passed.

But soon her promises seemed much too easy to keep. The woman wished for some difficult thing, some task requiring knowledge and precious skill so that she might prove the greatness of her love for the star.

Therefore she busied herself making *wasna*. Chokecherries were always ripe in the valley. Buffalo meat always hung in strips from willow branches. But she herself had to pound the two together and that seemed a worthy work. Her husband ate small portions of her food with gestures of pleasure and astonishment.

Well, but then he never ate enough to make a meal or else to nourish a body. And when he rose and left her in the evenings it seemed to her that all the *wasna* she had made remained in the cloud–tipi, left behind.

She made spoons from buffalo horn. She made two bowls from the burls of the black walnut tree. Into these she poured a savory soup which she brought steaming to her husband just as the sun was descending. He sipped and smiled and swore that there had never been a better preparation for his journey than this soup. Then he rose to leave.

"*Wicahpi*," she said, "do you love me as much as I love you?"

For a moment he gazed at her with his unflinching eyes. Then he said, "Unto whom do I give my days, *Wsu Sna Win*?"

"To me, *Wicahpi*," she sighed bowing her face.

So he reached and touched the point of her chin and lifted it that she might look at him. "From dawn to dusk?" he asked.

And she answered, "Sunrise to sunset and all the time between." And he smiled upon her such a bright warm smile that she could not help but smile back. Love for him ran like warm liquid in her breast, filling all the hollows, yes. Yes.

So she set herself yet more difficult tasks. She brought him moccasins of intricate beauty. She sewed leggings. She made a parfleche bag in which he could carry the *wasna* with him for his nighttime journies—and on that bag she painted pictures of her home below so that he might see the good things she willingly left for his sake and he might account her worthy therefore.

Oh, what delight he expressed for each of these gifts! He grinned and applauded and hugged his mortal wife and wore the leggings all day long. Often he pointed to the picture on the parfleche bag and asked her the meanings of things.

She felt very happy.

But every evening when he kissed her and prepared to go eastward he removed the leggings. He never carried the parfleche bag away with him. Always he wore no more than the loincloth and the burst of white feather at the back of his head.

What good was she then? What good was her work after all?

"*Wicahpi*," she said. The sharpness in her voice surprised her but she could not stop herself. "*Wicahpi*, do you love me as much as I love you?"

He smiled and said, "Unto whom do I give my days?"

In her heart a terrible question appeared: *Yes, but to whom do you give your nights?* Out loud she said, "Well, if you love me why don't you take my gifts with you when you go away?"

With genuine feeling he said, "One needn't use a gift to enjoy it. One need only receive it and I do."

She bowed her head and murmured, "*Wicahpi*, you don't even finish the food I bring you."

"No," he agreed. "It isn't necessary."

Softly she whispered, "You eat only for my sake then."

The star knelt down and embraced her. "It is a measure of my love for you, *Wsu Sna Win*," he said.

"*Wicahpi*, is there nothing I can give you that you need?"

He gazed upon her for a long time then placed his lips to her forehead and kissed her and rose up and went out of the tipi.

She did not look up.

She did not say good-bye.

The Lakota woman who once had laughed so eagerly now began to cry. "I am useless," she said. "I am a toy."

Suddenly she raised her face, her black eyes flashing with a dare. She looked ready to run a race against someone. "No!" she cried, that sharp sound in her voice. "No, *Wicahpi!*" She jumped up and ran out of the tipi. She went to a plum tree and broke off a strong branch and stripped it and fashioned a digging stick with that branch. Then she went exactly the way her husband went every evening.

At the foot of the eastern slope she found a wild turnip plant, luxurious with leaves. She kneeled down and thrust her stick into the ground and began to dig vigorously. When the plant was loose in soil she took hold of the crown and pulled, but the huge turnip popped out so easily that the woman slipped and nearly fell into its hole.

She scrambled backward. But then she crept forward and peered down. *Oiya!* This was more than just a turnip hole!

*Wsu Sna Win* could see the earth below in moonlight. She had punched a hole in the sky! She saw the watchfires of a tiny Lakota village down there and a ring of tipis and in front of one tipi an old woman bent down beneath a load of firewood.

"*Ina!*" she cried. "Mother!" But no one heard her and in that moment the wife of the Riding Star was so sad with homesickness that she thought of jumping through the turnip hole and falling down to earth again.

She wailed and lamented but she did not jump. She put the turnip back to cover her sin, and when the star returned to his cloud–tipi the next morning he found that his wife could not stop crying.

So he sat down and drew her head to his lap. "*Wsu Sna Win*," he whispered, "did you dig the wild turnip?"

"What?" She sat up horrified by his question. "No!" she said. "Can't I just be sad?" she shouted. "Isn't loneliness a good enough reason for sadness? You, *Wicahpi!* I am sad because of you! Every night you leave me! To whom do you give your nights?"

So that put an end to questions about turnips.

The star of the fathomless eyes gathered his wife into his arms and stroked her while she sobbed.

"Do you love me, *Wicahpi?*" she sobbed. "Do you need me? Someone should need me. Sometimes when I think that I am useless I just want to destroy things. Do you understand that?"

The star was silent a long time. Then he said, "*Wsu Sna Win*, there is an answer to your questions. There is a gift we each can give the other—one gift and two givers—which will make its givers necessary as long as it exists. Come. Let me hold you, Lakota."

And so it was that a mortal woman conceived in her womb the off-spring of a star.

Soon she was singing to the infant inside of her.

"*Hokshi cala*," she sang. "Baby, baby, someone to need me, and I shall dress and feed thee, sweetly."

Now when Rattling Hail Woman watched her husband mount the eastern ridge of the valley she whispered, "Baby, you will change your father. He will stop for you," she said, rubbing her stomach. "Surely he will pause for my pain and for your borning and he will love us. One night he will stay and love us both."

And so the woman grew big with child.

# 15

# Hokshi Cala: Baby

"*Wicahpi*," murmured the woman, smiling and tired, "do you love me?"

The star was removing from his braids two beautiful beaverskin coverings which his wife had made for him.

It was the evening.

He bent down and pulled back the flap of the tipi preparing to leave.

"*Wicahpi!*" she cried, "do you love me as much as I love you?"

He hesitated a moment then turned toward her, his black eyes calm and unchanging. She thrust out her chin and determined not to drop her gaze until he answered her.

Finally he said, "There is one baby, *Wsu Sna Win*, one gift and one love between us. Your love is mine, exactly the same."

"But you never *say* it!" she cried.

He wore no more than a loincloth and that burst of white feather. All her gifts were folded upon his pallet.

"Why can't you *say* it?"

"Does every thing that is need words?"

She went up on her knees and grabbed his wrist. "*Wicahpi*, will you love the baby?"

He bent and kissed the hand that held him. "My child, my blood," he said. "I will love it as myself." He plucked her hand away and turned and left.

"*Wicahpi! Wicahpi!* The baby is coming tonight!" she yelled.

No answer.

She heaved to her feet and ran out of the tipi screaming, "The baby's coming! Stay with me tonight!"

But the star had already spanned half the valley.

Without a thought the woman rushed after him. "I hurt," she wailed. "Oh, *Wicahpi*, I hurt so much. Give me this one night—"

Tirelessly her husband ascended the eastern slope. Then just as he vanished over the ridge the sun was snuffed behind her and she realized that she herself was at the foot of the slope.

Well! Then she would climb it too. Whether he liked it or not they would spend this night together.

She climbed. The way was exceedingly steep.

Suddenly a strapping pain seized her belly. It stopped her an instant and then it made her mad and she climbed with new fury. The baby was coming right now! Where was its father?

So the woman gained the top of the ridge and looked east and saw her husband running an open plain with such grace and speed that she was sad he had hidden his beauty from her. He was running toward a herd of buffalo, a vast herd all white, a hundred thousand buffalo, snorting, shaking their heads and stomping with the excitement of his approach, their strong horns darting lightning—every one of them albino, white in the dark sky, livid on the black plain, a violent foam.

Suddenly her husband fell to the ground and rolled and kicked. When he came up again and shook himself he was standing on four legs. He had become a buffalo as white as the others, a bull of tremendous size and strength, his brow a tundra, his horns forks of white flame.

Rattling Hail Woman covered her mouth and sank to her knees. "*Wicahpi*," she whispered.

This biggest of buffalos, clearly the *itancan*, wheeled around and began to gallop back toward the ridge where the woman was fixed, kneeling. The entire herd shuffled, lowered its heads and followed. Faster and faster came the leader, curved horns and a skull of brutality, straight for the woman that had been his wife. She could not move. She thought she would be crushed beneath the hooves—but that first buffalo suddenly sailed into the air above her, missing her, and she saw his eyes as he passed over, and in them was a horror she could not endure.

The buffalo's eyes were white as hailstones, cipher-white. Her husband's fathomless gaze was gone. These were blank eyes, frozen, sightless, terrifying eyes. She felt banished from him and abandoned.

The sight knocked her backward and then she was rolling down the slope and her water broke and her womb was contracting with tremendous force and hardness.

At the bottom of the slope she heard herself screaming. She could not find the part of her that was screaming, so she could not stop it. The pain caused her vision to go bloody. She set her teeth and hissed and the spittle ran down her throat and then, suddenly, a new thought occurred to her and her soul began to weep. Deep inside herself the woman wept, *Oiya, oiya*, for the thing she was about to do.

She crawled to the turnip she had pulled out before, and she pulled it out again. Here was her hole in the sky. She looked down and saw the little circle of Lakota watchfires. *Oiyaaa*, she said in her soul, her own mouth screaming still, but she had seen the *wanagi*-eyes of her husband, the ghost-eyes as white as death, and her mind was made up. What was to keep her here any more?

Thus it was that a human woman jumped through a hole in heaven and plunged down to the earth, feeling sorry for the baby in her belly, turning over and over, expecting soon to die.

"*Oiyaaaaaa!*" One can actually think while one is falling. One can consider both desires and disappointments. And Rattling Hail Woman wished it was her life alone she were giving away, not the life of the child of her husband as well.

But then out of the darkness came a swarm of lights, like whirling birds or burning bees. Stars! Stars with the voices of children! They plucked at her braids, they pinched the hem of her dress, and by marvelous bits of strength they slowed her fall.

In this way the small stars lowered Rattling Hail Woman down to the earth again and laid her on the ground in a good woods and then rose up to shed a pale light on what took place thereafter.

# The Rabbits Tell This Story

We knew the baby would be remarkable. His mother was making a sound like *Huh!* when we came into the clearing of the cottonwood trees. She was saying, *Huh! Huh!*—exactly like the buffalo cow when she is calving.

Well, and the two-legged woman had fallen from the sky. What do you think about that? And the stars came to watch this birth. These are remarkable signs, wouldn't you say? We knew the baby would be remarkable.

And didn't we see a little red cloud come out his mother's mouth?—blood red, a sacred dust? Yes. Like *pte*, the buffalo cow when she calves. Yes. We were ready for a wonder.

Poor woman, she could do nothing for herself.

So we came, seventeen or six of us or so. We licked her clean in the deeper parts. We nudged her legs to a good position. Some of us scooped a nest in dirt and lined it with fur while others stroked her belly, proud of the power in there. We knew! We said to each other, "This one will come as a four-legged does."

The woman opened her eyes and stared at us.

She said something in Lakota.

But we were very busy.

The baby's head was pressing against its opening, stretching that hole, but maybe the skin would burst, so we massaged it and some of us twined the baby's hair in our teeth and helped to pull and suddenly the baby squirted into the world and then that *hokshi cala* was crying so hard and it seemed to us that the stars were complimenting the strength of his voice. We licked the salty waters from his body and we bit the cord and we bit it again at the afterbirth. We buried the afterbirth but we carried the cord to his mother—

And don't you know! It was exactly then that the baby proved how remarkable he was.

We stopped and whispered in wonder: "Just like a four-legged!"

For that infant lifted his head and looked around. He saw things. Then he pushed his little rump up in the air and he straightened his hind legs. He flopped over seven or two times, but the next thing was, that baby was standing. Yes! And then he took some steps. Yes.

We cried. "Look! Like a four-legged! Right away he moves walking!"

So that was the only thing his mother said clearly before she went to sleep again. Just as she touched the cord she said, "Moves Walking. *Waskn Mani*," she said, proving that she was aware and in love with her baby. Everything would be all right.

And those words became the name of the child, of course.

We know. We were there. We saw his nativity.

And we have kept an eye on him ever since.

We expect great things from that boy.

# Part Three

# 16
# Wasna

What happened to *Waskn Mani* between his ninth and his thirteenth years is not a story. But in the Moon of Frost in the Tipi of that particular year (January) Slow Buffalo got sick and so the story begins again.

The old *itancan* had sneaked a large piece of *wasna* into his tipi. Since he had only three teeth left in his head it was foolish for him to eat such tough food but he was an old man with dreams and memories and sometimes he missed *wasna* so bad it made him ache.

So when he lay alone in the dark winter's night he took a big bite and immediately broke his third last tooth.

The pain of that bite shot up into his skull as if the bone were splitting apart. Slow Buffalo saw lights popping in front of his face and his vision ran red. He made no sound. He did not groan or cry out because he was ashamed of himself for sneaking the *wasna*. But that night the white knife of skull-pain descended through his body like an ice, a mortal chill, and he began to shiver and then nothing could make the old chief warm again. Nothing.

He said to the woman, his friend, "It started when I took a bite of *wasna*. I should never have taken that bite. That was a big mistake."

Now he ate nothing at all. He said it was because there were only two teeth left and he grinned. In fact, he had no appetite and the shivering made him very tired.

He went to the sweat lodge to pray and to become warm again. Instead the heat overcame him and he passed out. Two men carried him back to his tipi where he slept for three days. His breathing grew very faint.

When he woke up, here was the skinny Crier of the village, Standing Hollow Horn, crouched and staring straight down at him.

Slow Buffalo smiled. "*Hau*," he said and immediately his body broke into spasms of shivering. The skin below his chin shook like a chicken wattle. He had to stop smiling.

Suddenly the Crier jumped up and pointed at the *itancan* and yelled, "I know what you want!"

This was a very loud man. In order to make an example of quietness Slow Buffalo whispered, "What do I want?"

"You want a new robe," roared the Crier. He sounded enraged. "A robe with a ruff of wolf's fur," he yelled and then folded his arms across his chest as if he were ready to fight somebody. He pinched his lips and frowned like a black cloud.

"No," sighed Slow Buffalo, "I don't want a new robe."

"You see? You see?" cried Standing Hollow Horn. "You don't even wait to hear my reasons." He began to wave his arms around. "Wolf's fur never gathers frost," he shouted. "I know what I'm talking about. The winter frost has made you cold, but you will never suffer the frost again. Never! I will see to it."

Slow Buffalo peered up at the Crier, wondering why the fellow was so loud and angry. For a moment he thought that perhaps the fever was distorting his sight and his hearing. "*Hehlokecha Najin*," he said, "come here."

Abruptly the Crier knelt down by the chief. Slow Buffalo reached up and touched the skinny old man on his cheek and found that there was water there.

"Ah, Standing Hollow Horn, look," he said. "You are leaking."

Well, the Crier looked as if he were suddenly choking. With a strangled sound he jumped up and ran out of the tipi, whence the chief heard a long thunder of coughing. Then back came the Crier into the tipi, never looking at Slow Buffalo. He faced straight away from him and shouted a little speech: "Yes, a wolf's pelt will make a difference in your life. It will warm you and heal you once for all, and I am the man to catch the wolf that will save you. Yes."

For the second time he ran out into the night. This time Slow Buffalo heard a great crash followed by some wonderful curse words: "*Wan! Wan!*" Standing Hollow Horn had found a good reason for his anger. "Moves Walking, *chan*, you wooden-head, lurking in the dark! What? What? Stop that! What kind of a man is it that cries?"

"*Waskn Mani?*" said Slow Buffalo. He raised his voice and struggled to sound steady: "Is that *Waskn Mani?* Is he here?"

Shyly the boy put his head in the tipi. "*Ohan.* Yes, he is here."

"Good," the old man said. "*Waskn Mani*, please bring your grandmother to see me. Tell her that I am hungry."

The boy had not been in the chief's tipi for three days. Now he gazed without moving, his eyes bright with sadness.

"*Waskn Mani*, do you hear me?" Slow Buffalo whispered. He was losing strength. "Say to her, 'Your dear friend *Tatanka Hunkeshne* is hungry.' Go. Go."

The boy of huge black eyes nodded. It looked as if he wanted to say something but nothing came out and he vanished.

Outside the Crier began to shout again: "And then come right back so I can teach you how to make a wolf trap. Run!"

The boy at thirteen had become dark and lean and long. He had long nimble fingers, hair so long it fell to his waist, long watchful silences, forever a solemn expression on his face, eyes deeper than midnight. *Tatanka Hunkeshne* loved him—even as his grandmother loved him. But both also worried for him. Even those who loved him did not understand him.

He was of age, yet he did not fight. He did not hunt. As far as anyone knew he had neither counted coup on an enemy nor killed a single animal.

On the other hand, he stitched. Like a woman he scraped skins, tanned them, cut them and sewed them together. Like a woman he flattened porcupine quills between his front teeth. His work was patient, his clothing supple—and the beauty of his quillwork could make a warrior mute. *Waskn Mani* mixed a blue dye from duck manure, one kind of yellow dye from bullberries and another kind from buffalo's gallstones. No one had ever created such brilliance of colors. And his designs were so fascinating and so puzzling that young men thought the meaning therein must be some sort of insult and they offered to beat his head with a club if ever they found out that the joke was against them.

But the boy, even while they threatened him, simply gazed back with a seeming sorrow.

People who never get mad make other people madder.

And people who pity that madness madden them all the more.

That's why both the old *itancan* and *Waskn Mani's* grandmother feared for the lad. His soulful ways would get him hurt, if not killed.

There was an evil spirit in the band these days. The young warriors genuinely believed they had the right both to make and to execute threats. Their bloody success in the last four years had given them all a bloody swagger.

War parties from this single band had spread such terror over the earth that the bare news of their coming now caused whole villages of the enemy Crow to throw down their weapons, abandon their tipis and run. Far beyond the traditional territories of the Lakota other people heard that a new nation was emerging on the plains, a powerful *tunwan*. A nation? Hi ho, they were only a band! Nevertheless they possessed a name which, when they uttered it, shot dead the hearts of their enemies. Whisper that name. Sign it with jagged slashes through the air. Say "Fire Thunder" and straightway prepare for victory.

Thus it was that warriors had begun to ask, "Why fight only the

Crow? Why should such a mighty band with such a hero spend itself in small amounts on war parties and pony raids?"

They began to dream a new dream, a rash exciting dream, one not ever considered by the people of the plains before—for as the buffalo knew no boundaries neither should those who hunt the buffalo.

Yet, why not?

If they *could* then *shouldn't* they test the extremes of human achievement? Honor and glory never came of timidity and power would sicken in the breasts of men who did not use it. Soon they would spit blood.

So, then: panting, sweating, rolling their eyes at their own outrageous boldness they began to speak of territorial aggression. Warfare to gain the entire plains. "Why not? Why shouldn't the land be ours?" During the long winter nights warriors discussed strategies. They said, "Let's take advantage of the *Oceti Shakowin*." They were referring to the spring gathering of all Lakota bands, the Seven Council Fires. "Why wouldn't every Lakota warrior pledge his arm to one name and one plan? All would benefit! And who could withstand us when we rose up altogether as one nation?"

The idea dazzled the young men in Slow Buffalo's band.

They got faraway looks in their eyes and murmured with reverence, "For this reason *Wakan Tanka* has made us strong. It is our destiny."

They discovered profound affections for one another, each one praising his brother's prowess, all loving to gather, to talk, to dream: "No, no, not just the Crow. Fight the Shonone too. And the Nez Perce. Ha ha!—why not the Flathead and the Blackfoot and the Cree across the north! Hi ho, then we will go south: Cheyenne! Arapaho! The Pawnee—"

Fire Thunder himself sat and said nothing. He watched everything with a quiet benignity, his one eye as close to kindness as any had ever seen it—and a thousand warriors broke into song, feeling very happy.

"Listen to me, *Waskn Mani*," his grandmother said. She was speaking very softly just outside the old *itancan's* tipi. She had stopped the boy with her hand upon his shoulder. So bent, so short was she that his shoulder required a reach. But *Waskn Mani* bent down for her sake and listened.

"Perhaps Slow Buffalo is more than merely sick," she said. "More than *wicakuje*. Do you understand?"

The boy said nothing.

She began a persistent patting on his arm, though it felt like a poking because her fingers were as crooked as bird's claws. "He may be *waniyetu opta aiyakpa omanipi:* one of those who walk through winter darkness. Do you understand? A darker winter in this winter."

Still, *Waskn Mani* kept his countenance bowed and solemn, answering nothing.

"And for what I am about to do," she said, "shame no one boy. Honor us no less than you do now. Respect us still. When we grow old we grow to be babies again."

So she entered the tipi and her grandson followed. He crouched by the doorway. She went directly to the side of her friend whose eyes were closed, whose breathing was faint.

She knelt down and lowered her wrinkled face to his forehead and she kissed him.

He opened his eyes.

He attempted a smile. He said, "Do you mind, old woman?"

"I don't mind," she said.

A shivering seized his limbs. He said, "I miss what was. I miss the old days and the small band and a good fast ride on my pony. And the taste of *wasna*."

"I know," she said.

"And I think I am beginning to miss you."

The tiny woman nodded but did not answer in words. She reached into a parfleche bag and pulled out a piece of *wasna*. She took a little bite. While she chewed it she lay down beside the big-bellied chief and drew blankets up over the two of them and in the secret of the blankets removed her clothing so that her body was touching his.

Then she turned to kiss him.

But the boy saw that this was more than just a kiss. It was also a gift. For while their lips were joined together the woman passed soft *wasna* into the mouth of her friend and he who had but two teeth chewed and smiled and chewed some more and swallowed.

In this manner he had a good meal.

"*Pila miya*, old woman. Thank you, thank you—"

And soon he slept and did not shiver.

# 17
# Wolf Trap

That winter during the Moon of Frost in the Tipi wolves crept near the village and stared a while.

Slow Buffalo's band had set camp in a deep and narrow gorge where the cold wind could not blow and a stream ran some water even in extremest weather. The sides of the gorge were a sheer sandstone, perhaps sixty feet straight up. Only the wingeds could find a foothold there. But at its south end rocks formed a natural ascent to the surface and the stream made a beautiful ice-waterfall. In sunlight the winter was dazzling. In storm the gorge was dark. An enclosed darkness can sometimes cause a people to feel fearful and fore-doomed, but that is the exchange one makes for protection.

Then a wolf pack came prowling the bluffs above the village, four or five wolves on the wind-swept stone peering down at their two-legged cousins. They made the people nervous. *Waskn Mani*, on the other hand, wondered whether they had come to learn something about surviving the winter.

The boy gazed up at the yellow-eyed wolves, as lean as he was in this hungry season, crouching at the edge of the cliff, their tails slowly switching the air, watching. When he saw that motion he thought how much like the Lakota were the wolves, for they hunted antelope by waving their tails above tall grass till the curious creatures came close enough to be attacked. The Lakota did the same thing, crouching in prairie grass and waving white skins.

*Waskn Mani* looked at the yellow-eyed and whispered, "We are relatives."

Well, wolves loved their families, yipping and kissing and glad to be home after a long trip. Wolves honored their elders, feeding them when they were old and sick. And when someone died they mourned. They sang to heaven, to the stars and the moon and the deep and the mysteries. They knew the Creator even as the red people did. Both gave reverence to *Wakan Tanka*. Both worshipped.

In the night when *Waskn Mani* watched over the sleep of his grandmother and his *itancan* in the tipi of Slow Buffalo, the wolves sang and the boy's heart swelled with thanksgiving to hear them. "Relatives."

He looked out of the tipi. He saw their heads cast back to the moon and their long mouths rounded and their eyes shut tight. Then he covered his own face because their music made him cry.

These wolves sang a supernal harmony. They howled the high notes, the near notes, the sweet and keening notes. They modulated pitch to pitch, sending the weird song higher and tighter and wilder till the boy thought he would break his breast on account of the beauty and the unspeakable sorrow. He wondered whether one of the wolves was dying. He was hearing the grief of the universe, a lamentation altogether ghostly.

But then the wolves broke into fiery barks of marvelous laughter. At first *Waskn Mani* was shocked by the change, but then he considered how sorrow and gladness live side by side even in the same soul whether wolfish or human. And that is why his heart swelled with thanksgiving that night, and that is why he whispered, "Relatives."

But others in the village hated the howling.

It was for them the voice of winter lasting too long, the cold and the darkness far too long.

It was the savage world laughing at a people weak within their tipis.

Some warriors mounted the rocks at the end of the gorge and ran to attack the wolves. The pack glanced once at these men then melted like shadows. Suddenly the warriors felt exposed and frightened. They hurried home to their fires again.

But Standing Hollow Horn was determined. Neither warmth nor sleep invited him and he seemed to feel nothing but fury. All night long he cursed the wolves and worked on his trap.

"*Wan! Wan!*"

He chopped a hole in the hard earth making the bottom perfectly flat and lining it all with the paunch of a buffalo. He filled the paunch with water.

Next he wrapped thick buffalo fat around a flint-knife leaving just the point of the knife stuck out. This greasy package he lowered into his hole allowing a little island of fat to rise above the surface of the water—and in the middle of that island the knife-point like a serpent's tongue appearing.

That night the water froze into a solid block of ice.

Standing Hollow Horn, grim and skinny man, was nearly done.

Early in the morning he saw Moves Walking slipping from the chief's tipi.

"Ha!" he sneered. "Did a child enjoy a warm night, then? But I remember telling you to come right back to me to learn about wolf traps! Wooden-head!" He gave the boy a knock on the top of his skull but the boy said nothing. His dark face was unreadable, both sad and deep.

So the Crier felt sorry. "Well!" he said. "Oh, well, come along and help me anyway."

They went to the hole where the buffalo paunch was stretched out around its ice-block and staked to the ground. Standing Hollow Horn pulled out the stakes and said, "Grab hold of the edges. We have to lift the block and carry it. Ready, pull!"

Each heaved up on the buffalo paunch. It came out of the hole, drawing up the block of ice in whose center was fat and a knife-point.

"Come, now. Come."

Silently the boy obeyed.

The man in front, the boy in back, they walked through the village with the ice between them like a boulder in a blanket. They bore their burden upstream to the southern end of the gorge and then they climbed the stones to the top of the canyon. The old man squinted westward, blowing clouds in the bitter cold. "Over there," he said and he led the boy a short way across the plain.

"Here." They set the ice on its flat bottom. "You see?" The Crier pointed at yellow drill-holes in the snow.

In fact, *Waskn Mani* was aware that Standing Hollow Horn was showing him wolf-urine. But he said nothing about it. Worse, he *thought* nothing about it. His mind was far, far away. And then in that particular instant the Crier—as if suddenly relieved of much more than the weight of the ice—took a great gulp of cold air and broke into a coughing fit so violent that he sank to his knees gasping for breath. Mechanically the boy began to slap the old man between his shoulder blades.

For the rest of his life *Waskn Mani* wondered whether he might have been willfully ignorant. Was he deceiving himself by pretending not to know? Why hadn't he asked the Crier about his intentions? Why hadn't he interpreted the ice and the fat and the lethal knife-point waiting to strike?

But Standing Hollow Horn was so sure of himself and at the same time so seeming desperate, so anguished and pitiful that the boy kept suffering on the old man's account. He could never say such a thing out loud, of course, so he held his peace. He said nothing. He obeyed. His, too, must be the blame for treachery.

Together, then, the boy and the man set a murderous trap. And somehow the boy thought nothing of what he had done until he heard horror raise her voice in the darkness of the following night.

# 18

# "Beautiful Wolf, Don't Die"

That day a holy man entered Slow Buffalo's tipi, a *wichasha wakan*, a healer. He covered himself in bearskin, even his head and face so that one wondered how he could see anything, and then he began to dance and to sing. His power came from *Mato* the bear. This was a song she had taught him in a vision. He wore bear claws that clacked while he danced.

Only a few people remained in the tipi during this ceremony. *Waskn Mani* was among them and his grandmother too, of course, dear friend of the old *itancan*.

Slow Buffalo was sweating and shaking as if he were both hot and cold. Now he was groaning ceaselessly and it was hard to tell whether he was awake or sleeping. He spoke no words.

The singing grew louder and louder. The dancing shook the ground. By midafternoon a terrible pressure built inside the tipi like the heavy air before a storm. *Waskn Mani* crawled back to the wall and drew up his knees and trembled with genuine fear. This singing sounded like roaring in the mountains, like the roaring of an enormous bear.

And suddenly that's what was in the tipi with them: a bear full seven feet tall with teeth as long as knives, lips retracted, bellowing. *Waskn Mani* shrieked. No one noticed. The bear had dropped to four feet and was charging the chief. She drove her snout deep into the man's fat stomach and began to suck with wet ripping sounds. Slow Buffalo opened his eyes and his mouth very wide and seemed to be screaming but no words came out. Then the bear sat backward and all of a sudden it was the holy man again, wearing bearskin. He lifted the covering from his face and turned to the side and spat out a long green worm that curled into a tight coil. "There is the sickness," the holy man said.

Everyone felt much better.

The *itancan* sighed and fell asleep.

*Waskn Mani* got up and went outside. It was dark. He was surprised to find that the day had passed into midnight already. The village was silent, the fires low, the people sleeping, the air utterly still and cold, the moon making all the frosted tipis silver.

"*Pila miya, Mato,*" he whispered and he saw that his breath came out in a white feather. This moon was so bright that he laid down a shadow behind himself. "Thank you, Bear, for healing my grandmother's friend and mine."

Well, the pure clean coldness kept the boy outside a while. He walked the snow step by step very carefully, going nowhere, looking down to his moccasined feet: step, step, step.

He began to sing softly:

"*Mother, where are you? Ina, come home.*
*If I step on no twig, if I bother no stone*
*I will find you and save you and make you my own.*
*O mother, where are you? Dear Ina, come—*"

All at once he was hearing a savage snarling in the sky above him, gutteral, moist and deadly. A wolf!

Then came down a rain of angry barkings, many wolves, a pack of wolves—till one voice prevailed more menacing than all the others, a bloody insanity in that voice, a deep-throated growling, and the rest went yipping into the distance.

It took the boy but a moment to realize that he had heard a wolf–fight on the bluffs above. He glanced up and wondered what could divide such a good community. But then that fiercer wolf all by her-self began to lace her growling with giggles and manic moans, the sounds of an obscene feeding, and suddenly *Waskn Mani* recognized something much bloodier than fighting, and he knew of a certainty what was happening: someone was at the trap he had set! Someone was slashing herself to death and this was his fault!

He flew up the creek as fast as he could go. He scaled the stones at the end of the gorge screaming, "No! No!"

Oh, how could he have played so wicked a trick on his relative? How had he blinded himself to the horror of the knife-point?

He jumped out onto the flat plains and peered forward in moon-light and saw a pale wolf hunched at the ice-block, a huge wolf, her head slung low, licking the fat, shuddering all down her spine, her collar contracting with every swipe of the tongue. What? What? Each time she licked the fat she cut tongue-flesh! And what? She was bleeding but the blood was delicious and so she was gulping her own blood, drinking her life's–blood, letting the red run out. She was killing herself!

*Waskn Mani* rushed toward her, screaming, "Stop! Stop!"

She whirled, blood drooling from her jaw, and charged him, bark-ing. The fangs just grazed his forehead. Her snout was a foul erup-tion of flesh. The boy leaped sideways and immediately the wolf returned to the fat and the flint which was shredding her tongue.

For this is the trick of the trap, that a wolf will lick it for the fat but love it for the blood, craving the sweet blood, lapping the salt blood, draining herself until she dies. But since the ice has numbed her tongue she does not know her danger.

*Waskn Mani* rose to his feet, limber and light. He crept sunwise to a spot behind her, all the while gathering his long hair into his hands and twisting it into a rope. Ah, this wolf, mewing her pleasure, was so beautiful and so insane!

Now the boy began to run, long legs, long arms, the knotted hair held out before him. He sprang, he sailed through the air and landed bodily on her shoulders and yanked his hair between her jaws as if it were a bridle. He locked his legs beneath her belly screaming, "You cannot die! No, you will not die!"

She bucked and snapped and plunged forward but he did not let go. Guilt made this boy determined and very strong. He held her mouth half open with his twisted hair. He cried aloud that he was sorry for everything. He begged her to stop and lie down. She didn't. The wolf ran with astounding speed, madness in her yellow eye, greatness and endurance down her limbs. He shouted that she was beautiful, beautiful!—but she spanned the snows at a dead rate, crazy! Poor *Waskn Mani* bent low and laid his face against her neck.

"Beautiful wolf," he whispered, "please don't die."

Blood streaked her fur and spattered his cheek and she ran. She ran. She ran.

# 19
# Shunkmanitu Tanka

Before the dawn, before the wolf broke and collapsed, even while he was still clinging to her back in the bitter wind, *Waskn Mani* experienced a strange sensation, at first frightening but then consoling and kind. He felt suddenly as if he were riding *inside* the wolf. Not in her chest but in her spirit, as if he could see through her eyes.

And then her headlong dash made sense. She was escaping evil, an evil place, an evil thing.

And yes, she would stop in time. When she could go no farther.

She didn't think the stopping meant her death, but she couldn't be sure. Her living or dying seemed to be the boy's responsibility now. She didn't mind that. She felt entirely too tired to care for herself. Alone she would probably die. Alone she might even choose death. But she wasn't alone and she thought she liked this child—

Her name was *Shunkmanitu Tanka*. Yes.

Yes, and he could use it if he wished. And what was his name?

A good name. Who gave it to him?

Ah, yes, a virtuous woman. Yes, the wolf knew something about this woman. Yes.

But for now, goodnight. Goodnight.

So dreamy did *Waskn Mani* become in this sensation of deep knowing that he lost all feeling of cold and speed and it is very likely he fell asleep on the wolf's back while she was still running.

He couldn't remember the end of the journey.

He woke up in sunlight, lying beneath a great rock and encircled by the belly of the wolf, who was making a wretched sound in her throat with every breath but who was sleeping.

Now the boy did for her what others had done for him. He found a dried winter moss with which he wiped thick clots of blood from her muzzle and mouth. He washed her. Then he cut the dead flesh away from her tongue with the knife his *unchi* had given him four years ago. Long strings of skin, flaps and riven tissue, he cut it all away. He made the poor tongue bleed again a fresher blood from neater wounds and he washed it a second time. In the hidden pathways of little mice he found spiders' webs, an excellent medicine for cuts. He bound her with webs.

She woke. She gazed at him from a slant yellow eye but she didn't move. She was thirsty.

So *Waskn Mani* gathered snow and put handfuls in his own mouth. As it melted he cradled the wolf's head in his lap and bent down and put his lips to her lips and spurted water to the back of her throat. She watched him while she swallowed. She was hungry.

So he went out in the brilliant weather and looked for berries beneath the snow. Frozen crabapples of vinegar flavor. The tops of wild turnips in hard ground. Back beside her again he chewed these to a soft mash and kissed her and fed her thereby.

Suddenly the boy jumped backward, remembering.

"Your name is *Shunkmanitu Tanka!*" he declared.

Yes. Yes, it was.

He split his face with grinning. "I *knew* that," he said. "Yes and I think we are friends, aren't we?"

Yes. Each a *kola* to the other: a friend.

"*Hau!*" said the boy, his black eyes flashing, raising his right hand. "Hello, friend!"

With her yellow eyes, her broad and beautiful forehead, her ears erect, *Shunkmanitu Tanka* said, Hello.

So the boy felt glad. And so several days passed in that gladness and in healing.

But the wolf didn't like to eat a fruit mash. She wanted some meat. Therefore *Waskn Mani* made a spear from an aspen branch by sharpening the end in fire and then went fishing. With rocks he broke through the ice on a small lake and with the spear he stabbed the slower fish. This too he chewed for the wounded wolf. They ate it raw.

But then she grew tired of the fish, which was not her regular diet. Would the lad go forth and hunt? Could he bring her liver? A little kidney perhaps? Best of all, some muscle meat still warm and bloody?

Poor *Waskn Mani!* All at once his gladness passed. He sat in their den beneath the overhanging rock and didn't move.

The wolf said he need not hunt anything large. Let it be small, she said. A rabbit. A rabbit would do.

The lad lowered his face. His long hair hid him as though behind a veil. He whispered, "I can't."

Can't what?

"I can't kill another rabbit."

What is the matter with rabbits?

"It's not the rabbits," said the boy. "It's me."

Ah, then what is the matter with you?

"Oh, *Shunkmanitu Tanka!* I sinned by setting a trap for you. You felt that sin in your suffering. But what you don't know is that I sinned before by killing four rabbits, relatives of mine! I shot them with arrows. The fourth rabbit I shot through the throat and the blood came out her mouth and when she tried to clean herself she smeared blood everywhere and then she died."

This is the reason the boy cannot hunt rabbits?

"Yes. And nothing else forever."

Ah. So gentle a spirit. How old was the boy?

"Nine years old. It was four years ago, *Shunkmanitu Tanka.*"

Well, then. The boy has felt sorry for his sin a long time. And now he has confessed it. This is important since only the unconfessed and unforgiven sin destroys things, *Waskn Mani.*

The boy raised his face and divided his hair in order to look at the wolf. She was gazing at him as solemnly as he. She was not belittling him. In her eyes was honor and a sober respect and she seemed to be wise.

So he said, "What if a sin is not confessed? What if it is not forgiven? What then?"

The wolf, fixing him still with her steadfast eye, said: When the sin is great it breaks the circle of the world and when that hoop is broken then everything suffers. Everything.

The word she used for "circle" was *hocoka,* the same one by which Lakota refer to the circle of tipis in a village. Were villages and the world the same too? Could this be?

The boy said, "What do you mean, 'The circle of the world'?"

*Waskn Mani,* every creature is appointed to serve another. That's the *hocoka,* the sacred hoop. If someone for selfishness ceases to serve, the circle breaks and creatures go hungry. The more who hunger, the fewer there are to serve until everyone suffers. When everyone suffers the world itself may die. That's what happens when a sin is not forgiven.

Listen: Once upon a time our ancestor, the White Wolf, swallowed the sun. He had been a mighty fighter, a glorious hunter by whom the whole people of wolves were satisfied. But he grew proud in his greatness and decided he needed the sun for himself alone. This would constitute his most spectacular deed. Moreover, since heat and light would belong to him he alone would cause summer. None but he could grow green things or receive worship from all the peoples.

So that is what he did. The White Wolf leaped higher than heaven and swallowed the sun. Then the whole world suffered dark and cold and misery. Winter. The circle was broken. Every creature went hungry and none could serve another. That was the black road, *Waskn Mani*, where everyone is for himself with little rules of his own. Do you think this is the same as shooting a rabbit in the neck?

The boy whispered, "What happened next, *Shunkmanitu Tanka?*"

That which must always happen after such a sin. Somebody died.

*Waskn Mani* gaped. "Who died?" he whispered. "How?"

Well, if the hoop is not repaired everyone dies. This is the end of the world. But the hoop may be repaired if someone will give his life for the sin. The one who committed the sin may die unwillingly and that is punishment. Or another may choose willingly to give his life so that all the people might live. That is sacrifice.

The boy with wide black eyes repeated, "Who died, *Shunkmanitu Tanka?* How?"

The wolf crossed her forepaws on the ground and paused. She laid her long chin upon the joint of the upper paw.

Punishment, *Waskn Mani*, she said softly. The great warrior, the greater hunter, our ancestor, died. It was in the nature of his sin, for the sun burned through his back and cast his corpse to the earth where it is lying even to this day. The White Wolf is the frozen snows of the north. Nothing grows from his old flesh. He is a dazzling deadness. *Waskn Mani*, do you think this is the same as shooting rabbits?

The boy whispered earnestly, "I don't know."

Now she raised her great head. Her neck was strong, her throat collared in deep grey fur. Her eye flashed and she answered for the boy: No, it is not! No!—because you are sorry and because you have confessed and because I have forgiven you. No, *Waskn Mani*, your sin is different from the White Wolf's sin.

Suddenly the wolf stood up in the den, filling the space with her stature. The boy remained sitting. She whose tongue he had healed looked down upon him. She nuzzled the back of his neck then pushed the moist tip of her nose beneath his hair and touched the scar of his left ear and licked it. She licked it with a healed and merciful tongue. And then she said:

*Waskn Mani*, boy of the smoking eyes and the innocent face and cuts as bad as mine, I am hungry for meat. Let's go hunting.

"Hunting!" he wailed. "*Shunkmanitu Tanka*, hunting? To kill? Isn't this what we've been talking about? Won't killing break the circle?"

But the wolf was already outside rolling in snow, driving her snout through the cool snow, kicking the crystal snow so that it exploded and twinkled in sunlight.

Watch me! Watch me, *Waskn Mani!* Taking will break the circle but giving will strengthen it. Giving is serving. Watch me and learn that the sacred hunter asks for the life of her prey—

# 20

# The Conversation of Death*

The boy on the back of a wolf bent his knees to keep his feet from dragging snow. He gripped her fur at the withers. He felt a persistent tireless power all down her spine. He marveled that she should carry his weight as lightly as if he were but a cloud at her shoulder. They flew. She ran with an easy flap of her front paws and they flew.

*Waskn Mani* felt a fierce excitement. Her hunter's tension had entered him. Her quick scanning of the landscape—the left-right motion of her head—caused him likewise to catch the natural details around him and to read them for meaning. His heart hammered because of the hunting, yet his face was flaming. Well, and he also felt ashamed because he was hunting and he liked it.

The poor boy, a bracing wind in his face, the snow so brilliantly white even to the horizon, the speed that stung his heart with joy, the

---

*This phrase and its concept are taken, with gratitude, from Berry Lopez's *Of Wolves and Men*, Scribners, 1978

hunt so sweet and so horrible since killing came at the end of it: he
panted for a hundred reasons. His emotions whirled in confusion.
He wanted to cry *Stop!* He wanted the wolf to run faster. He didn't
know what he wanted.

Suddenly a black-beaked raven sailed low above them chatting in
twenty different voices, a talky bird, a gossipy sort. But this fellow
could see the land from above, so he and the wolf made an exchange.
The raven spoke of buffalo, the wolf of an *otuhan,* a give-away at the
end of the hunt, and both were satisfied. They parted.

*Shunkmanitu Tanka* now drove to the northwest with purpose.
Her mood changed, less merry, more severe. The very thump of her
heart came hard and declarative through her ribs to the boy's knees.
She was earnest now and he discovered that he himself was frowning. His long hair blew behind them like a cape.

Just at the top of a long rise the wolf slowed then stopped and
crouched. The boy slid off. He lay on his belly beside her and together they peered over the ridge.

There was a line of trees ahead of them, straight aspen and the
muscled cottonwood, darker bushes of the chokecherry, all leafless in
winter. This wood marked the path of a frozen creek. It gave no
cover.

Coming slowly down the creek were four buffalo, single-file. In
front, *Tatanka*, the bull, nodding his head hugely up and down. Then
two yearlings and the buffalo cow, *Pte*. Every five or seven steps the
bull would slam his snout against the creek-ice with such force that
he had bloodied the flesh. *Waskn Mani* gasped each time the bull
struck ice. His own nose ached.

The wolf said, Ponies and deer strike down with their hooves but
*Tatanka* uses his nose. The winters are hard on him and his family.

And she said:

Now watch! Pay attention, *Waskn Mani!* Learn this difference,
that murder takes a life but hunting receives that life as a gift and so
the circle is made stronger. Be silent. Stay here. *Wachin ksapa yo!*

She vanished over the ridge.

Almost immediately she reappeared below facing the buffalos on an angle ahead of them. She snapped into a rigid posture, her nose low, her ears laid back, her slant eye staring, her shoulders announcing the violence to come. *Shunkmanitu Tanka* was transfigured. Fangs sliding from a lifted lip, her tail in slow switch, she was a patient treachery and *Waskn Mani*, who knew her, felt the panic.

So did the buffalos. But the bull gave her one quick glance then turned and trotted up the far side of the creek. At a distance he bellowed for the yearlings. They stamped nervously between the bull and the cow. She, when she had seen the wolf, stopped and stared but did not run, did not move.

A second time with thunderous conviction the bull called the children and they obeyed. They sent their mother frightened backward looks but they scrambled after their father and then those three ran away.

The women alone were left, one as taut as a bowstring, the other brutal and shambling, but both alike in that they held still and stared at one another.

The buffalo cow made a deep sound: *Hunka.*

The wolf said, You see, *Pte*, that I am here.

I see, *Shunkmanitu Tanka*, she said. I felt your coming.

They did not speak for a moment. The whole snowy plains fell silent. No one moved. No one spoke. *Waskn Mani* did not breathe, for each woman stood in spare reverence not only for the other but also for the event at hand, life and death and life again in a valiant exchange. This, visible, was the circle of the world. This was hunting, *lela wakan*, very holy. With a steadfast gaze the wolf was asking for the life of her prey.

And the great cow did not doubt that she had the choice, or where was the gift otherwise? A noble creature requested her life and she was accounted worthy thereby, for her will and her wish were honored.

The buffalo cow said, *Shunkmanitu Tanka*, did you see my sons?

The wolf said, Yes.

Did you take their measure?

Yes, *Pte*.

And haven't I done well in my sons? Aren't they well bred to your eye and well raised?

Yes, said the wolf. They shall bring glory to their mother as long as they live and they shall raise their own children with her spirit.

Yes. Yes. Their lives shall surely honor me. My love is in them. *Hetchetu welo*, it is good. Yes. Yes—

Thus did the cow herself conclude the conversation of death.

And suddenly the language of hunting became motion alone, the rush of bodies and the skill.

*Shunkmanitu Tanka* bolted. The bowstring snapped. The wolf shot forth like an arrow over snow. She ran by a contraction of her stomach muscles, the flinging of her forelegs and the thrust from behind. She took wind in her jowls which bowled open.

But *Pte* did not stand still and wait.

The buffalo wheeled immediately up the creek and galloped for fields of snow, kicking a blizzard behind her. She kept her head low, ripping wind with her horns, driving her hind hooves high, weapons with which to strike a wolf. Her life was strong and courageous and lovely and worth the asking!

*Pte* bore left, never breaking stride. *Shunkmanitu Tanka* described a wide circle around her right side then dashed in and leaped straight for the buffalo's hams. She slashed them with her fangs then fell behind. The cow raised her head and bellowed. She was raining blood in the snow. Again and again the wolf drew alongside and tore her flanks, tooth and claw. So the rolling red muscle was laid bare. Yet she ran. The buffalo kept exploding the snow, making the deep snow a stumbling trouble for the wolf.

*Waskn Mani* was pressing both hands to his chest as if his heart might jump out. He did not blink his eyes. This panorama before him, the glory of both women, fixed his attention and his mind and his holy knowing forever.

Now the wolf raced far ahead of the buffalo, a sort of lonely romp. But then she whirled around and charged straight back. *Pte* could not turn in time. The wolf sprang at the buffalo's face and locked her jaws on the muzzle, crushing bone. She did not let go. The buffalo raised up her mighty head, flinging the wolf bodily into the air, but she did not let go. The buffalo planted her forehooves and whipped the wolf left and right like a rag. She cracked the wolf's length flat to the ground—but the wolf did not let go. This was the death grip. The buffalo tried charging forward, dragging *Shunkmanitu Tanka* under her low chest.

But then she stumbled and somersaulted into the snow and rolled to her side. The hunter's grip had closed off her wind. She was suffocating and bleeding and dying. Only when spasms began to seize her limbs did the wolf release her snout.

But immediately *Shunkmanitu Tanka* buried her teeth in *Pte's* belly. With her entire body the wolf yanked backward, backward till the flesh tore and the abdomen burst open.

The buffalo cow murmured, *Huh! Huh!* She knew. She was not ignorant even in the instant of her death. Softly she said, *Huh!* And then she died.

The hunt was over.

*Shunkmanitu Tanka* was very tired. She lay down to rest.

*Waskn Mani* too was tired but he could not take his eyes from the scene, the huge buffalo who had left such a long trail of blood in broken snow, the cunning weapon of a wolf, his friend, who lay beside her kill in quiet repose as if nothing splendid had just happened.

After she bestirred herself and ate and was satisfied by the meat, the wolf sat back on her haunches and sang to the sky. She sang the praise of *Pte* who had given herself with such glory away. Then she sang an invitation, first to the raven and then to others. Come! Come! It was a good hunt, she sang, and here is an excellent life to share with people of the plains. Come!

Thus she called wolverines and buzzards and magpies, coyotes, and even the tiny vole who loves the crop in a buffalo's stomach. This was the *otuhan*, the give-away.

The wolf sang, All come home now! It is more than I can eat!

Even so are wolves and the red, two-legged people alike.

Finally *Shunkmanitu Tanka* brought the liver to the boy. When he was finished eating she said, It is time for you to go home now.

And so they went eastward together.

*Waskn Mani* said, "But didn't the buffalo fight not to die? *Shunkmanitu Tanka*, how can that be a gift?"

The wolf said, No. She did not fight the dying. She fought me. And she fought very well, the measure of a worthy life. No, *Waskn Mani*, it is not the hunt which is sinful but the manner of hunting. Ask the hunted. Ask her. Ask her by name and obey the answer. So the circle is whole and holy. Just so.

They walked side by side into the night. The boy let his hand fall upon the wolf's neck and he patted her. They traveled a long while in silence.

Suddenly the boy went down on his knees in front of the wolf and seized the hair of her cheeks. He had just remembered something important. "You knew my mother!" he cried.

*Shunkmanitu Tanka* paused and sat down, her face dead-level with the boy's.

Yes, she said.

"You called her a virtuous woman and you said you knew about her, right?"

Yes. That is right.

"O *Shunkmanitu Tanka*, please tell me, please tell me about *mihun*, my mother, please!"

So the wolf sang a long sad song in the moonlight on pale snow. She told a story which made the boy bow down and weep. Then she consoled him by licking and whispering, *Kola*: friend.

He embraced her neck. He buried his face in the fur. So they were friends in gladness and in sorrow now and forever.

It was just dawn when *Waskn Mani* descended the rocks toward the village in the gorge.

He saw a man standing by the frozen stream, someone who wore no clothing in the cold morning, only a loincloth. He was alone.

Ah, see, it was Standing Hollow Horn, the skinny old Crier.

But as the boy drew near to greet him, he saw straight lines of blood running down the arms and back of the old man, and also down his chest. Standing Hollow Horn had gouged bits of flesh from himself and every gouge was bleeding.

So *Waskn Mani* started to cry. "Hownh! Hownh!" he wept. He could not help himself

Without a word of explanation, by the Crier's mutilation alone, he understood that Slow Buffalo, the only *itancan* he had ever known, was dead.

# 21
# Kola: Friend

In the Moon of the Dark Red Calf (February) Slow Buffalo died and the people of his band, the old ones especially, mourned.

Some of the women cut their hair. Some people on account of their grief slashed their arms with knives. Others gave bits of their skin in sacrifice for *Tatanka Hunkeshne*, offering sorrow on his behalf and suffering the bleakness with him. The blood ran in thin lines down from the cuts of their sacrifice.

Elders of the village directed that his favorite pony should be killed because they said he had a long journey to go over the *wanagi tacanku*, the ghost road south, and it would be better to ride than to walk. The ghost chief must have a ghost pony.

Somebody cut a piece of the old man's white braid in order to save it in a sacred bundle and then they wrapped his body in a buffalo robe. Not a new robe. This one had bald spots at the shoulders. It had no ruff. But it fit him at every joint and curve. The robe and the man had loved each other a long time.

They carried the *itancan* up from the gorge to the snow-plains, to the cold and the wind and the white sky. People were weeping as they went.

Here was a scaffold built on four long poles above the ground. It looked like a skeleton on four legs.

The young men who carried Slow Buffalo over the fields of snow now raised him as high as their shoulders and placed him on this scaffold. Some people were sniffing but then one man began to sob so uncontrollably that he pulled his robe over his head and went away. This was the Crier of the village.

They tied Slow Buffalo's personal bundle to a leg of the scaffold. They left a small parfleche of food on the snow below, a sincere gift, nourishment for his journey. It was *wasna*.

In a little while the people began to depart with their heads bowed down, holding their robes at the throat because of the bitterly cold wind.

So then there was no one left by the burial scaffold except one old woman whose face was deepened by a thousand wrinkles.

She stood absolutely still at one corner of the scaffold, herself bent down by wind and sorrow, by age and by bad feet.

The winter sky was low, unbroken, a smooth grey roof that stretched to the round edges of the earth, bitter and bleak and cold and grey. Likewise the snow lay flat and grey even unto the horizon. Between the cloud above and the snow below there stood these darker figures, a man and a woman, she on her feet, he on his back on a scaffold high in the wind.

And snow was whitening the side of his buffalo robe where his stomach mounted up. It had begun to snow.

And this too: the snow caught on the eyebrows and in the cracks of the old woman's face. It melted into droplets.

When she spoke her breath came out white and the wind pulled it away. She said, "*Tatanka Hunkeshne*, how do I face the rest of my years without you? Did you mention this before you left?"

She looked up and noticed that the top of his head was uncovered. There a feather was shivering in the wind. She lifted her hand and opened the robe at his face and touched his cheek with her knobby knuckles. "You don't mind the cold any more, do you?" she said. "You are yourself the cold and the wind now and soon you will go soaring in an eagle's belly. Well, well, God have mercy on you, old friend. But I am here and I am cold and my poor feet are hurting. Huh! Huh!"

Suddenly she buried her face in her hands and her shoulders shook. Then her voice came out in a small squeak. "O *Tatanka Hunkeshne*, who remembers that we used to laugh together, you and I? Who can believe that our bodies were young once and loved to run, and I was straight and swift and you were handsome with all of your teeth? Who knows this now? *Kola! Kola!* Friend to me through all my ages, no one remembers but me. We cannot sit down and remember together any more. And all of our people have passed. How shall I remember alone? Huh! Huh! How shall I face my years without you?"

She made a fist of her right hand. Even in the blowing snow she began to pound him on his forehead, tiny hopeless hammerings. "When Black Elk died you sat with me. But now it is you who are dead. So who will sit with me now?"

That feather vibrated in the wind, making a sort of moaning sound. The woman glanced up. "*Tatanka Hunkeshne*, forgive me," she cried with a sudden shame. "I don't hate you. I am only just a little upset." She opened her hand and stroked his face. "You have such a wonderful nose, old friend. The most handsome nose I have ever known." Now she pulled the robe back over his face and tucked the feather in, covering even the top of his head, the thin grey hairs.

"Please don't mind if I go away now. It is almost night. I have to find my grandson. And my feet hurt. I will sing a song for you tonight. I promise—your own brave song, some courage for the journey, huh! Huh! Huh!"

So the small woman turned and trudged the snow back home. She was the only figure upon the plains, tiny and bent and lonely and dark in the dusk. Because of the wind she held her robe tight at the throat.

◦ ◦ ◦

That night in the middle of eating *Waskn Mani's* grandmother suddenly began to talk. She had entered the tipi in silence. She had heated the cooking stones and boiled water and made a soup all in silence. But then—just when her spoon was halfway to her mouth— she looked at her grandson and started to talk.

"Hi ho! The cheekbones of your beautiful mother," she said. "Boy, you are becoming very handsome. How old are you? Thirteen? My, my, my. Time is racing away from us. But you! You! Look how tall and strong you are! Things are changing. Everything is changing, *Waskn Mani*. See?—you are almost a man now. Do you remember when we used to watch the swallows together? Huh! Huh! We call that fork- tailed bird *upijata*. But I am not thinking of his tail right now. I call him *pshica*, the jumping bird—huh! Huh! I call him the jumping bird because I am thinking of *icapshipshi*, how a whole flock of birds will suddenly scatter when something comes to frighten them. Change! Change, *Waskn Mani*, change! That's what I am thinking about. Huh, huh! Do you mind that I am talking so much? I can't help it. And I said I would sing a song tonight for Slow Buffalo, but I can't. I can't. Do you mind if I put this spoon down now? I'm not using it any more. I'm not very hungry. I don't know why I held it so long. Oh, *Waskn Mani*, I am so sad, I am so sad. Do you mind if I cry for a while?"

# 22

# Transfiguration

Fire Thunder was furious, mute and furious.

Betrayed by his own voice! Only when the emotions caught him by surprise did his voice slip into that high hateful baby-whine. Fire Thunder could speak as well as any man when he was in control, but the nearness of Rattling Hail Woman, young and tough and plainly happy—the nearness unmanned him. Her beauty, especially her woman–scent beneath his blanket, stunned the man in his heart and so it was the baby that spoke. He squeaked. He had made his name sound like the cry of a meadowlark.

The man melted in humiliation.

But then, when one by one the people of that entire village began to laugh, humiliation hardened into fury.

Fire Thunder strode to the edge of the encampment, dropped his blanket, grabbed a bridle and weapons and a nearby pony and rode away to the west.

Without a conscious thought he tied his braids behind him. The gesture itself decided his purpose: he was going to war. Alone. Rage empowered him.

He galloped through the night to the closest Crow encampment and just at dawn, in exquisite silence with an economy of motion, he murdered the guard and slipped away with seven ponies.

But the fury in his belly was burning still.

He rode the next day to another Crow village. He did not speak. He scarcely thought. He acted. He fought. He hunted. He lived outside himself at the rim of his flesh. Rage whetted all his senses and taught him a canny attitude, that if he banked the anger it would become an exhaustless source of strength. Like fate. So the warrior learned confidence and silence at once. He did not *need* to speak. Silence imparted power.

So, then: Fire Thunder, his manner and his method.

He hit the enemy villages always before the dawn, swift and restrained and raging. He felt pleasure in his veins at every raid. His bone and muscle were, he discovered, a beautiful machinery. Guards died without protest and he took at least six ponies with every raid.

This was the start of the stories of Fire Thunder. Even before he returned to Slow Buffalo's band the Crow knew his *wochangi*, his power and influence, for he extended his raid through several months without being seen by any living man. Therefore they spread the word of a ghost warrior who took ponies in perfect silence. Swift afoot, swifter with arrows, more quiet than the owl, he descended and killed and departed as though he were someone's nervous dream in the night.

And he liked the danger. It was the same as food for him.

But then he entered a Crow village that had prepared for his coming and in this place suffered such mortification that he was never the same thereafter. Until now the man had displayed superior skill, the best of warriors, but when he left the village of a Crow warrior named Cold Wind, Fire Thunder was another sort of being altogether.

Cold Wind, chief of the dog-soldiers, had surrounded the pony corral with a fence of dried brush and then had commanded twenty dog-soldiers to hide on the side of a hill. There they lay all night long, their arrows bundled in grasses and pitch, ready to burn.

Fire Thunder crept to that corral as secretly as to any other and melted through the brush fence in perfect silence. In fact, no one either heard or saw his arrival, not even the marksmen on the hillside, but dogs had been lashed to the legs of the ponies and when the ponies started to stamp the dogs started to bark.

Immediately Cold Wind's men lighted their arrows and shot at the brush around the corral. A bright circle of fire rose up in the night and the single Lakota was caught shadowless in the center, crouched among the ponies.

The glare blinded Fire Thunder. He stared into blackness, blinking like a fool. Worse, the sudden realization that people had been aware of him before he was aware of them embarrassed this warrior and made him feel naked. Someone else was in charge, not Fire Thunder! In that instant he lost confidence. He couldn't make his body work. He could not shoot back. And there went up into the night a strange bleating sound: *Eeeeeeee!* Fire Thunder felt panic. He willed himself still. He would not move in panic. He feared the effect. He was a pitiful poor beast in the center of a wild fire, helpless!

The Crow warriors had every right to believe in their advantage. Cold Wind leaped up and whooped and led them down the hill and around the corral, a solid surround. The Lakota was in light. They were in darkness. But they didn't wish to wound their own ponies so they laid low and waited for their ghost–enemy to attempt his escape—maybe by flying over fire? They would kill him when he did.

But he didn't. He did nothing. Ponies were stamping all around him, terrified by the flames, and the dogs were baying and biting at the ropes that bound them, but that warrior stood fixed as if charmed or else unspeakably brave, his arms spread wide, his eyes reflecting fire.

What kind of a plan was this? What kind of magic? Well, it is better to take the initiative, especially on home ground. Cold Wind signaled for a charge, all the dog-soldiers at once.

Fire Thunder for his part was trying to figure out what was making that weird bleating sound, *Eeeeeee*, in the midst of the animals. It seemed that the one-note song might hold some secret. If he could find its source he would learn something strong.

But then the Crow were charging him. From four directions they poured over the burning fence of the corral, yelling and shooting. Fire Thunder heard the buzzing of a hundred arrows.

One arrow hit his left eye, pierced it and stuck there.

Fire Thunder actually saw the warrior that had shot it, a grim young man with the black sun tattooed upon his forehead.

And suddenly he knew who was making that weird high sound and he shivered with horror because it was himself. He, Fire Thunder, had been screaming through his nose like an infant. *Hokshi cala!* Oh, a cold heat took his heart in that moment, the white rage of humiliation, and he began straightway to perform prodigious feats, astounding the Crow warriors who were attacking him.

He grabbed the shaft of the arrow that stuck from his left eye. With a tremendous yank he pulled it out. But he tore out the eyeball too. It popped from the socket still stuck on the barb of the flint like a bloody plum.

For Fire Thunder the entire world slowed down now. Sound died. His sight went red. The gorge rose in his throat and his flesh went slack with loathing.

He felt no pain. He felt instead a mortal shame. Fire Thunder had seen his sight go away on the point of an enemy's arrow, the eye ripped from his head, and he saw himself thereby disfigured. Monstrous and dishonored. *Eeeeeeeeee—*

Oh, that ridiculous squeal, the brat inside of him!

So then it was that a pure, luminous hatred burst and ran through this man's veins like a white blood, hatred so cold and sweet it felt like delight. In his face it became a mechanical calm and he ceased screaming. In his heart it was a wrath so magnificent that his spirit seemed to leave his body and look down from a high place.

And this is what his spirit said: *No one shall live to bear witness. No one.*

And this is what the Lakota did:

He murdered the first Crow to fly at him. He seized that warrior by his long hair and snapped back his head and thrust the arrow with its bloody eyeball into his mouth, through his throat and out the back of his neck, killing him.

One arrow had taken his left eye. That same arrow killed a Crow.

Other warriors hesitated in astonishment. The man with the black sun on his forehead stood motionless among the wild ponies, admiring the brave thing he had just seen. Fire Thunder seized the advantage and began to shoot arrows with silent insanity, one and one and one, utterly fearless, perfectly accurate, an efficient killer bleeding from his empty eyesocket down his cheek so that the blood laced his left arm, a cold man killing his enemy, turning round and round in a radius of deadly arrow points and killing his enemy dead.

He thought to save the tattoo of the black sun as his final target. It would be a signal that he knew, he knew—this warrior knew exactly who had stolen his sight. But when he looked again for the black tattoo the man was gone. So: the whole herd of ponies was bucking and kicking with such terror that their sharp hooves had stamped the dogs to death. So then: they must have accomplished Fire Thunder's vengeance for him, slaughtering his first attacker.

So he cut one pony free and leaped astride its back and whipped it to his control and cleared the fence of fire and charged the rest of the warriors who were running from his fury. Those he didn't shoot he attacked by hand until it seemed to him he had rubbed out the entire band. He was scarcely breathing hard. He was peaceful. He cut the throat of one last victim and tied that body by a long rope to his pony and galloped into the fire that surrounded the corral, dragging the corpse straight through the middle of the blaze, scattering sparks and bright coals and ash into the night, setting the Crow ponies free and then, without a pause for rest, driving them homeward.

Thus Fire Thunder came home with an unusual prize, a bloody

herd of Crow ponies, bloody because they came dragging behind them the horrible corpses of dogs and warriors disfigured beyond recognition.

And thus he returned transfigured.

Mute and mysterious, from that day forward he puzzled the people he moved among. Lightning, yes, bright lightning—but a silent thunder.

He told no stories regarding himself. He sang no songs. The Crow spoke long about a certain *wakinyan* who had attacked them, slaughtering people even while singing sweetly like a girl: a beautiful voice, they said, a bloody eye and a prairie of dying around him. A circle of death. But Fire Thunder neither accepted nor disputed the word that followed him home. He set his mouth in a straight line and said nothing and people began to call his jaw *inyan*, stone.

Over his left eye he wore an otterskin headband ever thereafter, like a slash across his face. He never removed it.

Never again did people see the whole of this warrior–hunter: a piece was concealed forever. The right eye, the only eye, had become a black ice. Obsidian. So people of several nations wondered, "What laws does he honor? What rules does this warrior obey?"

From that time forth Fire Thunder was indefatigable. Against an enemy he could ride four ponies to death, always leaping to a fresh mount when the last one expired. He could decapitate a man with a single blow. He would shoot arrows with such speed there were always three in the air: one and one and one. Or he would suddenly stop in the middle of battle and turn his back and walk away, arrows tearing the air at his ears, his face a mask of perfect serenity.

What prayers does this one pray? What visions has he seen to be given such powers and such protection?

*Ah, Fire Thunder, who are you now?*

He became an enigma among the people. Slow Buffalo's band saw it, as had the Crow before them. All the hunters on the plains began to see it. In time the whole world stood in awe of this one.

But why had he chosen to come back to Slow Buffalo's small band when there were others of more glorious reputation? Surely, any other *tiyoshpaye* would have been glad to receive him. Many said so, inviting him.

Moreover, why would a proud young man go back to the people that had scorned him with their laughter? Why return to those he had lived among but a few months?

Well, Rattling Hail Woman. Because of her.

Or so the story goes.

# 23

# Courting

They said, "She is not here," and then they were surprised to see the man was visibly distressed by their answer.

This brief exchange took place several months after Fire Thunder's spectacular return. He had without much noise given away most of the ponies stolen from the Crow, making many people happy and binding their hearts to his thereby. People spoke highly of Fire Thunder. He was young. He must, according to his silences, be humble. He was a dreamer surely because he disappeared from the village for days at a time always alone.

And then one night he began to leave ponies tied up outside the tipi of Rattling Hail Woman's mother.

Well, the people didn't actually know whose ponies these were since they came in the darkness more quietly than the owl flies, one pony at a time, one new pony every night.

But of course Rattling Hail Woman wasn't home. And her mother didn't know what to do with the ponies. Out of compassion she fed and watered them. Otherwise they stayed tethered in front of the tipi increasing in number until they were fourteen.

Then on an early spring evening the people saw Fire Thunder standing by the small herd staring gloomily at the tipi.

Some women came and stood beside him. "*Hau*, Fire Thunder," they said.

For a while he said nothing. But then in a voice so soft it was barely audible he said, "How many ponies does it take?"

"Ponies?" they said. "Are these your ponies then?"

He whispered, "How many ponies is Rattling Hail Woman worth?"

"Oh," said the women. "Oh!"

The muscle in Fire Thunder's jaw began to work. His nostrils widened. Apparently it required some effort for the warrior to be speaking these things. He whispered, "How many ponies must I bring before she comes out and accepts them?"

"Poor *wichasha!*" the women murmured among themselves. "He doesn't know." And then they said directly to Fire Thunder, "Sir, we are sorry, but she is not here."

The young man gasped and they were surprised by the strength of his reaction. Slowly, with cold articulation, he asked, "Where is she?"

"Well," they said, "we don't know."

"Has she gone away . . . with . . . a husband?"

"Well, it isn't likely because we heard no such thing. No gifts were given. But we don't really know."

"Is she," he whispered glaring at the ground, "dead?"

"Fire Thunder," the women said with genuine sympathy, "we wish we could tell you something true. But we can't. Why don't you ask her mother these questions? Maybe she knows something."

The young warrior had a scared look in his eye, something they had never seen before nor ever would see again. Out of respect the women bowed their heads and left him alone. The whole camp was wet from a spring thunderstorm that afternoon. Fire Thunder waited a long time without moving. Then he lifted his gaze to the tipi and reached out and scratched the flap.

Rattling Hail Woman's mother looked outside, her face already beginning to wrinkle from hard work and the dry sun and disappointment. She saw the young man and came out and stood up slowly.

Fire Thunder nodded a greeting and whispered immediately, "Where is she?"

The woman searched his features with sharp eyes, the beaverskin headband which divided his skull in two, his great jaw and hard chin. The warrior did not repeat the question but neither could he match her stare. He lowered his eye.

Finally it seemed as if the woman made up her mind to speak. "You mean Rattling Hail Woman," she said. "Well, she is gone. Just as you were gone. For many months I thought she might have gone away with you. I was hoping with all my heart that she was somewhere with you. But then you came back and I saw that she was not. That makes me feel very sad because now I know that I do not know where she went."

The woman and the man stood side by side in silence.

Then in an odd flute-like voice the man said, "Mother, is she dead?"

Again the mother of Rattling Hail Woman took her time as if deciding whether to answer the question. At length she said, "One night I dreamed I heard her voice. She said to me, *The Spotted Eagle is coming to carry me away* and in my dream it seemed to mean that, yes, she was dying. When I woke up the next morning Rattling Hail Woman was gone and she never came back. Fire Thunder, I don't know. I don't know. Maybe she is dead. Maybe it was a foolish dream, a false and fearful dream. I don't know."

Without another word the young man turned and walked back to his own tipi. He went inside and there he sat with his back to the door for five days doing nothing. Thunderstorms passed, but the man paid no attention. He didn't close the smoke flaps of his tipi.

On the morning of the sixth day he roused himself and came out. He went to the tipi of Rattling Hail Woman's mother where he untied one of his fourteen ponies and pulled a bridle over its head.

Leading this pony behind him the tall warrior stalked through the entire village looking left and right with his single eye until he spied the small girl whom people called Red Day Woman. She was lying belly-flat in a puddle of mud, her legs bent back like a frog's, her chin propped on two palms, the middle fingers of her right hand stuck in her mouth, staring.

Fire Thunder bent down and touched the top of the child's head which was caked with old winter dirt. All at once he slipped his hands beneath her shoulders, picked her up and put her on his pony. She sat there saying nothing. As far as anyone knew, the fat slant-eyed child had never said anything.

Ever since she had appeared in Slow Buffalo's band the people had let her alone because they thought she might be *washtay*, good luck. It was well known that *Wakan Tanka* would sometimes put his spirit in certain children and send them to live among ordinary folk. For this reason a queer child was permitted to wander wherever she wished among the Lakota, to break the small rules, to sleep anywhere, to eat whatever she reached for. And the people would often pet her as they passed in order to receive a little luck. But they did not love her much because they could not understand her. Rather they were somewhat afraid of her.

Well, but Fire Thunder showed no fear of Red Day Woman. He put her on his pony and took her for a ride that day, leading the animal no faster than a rolling walk. Little girl, little girl, she wobbled and drooled and began to smile. She did not protest. The man himself wore no expression in his face. A straight grim mouth. He might have been going forth to hunt something.

At some distance from the village they came to a pond. Fire Thunder lifted the girl down and carried her into the water. While she kicked and splashed and laughed right heartily he bathed her. He washed her hair. Then he placed her on the bank facing the water and with the rough side of a buffalo's tongue he brushed her thin hair straight and smooth.

Red Day Woman sat in the grass like a chief's daughter. She gazed demurely down into her lap. She seemed to be listening to soft words. Fire Thunder was kneeling behind her now, first cutting her hair to an even length and then braiding it. Very thin hair. Her braids looked like mouse tails. Finally the giant dipped his finger in an ochre dye and painted the part down the middle of her head a pretty red color.

Gravely, then, he came around to the front of the child and sat cross-legged, peering at her with one eye. She grinned back, her own eyes tightening down as sharp as two darts aiming for the flat of her nose. Her tongue came out when she smiled. The man did not smile. His jaw was *inyan*. Stone. The muscle pulsing.

In a little while he stood up and walked to an old cottonwood tree. He peeled away a large section of the outer bark and with the edge of his knife scraped the white woody surface beneath. Soon a foam came out of the wood—new sap, the rising sweet sap—which he caught on his knife and carried to Red Day Woman. She ate the food with giggles and glee, thrusting her tongue out both to eat and to laugh.

When she was full she poked the two middle fingers of her right hand into her mouth and lay down by the pond and immediately went to sleep.

Fire Thunder sat beside her till nightfall.

His pony cropped grass.


Suddenly Rattling Hail Woman was home again. No, she had not died after all. Nor did she return in the company of a husband. But there was a cradleboard on her back and a black-eyed baby in it, an infant alert and watchful.

One morning as she went walking among the tipis with her mother she happened to utter a word and suddenly Fire Thunder flew out of his lodge gasping, "You!" His one eye was big with looking, his other eye covered with that slash of beaverskin. "You!" he choked.

Rattling Hail Woman stopped and turned toward him. There was no laughter in her face. She seemed many years old, darker, melancholy. But neither was there fear or scorn in her face. She looked with genuine kindness upon the man.

"*Hau*, Fire Thunder," she said. "Yes, me," she smiled. "It is me. I am home."

The warrior's cheeks deepened their color. He opened his mouth and closed it again. The muscle in his jaw began to work. Then his eye narrowed and he stiffened, peering over her shoulder at the cradleboard. A tiny squeak escaped him. "You have—" he whispered. "You have—" He spun around and rushed back into his tipi.

That night all thirteen of the ponies that were tethered in front of Rattling Hail Woman's tipi disappeared.

By the next morning Fire Thunder likewise had disappeared.

After a month he was back in the village, staring, saying nothing. His herd of ponies had tripled in size. None of these prizes found its way to the tipi of Rattling Hail Woman but sometimes Fire Thunder himself did. He would stand among some trees chewing on his empty mouth. The warrior was losing weight, growing gaunt.

Then one day he saw Rattling Hail Woman sitting under a plum tree alone. He took two quick steps toward her—but lo: she was nursing the infant. She had cradled his head in the crook of her left arm and tucked his face close to her full breast, pressing a finger upon the flesh beneath his nose so that he could breathe. He was making sweet smacking sounds and she had bent her head above the boy with a complete and crushing love. Her left braid brushed the baby's forehead.

"*Hokshi cala*," she murmured softly. None but the babe and the warrior heard her. "*Hokshi cala*, how I love you."

Fire Thunder uttered a cry of anguish and ran away.

This time he was gone for several months together.

When he came back, driving ahead of himself a herd of more than five hundred stolen ponies, the men of the village cried "Hi ho!" and praised his prowess but the women felt pity because the young giant was turning into bone. He was suffering. He was clearly sick.

Therefore for his sake they took courage and gathered outside his tipi where he sat with his back to the door. They began a conversation together—exactly as they would when they lay in their own tipis at night and talked through the walls.

"Well, we don't know whether it makes any difference to Fire Thunder or not," they said. "Who can tell? *Tatanka* tells no one what he is thinking. But so far as we can see there is no father for this baby. There is no husband for its mother. None at least that we can see. No father in sight—"

That same afternoon Rattling Hail Woman went to the stream to fill her flasks with water. There she knelt by a still pool and pushed the skins underwater, singing softly and sadly to the boy on her back. "Shoosh, shoosh, you musn't make noise where the bad one might hear you. *Waskn Mani*, do not cry."

A pebble clattered across the stones at her left. She looked up and saw nothing then bent to the water again.

Another pebble plunked in the pool. Now Rattling Hail Woman stood up and turned around.

There behind a bullberry bush was the fierce face of Fire Thunder, all the rest of his body concealed. Perhaps he was crouching down. He was like rock in the underbrush. In a deep voice he said, "I am coming to visit you tonight."

Right away she said, "No. Don't. You can't."

The man blinked and hesitated. But then he rose to his full height and dwarfed the bush. He frowned with a greater ferocity and said, "Yes! Yes, I have said it and I can. I will come at dusk. How many ponies? A thousand?"

She would have said, "None—"

But he vanished.

The baby started to cry.

The woman stood with her back to the stream and raised her hands in a gesture of helplessness.

"Oh, baby, don't cry!" she begged. "Please don't cry!"

Amazingly the infant fell silent, wide-eyed, watchful, sleepless, steadfast, dark and silent.

That night Fire Thunder strode through the village leading fifty ponies behind him. There was a blanket over his left arm and a scent of sage so strong that even the ponies were sneezing. His braids were newly woven, glossy and straight. He wore leggings with fringes. His eye was fixed forward, looking neither to the left nor to the right.

When he came to the tipi of Rattling Hail Woman both he and his herd stopped dead. He said nothing, waiting. He blew no flute, he called no name, he made no sound at all.

Rattling Hail Woman did not appear. The tipi glowed orange from the fire inside but no one was moving there.

Soon the ponies began to whinny and stamp. The entire village knew that Fire Thunder had come courting. But Rattling Hail Woman acknowledged nothing. She did not come out.

Finally a shadow slipped to the tipi door and her mother crawled out. "Fire Thunder, go away," she said. "It would be best if you left each other alone. *Wsu Sna Win* does not want to see you."

Instead of leaving, however, the man pulled his blanket over his head and declared from the darkness, "I wish to talk with your daughter, not with you. Go get her."

The woman said, "We don't need any ponies. Please go away."

But the warrior stood like a tree, saying nothing.

Suddenly Rattling Hail Woman cried from inside the tipi: "You do not know what you are asking. Go away."

Immediately, as if caused by shock of that cry, there went up into the night a wailing so sorry as to break a woman's heart, a sweet and piteous pleading. It might have been a frightened child except that it formed a grown man's words: "Rattling Hail Woman, Rattling Hail Woman, come out and talk with me."

"Ah, Fire Thunder!" she called. She knew whose this voice was. There was silence for a moment and then in anguish she cried, "It is no use, our talking together."

"Don't humiliate me!" he begged beneath his blanket. Though the man remained as straight as a tree that falsetto voice skipped higher with every word. "Honor me, honor me!" he whined. "At least you can come and tell me why talking is no use."

So the woman crept from the tipi on her hands and knees. She stood up in front of the warrior whose head was hidden. She bowed her own head in a seeming weariness.

He said, "Why is it no use?" His knees had begun to tremble.

She said, "Because—"

But he wailed, "Come under the blanket with me!"

She said, "No."

He fairly screamed, "Why not?"

She whispered, "It is a gesture I cannot make."

He tore the blanket from his head. "Why not?" he pleaded, his single eye moist with emotion, the headband a black slash across his face. "What is the matter with me?"

She raised her face and said, "I have a son."

"I've seen him!" the warrior declared. "But I have never seen a father for him. Rattling Hail Woman, marry me and I will be his father."

"O Fire Thunder!" The woman's broad forehead shattered. She clasped her hands together. "I cannot."

"Why?" he roared. "What is the matter with me?"

"Nothing!" She covered her face. The sobs came up in spasms.

"It's the way I look, isn't it?" he squeaked.

She couldn't answer. She sobbed.

"Yes, it has something to do with my looks!" he cried in a voice reduced to peeping. He too had begun to heave and sob, a violent sort of sorrow.

"No," she whispered. "No, no, no, there is nothing—"

"Nothing? Do you mean that?"

"Yes."

"Then marry me! Rattling Hail Woman, marry me!"

She kept her face covered. Her body sagged. She shook and shook her head.

"Why not? Why won't you marry me?"

"Because," she cried. She lifted her face. Her eyes flashed green with intensity. The effort to speak made her voice a screechy thing. "Because the boy *has* a father! Because I am already mar—"

"No, don't say it!" the poor man shrieked. He put a huge hand over her mouth. "Don't say it!" Then he dropped to his knees and wrapped his arms around her legs. "I love you, I love you, Rattling Hail Woman, I can't help it, I love you—"

She was trying desperately to drive him back, hitting his skull with the heels of her hands. She threw her head to the side and cried, "I am already married! I have a husband!"

"I see no husband!"

"But I see him. Every night I see him."

"Liar! No man enters your lodge at night!"

"I see him through the smoke hole," she wailed. She was beating him with fists. "Fire Thunder, he is a star—"

"*Oiyaaa!*" the warrior wailed. "Now you cut with a tongue like flint! A *star*? Oh, how you must despise me!"

"No, I do not despise you—"

But in that instant her finger hooked his headband. The covering was torn from his left eye. It snapped away. Fire Thunder was naked before her.

Both of them froze in a ghastly silence.

Rattling Hail Woman gaped at the empty socket. She saw into the black gap beneath his eyebrow, tendons and small muscles writhing there like worms. Her jaw dropped. She whimpered.

And Fire Thunder recognized the loathing.

"*Winyan!*" he whispered. His voice was a death-wind. Passionless. "Woman!" he breathed. "Oh, you woman!"

Slowly he rose to his feet. He drew back his right hand and in a sudden motion struck her backward to the ground. A smile walked across his features. The lids of his left eye sucked inward. Fire Thunder turned, glanced at the nearest pony, bent his arm and with a blow from his descending elbow broke its neck. The animal slumped like mud to the ground. Yes, yes, and with that same arm, raised and straightened, he pointed at the woman on her back before him.

Rattling Hail Woman watched in solemn silence. Her own expression had composed itself. She was neither sobbing nor crying now.

With an enormous forefinger the warrior pointed directly at the woman's heart and whispered, *"Chante ishta."* They both knew precisely what he meant.

And so they separated as if in peaceful agreement. He returned to his tipi. She rose up and entered hers. She gathered her child into her arms, the black-eyed *Waskn Mani,* and hugged him hard to her breast.

There was no need for thought. There was no time.

"Child," she whispered, "stay with your grandmother, do you hear me? Obey her. Love her. Honor her. One day I will return and praise you for the strong son you have become. I love you, *Waskn Mani.* I will always love you," she said.

So she kissed him in the firelight, her own eyes bright with a water—and this is the beauty he ever remembered, the brimming woe in her black eyes, the deep solemnity of her expression.

She handed the boy to his grandmother. He did not cry. She was glad. She put food in a parfleche bag, took extra moccasins, whispered an earnest farewell to her mother and left.

In haste and in fear Rattling Hail Woman fled Slow Buffalo's band that night. Nor did she stop the following morning. She kept running. She ran with strength and an increasing serenity. She had altogether ceased her weeping. There would be no more crying now. She ran for the mountains and high ground, in order to be closer to the star, *Wicahpi,* her husband after all.

# 24

# Scorched Mountain Woman

By morning the hunter himself had gone in search of his prey.

He was smiling. Hatred had resolved itself to an elegant thing within him. Wrath had found its finest focus—and he, Fire Thunder, would never love again.

He darted his good eye restlessly over the landscape, seeing everything, missing nothing. Patiently he tracked the passage of the woman.

He spied the slightest depression in sedge, interpreting it. If a pebble was moved but a bit from its bed he saw it. All the world was a writing before him, signs scribbled in *maka*, the earth. Here was a black strand of hair—since hair is falling all the time but fear and worry speed the loss. He lifted the strand to his nostrils and sniffed and recognized the scent of Rattling Hail Woman.

Thus he followed her.

Fire Thunder's quivers were full. His knife was sharp. He was prepared for a long hunt. He had *wasna* and moccasins and rage, a banked and lasting rage. It felt good. He had not felt so good in more than a year.

Here is how closely he observed the world:

He saw a robin land high on a cut bank. She hopped twice, pecked something, then fluttered off.

"That robin," he said, "found wolf hairs for her nest. A den is up there—and if the wolf is losing hair then she is nursing young cubs. Hi ho! Then cubs are up there too."

He climbed the cut bank and found things as he had expected. Three cubs came cheerfully from their den to him, yipping little greetings. He picked them up and snapped their necks and sliced their bellies with his sharp knife and ate their livers raw.

And so he survived from day to day.

He shot an elk. He ate her brains uncooked because he was stalking secretly and intended to build no fire until the end.

On the fourth day he suddenly caught sight of Rattling Hail Woman miles ahead of him moving through the foothills of the mountains.

His hunting intensified.

There is a drum that beats. This is a deep and soundless drumming that attends the horrors of this world.

It may be the spirit's warning to those about to commit the sin, booming the low note, *Don't!* It may be a hard *beware* to the victim, increasing her fear and driving her farther away. But often the sinner won't hear what always the victim does.

This drum began now to beat in grandmother earth.

Fire Thunder spied Rattling Hail Woman as she stood full height on top of a hill. She turned. She must have seen him too. She sprang from rock to rock away, leaping as lightly as a goat.

*Well, and that's what she is!* he thought with admiration. *A goat!* He was thrilled with the skill of his quarry.

The hunter knew where he was going now. He gave up caution for speed and he ran.

When he arrived at the hill upon which he'd seen her earlier, he found her trail and followed. He exalted in the precision of his one eye. He rejoiced in the endless energy of his young body. As fleet as the goat himself he ascended the mountains after the woman.

At one place among the fir trees he surprised a nest of rabbits who scrambled in seven directions as fast as blinking and it occurred to him that if the woman could be a goat she might as well be the rabbit too and he laughed. He was delighting in this chase.

He saw a doe go bounding ahead in beautiful arcs higher and higher up the mountain.

"*Winyan!*" he roared in a deep voice, the voice of a strong man self-possessed, a hunter—and the thunder echoed up stony escarpments. "Woman!" he roared, "I know now what I am going to do!" He laughed aloud and in taunt continued to reveal himself: "Play all the roles," he called. "Leap skin to skin and beast to beast! Change to any form, it does not matter. I will kill them all!"

Now by a constant cutting off, by dashes and shouting and threatening death, by stomping the mountain in terrible fury, he drove her. The one-eyed warrior drove all the four-leggeds before him up the mountain as long as there was daylight left. He drove them while the drum which he did not hear kept beating its warning. He drove them to a final stand of fir whose top reached up to the timberline, on either side of which was rock, a sheer precipitous rock, at the front of which he took his stand roaring, "*Winyan! Winyan! Woman!*"

And then in the night he struck fire to dry moss. Smoke curled up before the patient hunter. A red glow burst into licking flame.

Fire Thunder bound his arrows in bundles of grass and in pitch. He ignited the grass. And then he began with distance and accuracy to shoot his flaming arrows upward.

They were lightning bolts. They whispered as they went. One and one and one the smoke and the tearing fire, they wove the borders of this isolated forest in a lurid light. He circled the forest with fire. He fenced it in a black flame. And finally from the highest regions downward he brought the burning to himself, arrow and arrow and arrow.

This fire vomited smoke. It terrified the four-leggeds and drove them down, crashing the underbrush, running for their lives. The deep drum drummed its delirium.

One by one the animals broke from the forest in front of Fire Thunder. One by one he shot them dead. Hatred impersonal, universal, indifferent and placid. He seemed to be observing the slaughter from above in cool scrutiny, an emotionless separation. No more sorrow nor sickness. No misery, no delight. In perfect silence he released his arrows and killed the creatures in their hearts: rabbits and deer and antelope and goats and lions, the chittering squirrel, the jointed moose, the bear and elk and marten and wolverine, porcupine, fox and mice. None were too small for his despising. None escaped. Not one. For the woman would surely die among them.

So the mountain itself was dead. In the end its streams ran red with the people's blood and the people's bones were left at the foot of this forest as a mortal rubble. A border of mortality.

By morning's light the forest was a smoking char on the face of the mountain. Black. It never grew green again. And soon the Lakota saw a peculiar sight where the forest had been: the fire had formed a huge black figure on the high reach of mountain rock. It looked like a woman caught in anguished supplication, her arms beseeching heaven, her braids flung wild about her head.

A sense of old sadness clung to the place and a smell of bitter ash.

The Lakota said lightning had caused the fire and because of the shape of the burn they began to call this place *Scorched Mountain Woman*.

# Shunkmanitu Tanka Tells This Story:

He killed my suckling children. He broke their necks then ate their livers. I found them by the den, their bodies uncased.

So that is how I came to know of the treachery abroad.

I followed his scent. He was traveling westward to the mountains at surprising speeds. Then there was a second spore below his. He had the stink of dry sweat. He dropped an acid scat like a man afire inside himself. The other smelled of ripe dark cherries and these are the things I can tell you about her: she ran barefoot. But her step did not falter. She ran lightly and strong and straight. And this too, *Waskn Mani:* there was no fear in the woman. None. She ran swiftly and with confidence.

When I arrived it was the night and the whole mountain in flames. I came too late. But I saw him then and I know him now and his name is Fire Thunder.

He seemed a shadow–man moving between the burning and me, a creature as big as *wakinyan* but bound to the ground. He was killing my cousins in silence. Even his spirit did not speak. Nothing. It was a mute business with him, this slaughter.

Only when he had finished did he utter a sound.

He raised his arms to the mountain and cried out in a pretty voice, "Rattling Hail Woman, whichever was you I have killed her. If I have taken all then I have taken you."

That is what he said.

Hers is the name he called. Rattling Hail Woman. Hers.

*Waskn Mani,* I am sorry. Yes, yes, in my traveling I have met your mother, lovely and dark and brave and good and I myself perceived the sign that was her dying, which the Lakota call *Scorched Mountain Woman.*

I mourned her there. I lingered below her likeness for three days, singing laments for your mother and for my children and for the multitude of our relatives, all murdered by one man.

Murdered, little brother. He did not ask. He did not honor. He did not serve nor was he served. He walked away with nothing except a haughty spirit, silent inside himself.

And what do you think? This is what I think: I think that soon he will want to swallow the sun.

# 25

# Hocoka

In autumn the sound that the wind makes on the prairie is a vast rattling, a scolding whisper as wide away as the horizon, and the smell of the air is the smell of dry sticks breaking.

In winter the wind snakes and hisses, blowing snow over snow.

But in spring the wind makes a soft sound, a pliant and moist murmuring sound whose smell is all green. Moreover, one can see the hand of this wind as it strokes the tender grasses, flattening whole fields then raising them up again.

Respect the autumn wind: its knowledge is full and final.

Fear the white wind of winter: it can kill.

But love the vital winds of spring.

*Waskn Mani* loved the endless sweep of green land in the spring and the sea-blue sky through which the enormous grandfather clouds came riding from the west, grumbling and muttering then crashing with commands and sending *wakinyan*, the thunderbeings, down to earth with their bright judgments.

The name for spring is a good one: *wetu*. It thinks about sap rising in the trees and blood in young men's bodies and springs of water in the flesh of mother earth.

Early one spring morning *Waskn Mani*, thirteen years old, was walking on the high plains alone, thinking. There was much to think about.

Then here came a man from the direction of the village, so the boy sat down to wait. A person can see several distances across the plains. There was a while to wait. At first the man was only a small dark figure because the sun was rising behind him. But then *Waskn Mani* saw that it was Standing Hollow Horn. They had not spoken together since the *itancan* died three months ago and the few words which the crier *had* said sounded mostly angry.

While the old man was still far off he pointed up to the sky and made gestures for *Waskn Mani* to look upward too. Circling on great wings were three buzzards. Standing Hollow Horn nodded furiously. *"Heca!"* he yelled. "The buzzard! When the buzzard comes back to stay you know that spring is here, right?"

Soon he came trudging near to the boy.

*"Hau,"* he said.

*Waskn Mani* said, "Hello."

Without stopping the man gestured again, meaning *Walk with me.* So the boy stood up and went. But they both remained quiet a long time. Only the wind spoke.

Suddenly a meadowlark beat its wings and burst from the grasses. It flew straight up from the earth to the clouds crying, *"Masteko! Masteko!"*

"Do you understand what that bird is saying?" the old man asked. "He is a good sign. He sings *Masteko, masteko, I like the warm air,* meaning that we shall have good weather for several days now. I learn from him. I know that tomorrow morning I will wake the village very early and we will start our journey to the Seven Council Fires. It is time."

Standing Hollow Horn fell quiet again and they kept walking.

He said, "Moves Walking, you should be able to interpret what animals say. *Wachin ksapa yo*," he said and then he was quiet again and they walked.

He said, "Do you know that the young men of our band want to paint their faces black and go to war? *Wan!* What are these fools thinking?" Thus they walked chiefly in silence punctuated by these disconnected comments of the skinny Crier. He was not coughing. Maybe the spring wind eased his breathing as much as it did *Waskn Mani's* spirit. But the man's face grew fiercer the farther they walked. "*Wan!*" he whispered, "*Wan! Wan!*" as if he were struggling with something in his heart.

So *Waskn Mani* took courage and said, "Grandfather, did you come out here to tell me something?"

Abruptly the old man stopped, squinting westward. "No," he said. "No. Except maybe that I like it in spring when the tender grasses begin to show their little faces."

Such soft words! To the boy they sounded so odd in the mouth of Standing Hollow Horn that he grinned. "That?" he said. "You came to tell me that?"

"Yes. No. Well—" The Crier cleared his throat. He thrust his head forward on its long stalk of a neck. He looked like a crane. "Well," he said, "well and maybe that I don't blame you any more about the wolftrap. Perhaps a ruff of wolf's fur would have made no difference. Perhaps Slow Buffalo was going to die anyway. Perhaps he wanted to die. Who knows? So I came to say, I want to say, well, you are not bad, *Waskn Mani.* You are not a bad boy. No, I think you are a good boy. So if God has a job for you to do you better do it and don't ask questions."

Immediately the man turned and began to walk back to the village.

*Waskn Mani* gaped after him, forgetting to follow, and soon Standing Hollow Horn was a little dot in the distance.

It was just as he had promised. The next day even before the dawn the Crier came walking through the village and shouting: "Co-o-co-o!

Co-o-co-o! Get ready!" People started to stir. The air grew sharp with excitement.

Passing the tipi of *Waskn Mani* and his grandmother, Standing Hollow Horn cried, "Take it down! Down!"

In a twinkling the boy went to work. He scurried up the tipi unpinning its hides and calling to his grandmother, "*Unchi*, hurry! Let's go! Get up! Get up! It's time to go!"

His heart was very happy. They were going to the *Oceti Shakowin*, the Seven Council Fires, and there they would find one of the best things a Lakota can think of: more Lakotas!

The boy lowered the tipi hides like skirts around his grandmother. He spread them flat on the ground and gathered all their possessions together upon these buffalo hides then rolled them tightly into a great carrying case. He lashed the tipi poles at one end and fanned the other end to form a widening frame. He tied the rolled buffalo hides in the center of this frame and in this manner had finished making the pony-drag even before his grandmother had stood up. She was sitting on her bedding still—except that she was in public now, no tipi around her. She was leaning forward and rubbing her feet.

Other families had already eaten their breakfast. Children raced everywhere throughout the collapsing camp, squealing with glee.

*Waskn Mani* knelt down by his little grandmother.

"*Unchi*," he said, "I am going to get the sorrel pony from the corral now and then I am going to come right back. Will you be ready when I get here?"

She didn't answer. The boy rose up, glanced backward as he went but he couldn't wait. All through the village people were preparing to go, winching rawhide ropes, clattering long poles, clacking the wooden weapons together, stuffing parfleche bags and throwing them over the backs of ponies, and the ponies were stamping and blowing and the dogs were barking and dashing through the ponies' legs.

The old sorrel had been a gift from the *itancan* years ago. In spite of her age she understood the excitement and came willingly back with the boy.

But his grandmother had not moved. Her legs stuck out like sticks in front of her. Her poor feet aimed at each other, odd lumps. She looked sad.

*Waskn Mani* kept glancing at her as he bound the pony-drag to the shoulders of the sorrel. Finally all his work was done. There was nothing left to do but go. Moreover, other families had already begun to move into line—but still the wrinkled old woman continued to sit in her grim silence.

"*Unchi? Unchi*, we must go now," the boy said. He knelt beside her and touched her back. "What is the matter?"

"Maybe it's my feet," she said.

"Then I will lift you to the drag. You can ride," he said.

"Maybe it's my grandson," she said. "Maybe he is forgetting about me."

That struck the boy with such force he gasped. It had never occurred to him that he might be doing something to hurt his *unchi*.

Well, and she must have heard his gasp because she turned now and gazed at him from under hooded eyelids. "You will forget me one day, you know," she said softly. "Not because you do not love me. But maybe God will have a job for you to do and then you will be too busy for your grandmother."

Truly, even in the midst of the morning's excitement the boy's black eyes began to swim in water. Her words troubled him. He was feeling guilty and he did not know why.

She squinted the harder then lifted her hand and stroked his hair. "No, no, best boy beloved. *Hokshichantkiye*, no," she whispered. "You are too serious. I am sorry. You are not the matter with me this morning. No."

The tiny woman heaved a sigh and looked away.

"One of the Seven Council Fires lacks a chief," she said. "When we all gather together they are going to choose that chief. People will rejoice. They will praise the glory of the candidates. They will take pride in being Lakota—

"But their joy will be my sadness, *Waskn Mani*, because to me the old *itancan* is more real than any living hero. Every glad 'yuhoo' the young men cry will be a sorrow inside of me.

"Choose a successor to the chief? *Ohan.* yes. They must." She reached forward to rub her bad feet. "The band cannot go on without a chief. But choose a successor to Slow Buffalo who loved *wasna*, after whom there is no other friend for me? *Onshika, onshika!* Pitiful. How can I go on then?"

Suddenly she straightened up and gathered the boy's long hair in her two hands and buried her face in it, and her shoulders shook a while. So he patted her back.

Then she pulled away and leaned her weight upon him in order to stand and so he led her to the pony-drag.

"Yes," she said. "You look more like your mother every day."

By reading the signs six Lakota bands left their different winter grounds all at the same time. They began to travel toward the same valley, the same river, the same bend in that river.

And the seventh band, Slow Buffalo's, likewise went forth in a long line across the greening plains, walking and riding and talking, a jubilant people, a wonderful multitude after all.

The scouts went first on foot, returning now and again to say what they had seen. The elders came next, the ones who made decisions based on the scouts' report. Then the Crier. He announced these decisions to all the band. And the people followed family by family.

Along the flanks of the families rode the richness, the strength and the size of the band: its young men, the hot-bloods, warriors who drove their ponies up and down both sides of the procession, ready to fight or else to hunt. Add to the side–riders a rear guard and there were nearly a thousand brave men. Oh, they were a boisterous company! They trembled and shivered because of the war they had planned all winter long. They bristled with the weapons they had made in the dark hours. They trusted the measureless glory of Fire Thunder to persuade the Chief Society in its choices. *All* Lakota would paint their faces black, a mighty nation!

These young men saw no sweetness in the spring.

They dreamed instead a bright new thing, Territorial War.

And so the men of this band were different from the other six in that they looked past the *Oceti Shakowin* toward a more future goal. The gathering of the Seven Council Fires was a means to a greater end. With focused energy, then, they traveled today and tomorrow and the next day, stopping in the evening to eat and to rest, setting the tipis near water then breaking camp the following morning and riding on. On. Like an arrow with but one point and one target, on!

Throughout the journey *Waskn Mani's* grandmother never dawdled again. She had seen a fire in the eye of her grandson, the same keen joy his mother had once displayed in the good red and blue days of the past. She did not feel his joy. Neither did she understand it because it had a mystery about it and a complexity. This joy did not produce smiles or laughter, as with *Wsu Sna Win*, but rather a sacred intensity as if he were thinking hard in a foreign language or else listening to *Wakan Tanka* in his heart. Such constant thinking made the boy seem almost a man. Almost holy. *Waskn Mani* did not look at the hills and trees as they traveled. He seemed to look *through* them. And he breathed with a lunging ferocity as if the air were rich and tingling.

Ah, the child had some secret in him, some knowledge so deep that even he might not know it was there.

This is what caused his grandmother to say that God might have a job for him to do. Moreover, this is what caused her to *keep* saying things to him these days, as if she were trying to hold onto her grandson. The old woman had seen the same distraction once before—in her daughter just before that one disappeared.

"*Waskn Mani?*" she said from the pony-drag on the seventh day of their journey. "*Waskn Mani? Hokshichantkiye*, boy of my heart, are you still here?"

Of course he was here. He was walking beside the old sorrel. But who could tell what was in his face? She only saw his back and his hair.

"I am sorry for the little joke I made before we started out, when I said that my grandson might be the matter with me. Do you forgive me?"

It seemed that he nodded.

She said, "I do love you, *Waskn Mani*. Even as much as I loved your mother I love you. No less. Do you believe this?"

This time he turned to look at her and she was glad to see his face. "Yes," he said. "Yes."

The boy had bound his long hair in a headband. His cheekbones had risen like cliffs beneath his eyes, which themselves were like black suns arising.

"*Unchi*," he said, "you have apologized to me every day since we left. Why do you say sorry to me? Even Standing Hollow Horn did the same. At least I think he was apologizing—"

The woman grinned. "That old Crier did the same as me?"

The boy nodded.

"Ha! Well, maybe it's growing old that gives us the same notions, I don't know. Maybe *Hehlokecha Najin* isn't such a noisy fool after all. He married once, did you know that? Have I ever told you that before? Yes. He used to shout at her too, as he shouts at everyone. Black Elk and I heard the shouting through the tipi walls. But there were no children. His wife died while she was trying to bear the only baby Standing Hollow Horn might have had. He carried the mother and the baby to the same scaffold. Yes, and Slow Buffalo stood beside him for three days. Yes. She was a gentle and lovely woman. Her name was White Cow Sees and she was my only blood sister. Yes."

At the front of the band's procession there now went up a great shout. The old woman recognized it: a roar of greeting and welcome together.

People began to spread out along a wide ridge. They were clapping their hands and waving. Young men charged their ponies left and right yelling, "Yuhoo!"

Swiftly, with a growing excitement, *Waskn Mani* led the sorrel right up to the ridge and looked over. He gasped for joy. He nearly dropped to his knees in worship. Instead he came back to his grand-

mother whispering, "Come, see! *Unchi*, come and see this!" He lifted her to her feet then led her to the edge and pointed down into the
river valley before them.

"*Unchi!*" he cried. "Oh, *Unchi*, look at us!"

The valley was filled with Lakota. Their tipis went on and on along
the riverbanks, both sides, three looks maybe four looks away. Too
many tipis to see in one look. Thousands of tipis, a forest of white
tipis, people moving everywhere among them like ants on a huge hill,
and ponies corralled and dogs barking and children racing, children
laughing and running everywhere.

"*Unchi*," the boy whispered, his eyes flashing with strong feelings,
"such a people we are! Such a wonderful people!"

Some scouts below saw this seventh band arriving. They jumped
to their ponies and began to ride up a winding path to welcome
them. They made their mounts prance for gladness and they waved.

Far back in the center of everything, just where the river made a
large and lazy bend, a big lodge had been built very long by the coverings of two tipis. This was the *tiyokihe*, a place of high ceremony
and honor because in this lodge the seven councils would meet to
conclude grave decisions for all the people. The Chief Society would
sit in there.

*Waskn Mani's* grandmother put out her hand and touched the
shoulder of her grandson.

"What do you see?" she said.

"Lakota," he whispered, unable to tear his eyes from the valley.
"Lakota, almost as many as the buffalo!"

But she said, "What else do you see? *Waskn Mani*, look at the
design of things. What do you see?"

He sharpened his gaze and thought a while. Then he said,
"Circles. Is it circles, *Unchi?* I have heard of the circle they call
*hocoka*."

"So," she said. "Good for you, *Waskn Mani*. Yes. You are looking
at the hoop of the people, the sacred hoop, *cangleshka wakan*. It is
the same as the hoop of the world. In a sacred manner all hoops are
the same hoop. Do you understand this?" she said, trying hard to

pierce him with her own looking. "You and I, we make a tiny circle together, yet it is one with all others. Do you understand?"

Still gazing into the valley with his grave, black and shining eyes, he nodded.

"I love them, *Unchi*," he murmured. "I love this people so much. So much—"

She reached up to his cheek. "I know this," she said. "I have seen this in you."

At her touch he turned and looked. He saw her and he frowned. "Grandmother," he said, "why are you crying?"

The old woman bowed her head and made two fists. At first she laid them upon his breast and then she began softly to beat him. "Because I am scared of what God might ask of you," she said.

"What? What are you saying?" he whispered.

"Or else because my feet hurt," she wept, still beating him. "Or else because it is what old women do. They cry. Shut up and don't ask questions." She stepped very close to him with her head still down. "But once, *Waskn Mani*, once before we go, would you please make a circle also of our hugging? This once?"

Just then the scouts came riding over the ridge, waving their spears and yelling, "Yuhoo! Yuhoo!" This was their welcome to Slow Buffalo's band, the greatest of all Lakota bands and the last to arrive. Now all seven bands were here.

"Did Fire Thunder come with you?" the scouts asked. "Is Fire Thunder coming this year?"

# 26
# Waga Chun: The Rustling Cottonwood Tree

Always the Lakota came to their Seven Council Fires ready for talking and smiling, news and food and good visits. By spring it had been so long since they last had seen each other that many things would have happened good and bad. Much to talk about. Stories to tell.

So every day the adults traveled to different camps throughout this great nation of relatives, a village so wide it took a day to cross it walking. They told stories by family fires, sometimes slapping their knees and weeping with laughter, sometimes falling silent when they heard of a friend or a relative that had died.

Slow Buffalo had died.

"Who will take Slow Buffalo's place in the Chief Society?" they said. This same conversation was repeated in almost every band and every camp.

"Does anyone need to ask?" they said. "It seems as if that band has already picked its next *itancan*."

"*Hau!* You are right. I have heard them call themselves by another name."

"Well, the men do. The hot-bloods do."

"Fire Thunder's Band, they say of themselves."

"Aye, so they say. But will the Chief Society agree and appoint the same one?"

"What if it doesn't? What then?"

During the Seven Council Fires young women and crimson-faced young men took advantage of the closeness. This was a very good time to seek marriage outside of one's own band. Rightly is the spring called *wetu* for the pumping of blood. Men blew on flutes till they were dizzy. They sang songs meant to make the women dizzy too and the shy women came to stand with them under blankets saying nothing. Courting.

Children darted everywhere among the tipis, shrieking in glad freedom. No one was supposed to scold them now.

Some excellent sage grew on nearby hills, dusty green among the darker waves of sweet grass. Women went out in groups to gather it, always leaving a little tobacco wherever they picked sage because this was a holy plant for which one should give thanks.

People made anklets and bracelets from the sage and crowns for their heads. They were preparing proper adornments for the Sun Dance. They made whistles of the eagle's bones and sacred fans of his wings.

The river that flowed through the valley and the village made a large bend just in the center, the *hocoka*, a lazy loop that embraced a flat open space. Here was that double-large tipi in which the Chief Society would sit, the old men whom people called *Tezi Tanka*, the "Big-Bellies," because of their size and their authority.

Here, too, a great circle had been constructed, a fence and a round bower of green boughs which gave shade to the outside of the circle, the Mystery Circle now waiting for people to come and dance, the sacred Sun Dance circle in the center of all the circles of the Lakota.

Fire Thunder's men intended to dance the Sun Dance this year—all of them and no exceptions. They planned to pray for victory over the nations of the plains. Nor were their plans and their prayer a secret. Warriors of other bands likewise had begun to indicate their desire for such a bloody and glorious contest. And all who pledged to dance—more men every day—all now sat in sweat lodges, naked, hunched down around the rosy stones, shouting songs to *Wakan Tanka*, begging that great grandfather to oversee their marvelous endeavors and conquests.

It was in this way that the obsession of one band began to spread through a nation. When some talk with complete conviction and the promise of reward—and besides that with fire and kindness and clear invitation for their brothers to join in the triumph—well, others listen. Their brothers listen and even silence can be taken for approval. Who disputes the thundercloud after its rain has begun to fall? Too late. Get wet. Become one with the wind and the water. Choose to enjoy what you cannot choose to avoid.

*"Ho Tunkashila Wakan Tanka!"* the men shouted in their sweat lodges, a roar of singing so magnificent that young boys lurked outside the low closed lodges and wept that they could not be inside. Glory was in that darkness! *"Ho Ate Wakan Tanka*, we are sending a voice, we are sending a voice! Put stone in our faces, changeless and steadfast our will, firm our purpose, courageous our going, victorious our coming again! Put in our arms the powers of the universe! Grow in us the claws of *mato*, the eyes of *wanbli*, the horns of *tatanka*, and place in our palms the lances of the *wakinyan*: lightning!"

Oh, this was thrilling talk! Those who sang such songs did not also mention matters of personal humility. They did not remember that the door of the sweat lodge is small in order to force a man to bow low and thereby to indicate that he is nothing next to *Wakan Tanka* unto whom he prays. Indeed, it was that very boldness, that monumental self-assurance, which felt like a new thing to men of the other bands and which caused them to consider in their hearts how they too might participate in the outrageous glory to come.

These Lakota men began to experience a sweet distinction from all the other nations. They *felt* like a special people, and that feeling was good, very good, so good that it became its own conviction: what one feels so deeply must be true.

"We are picked by God. Chosen."

"It is a destiny."

"Why should we make a conquest of the plains? Well, why should we *not?*"

"We shall do it because—

"—because we *can!*"

"Aye, we shall do it because it is what we *can* do. It is who we are. Being is in doing. If we do *not* do what we can then we deny what we are. We reject what God made us to be and that is bad. It is bad to scorn the gifts of *Wakan Tanka.*"

Destiny.

And so the number of sweat lodges multiplied because the number of men preparing to dance kept growing every day. Fervor filled the hot hearts. Song swelled in the center of the camp. Many men were very happy. They looked fierce for happiness.

They said, "Is Fire Thunder coming this year? Will Fire Thunder dance?"

And they roared, "*Ho Tunkashila Wakan Tanka*, we are sending a voice! We are sending a voice—"

In the center of the dance circle a hole had been dug to the depth of a man. The fresh earth was piled in a hill just west of it. This hole was for the foot of *waga chun*, the rustling cottonwood tree who had yet to be cut down and carried here where he would be lifted to stand in the center of dancing. Then he would become *wakan*, sacred, bearing the prayers of the people to heaven.

The tree himself had already been chosen, a straight tree, tall and strong. His leaves were a comfort to the Lakota because the shape of them was exactly like the buffalo coverings of Lakota tipis. Old people said that the cottonwood had taught them that shape in the first place. He was a generous tree. He deserved to give his life to the center of the sacred hoop.

On the proper day, therefore, the young men came out of their sweat lodges and dressed and gathered with the entire nation to pray, then all of the people ascended the side of the valley to the place where *waga chun* stood waiting to be cut and caught.

The Lakota people covered the hills like grasshoppers. They were beautiful in many colors. But they were also one, one mind and one body under blue heaven—and even those too far away to see the ceremony knew what was happening.

An old man was handing an ax to a small girl. It was very heavy in her hands but bravely she stepped up to *waga chun* himself and drew the great ax backward and swung at the trunk of the tree. She missed. She lowered her face in embarrassment but the people laughed. Ah, they loved the child as much as the tree. So she grew bold and swung again and this time the ax took a tiny bite of bark and the women made the tremelo of praise, so all the people down the hill and into the valley knew that the cutting had begun.

Certain strong men now took the ax and with mighty swings chopped into the white meat of the tree. It was indicated in which direction he would fall, so then other men marked that place by standing in a double line that reached away from the base of the cottonwood as far as the tree was tall. Two by two these men held poles between them. They looked like a ladder made of people.

*Chop! Chop!* The ax sounds boomed through the wood and the valley. The cottonwood shuddered. His leaves made a whispering music not just because of the wind but also because of the bites at his ankle. The deeper the ax head cut, the more his branches trembled and the louder the song of his leaves.

*Chop! Chop! Chop!* When it became clear by his slow swaying that the tree was about to topple, all the men in line below him lifted high their poles. They were preparing to catch *waga chun*. That sacred tree must never touch the ground! Indeed, first they would catch him and then they would carry him down into the dance circle, never dropping, never dragging him, but holding him high and holy all the way. Thus would they honor the beam that reaches from earth to heaven, *chan wakan*, the pole that pierces even the center of the universe.

*Chop!* There was one final mighty strike. The tree let out a splintering groan—

But in that same instant the people who stood at the bottom of the hill began to cry out and point to the far side of the valley.

"Fire Thunder!" they were screaming. *"LOOK! FIRE THUN-DER!"*

Everyone looked.

Yes! On the high ridge, mounted yet higher on a pony as still as stone, regarding the whole Lakota nation as though he and they were an equal balance, one-eyed, grim and silent and muscled:

Fire Thunder. He had come.

So when the cottonwood cracked from his stump and came tearing down through the canopy of the forest, many men below him were caught by surprise. They sprang back in terror, fearing to be crushed. Those left behind were too few to catch the giant and *waga chun* hit the ground.

# 27

# A Contest

Many games were played during these days. Many strenuous contests were held among the young men, some merely for fun but some made brutal for a serious testing of skill and courage. The results would be remembered for a long time to come.

By one such contest an obscure boy suddenly made a name for himself among the seven bands—though whether he actually won the contest was furiously disputed and no one knew what to think of him, whether to praise him or fear him or mock him. Well, but this is what they did do: they told the story for years afterward.

One morning a hundred men gathered at the bend in the river for a shooting contest. Each had seven arrows, every arrow made by that man's hand. Across the river targets had been set at various distances. These were pieces of rawhide cut in the shapes of animals, some so far away that their position had to be explained: "It's by that boulder, just at the tip. See?"

All day the long-distance marksmen eliminated themselves. By the middle of the afternoon there were ten men shooting, always seven arrows at a time. Soon there were four—who sent their arrows through great arcs out of sight, yet who could strike the figures in their hearts. Ah, the Lakota were proud of their expert relatives! Men roared. Women made the tremolo of encouragement. Children stared in astonishment. Soon but two were left and finally there was one man whose shooting was farther and more accurate than anyone else's.

But this man was not yet declared the winner. Rather, he had earned a place in one more contest.

Everyone, even this marvelous shooter himself, turned toward the double-long tipi where Fire Thunder sat in calm indifference. They all smiled for there was not one Lakota heart which did not know his reputation.

They said, "Let Fire Thunder try."

And indeed, he rose and came forth. This last warrior deigned after all to try.

So the rawhide image of a goose was shown to each contestant then carried so far away that certain men had to hide near it in order to see if it had been hit.

The best of the rest of the men, the winning shooter, went first. He released each of his arrows with careful deliberation. A shout went up at the target: "All seven! Ha ha, all seven arrows have found the belly of a single goose, ha ha ha!"

People cheered. It was a good day filled with excitement and wonderful display. And it wasn't done yet. Hi ho!—how could Fire Thunder improve upon such shooting?

Well, that mighty man stepped forward, a cottonwood for height and strength: he always seemed taller when he passed near a person than that person had remembered, his eye colder, his muscles more like ropes. Fire Thunder strode to the edge of the river, drew an arrow from his quiver, notched it and prepared to shoot.

Exactly then a boy appeared beside the man. He must have distracted Fire Thunder because the arrow which he released tore water.

*Ahhh!* People felt an immediate anger toward this boy. Who was he to destroy the moment? Why was he here? To *what?* To *shoot?* He wants to shoot? *Now?*

He was lean and stripped. Yes, like every other contestant he carried a bow and seven arrows. His face was calm and solemn, his eyes huge with watching, his hair so long it fell in a black rain over his shoulders and lower than his waist.

Fire Thunder, on the other hand, had lost his calm. His eyebrows drew together, his nostrils flared.

Small signs, but the people read them and began to berate the boy. "Get out of here! You have no sense. You're a distraction. Besides, you're too late. Don't you see who is shooting now? Get out of here!"

But here came the first surprise of this story:

Fire Thunder himself raised a hand to silence the people and in a voice as soft as the river's flowing—lo, how swiftly the man regains his cold obsidian calm!—he said, "Let the *atkuku wanice* take a turn."

He said, *Atkuku wanice*. Well, perhaps he knows this *hokshila*. Perhaps he wishes to teach someone humility. So the people said, "Let him shoot. Why not?"

Then came the second surprise:

Great Fire Thunder suddenly drew and shot not over the river but straight up into the heavens, six arrows so rapidly the first was still rising when the sixth leaped from the bow. Then he placed his weapon on the ground and said, "Flying north at the top of the sky are six feasts for six bands of Lakota."

Though everyone else kept gazing upward he did not. He fixed the boy with a steadfast, expressionless stare. Like a serpent. No longer wrathful. No longer anything. Ice.

"There!"

All at once, nearly choking on their astonishment, their heads cast back with looking, people were pointing and shouting, "There! Look there!"

Down from the blue sky came two bodies tumbling round and round, four bodies, then six—geese! Their long necks flopping, their wings torn loose in the wind, some were thrashing, some dead, each with an arrow protruding, arrows painted with no color at all, no adornment, as was Fire Thunder's custom. These geese hit the ground with great thumps. Big birds. Five of them lay still. Fire Thunder walked over to the sixth, whose feet kicked sideways in the dust, and crushed its head beneath his foot.

Oh, what a wild cry went up after such a remarkable performance, a hooting, people beating one another on the back. None but Fire Thunder had even *seen* the geese in heaven. Yes, yes, this was a good day.

But that warrior, forever fair, raised his hand again and stepped backward, offering the field to the black-eyed boy. Ah, yes, the boy. People had forgotten about the boy. Well, maybe this would be entertaining. A joke, a little laughter. How could anyone do better than Fire Thunder, let alone a boy of no repute at all?

There were women among the observers who felt pity for the child. He did not seem arrogant to them. It didn't look as if he deserved to be humiliated.

Well, but he didn't hesitate. He shook his hair back. He took a position in the center of the open space and laid down his bow and raised his hands to the blue sky and—here was the third surprise of this story—he prayed.

He called in a sing-song voice: "*O Wanbli Galeshka*, are you ready to die? Am I worthy to receive your life? Surely it is a glorious life. Would it give you honor to grant me that life? If so I ask for it. If not I could not take it with a thousand arrows. I beg you, remember my mother with mercy."

People looked upward. There was no eagle there. They looked back at the silly boy and began to grin.

"Who is this? Which band is he from?"

But the boy had already notched a long arrow and had drawn the sinew of his bow so far back that his thin arms trembled.

Then he shot. The arrow went with a whine and seemed in fact to gather speed the higher it flew—until the silence of the round sky swallowed it.

The boy leaned on his bow as if it were a walking stick.

People glanced up and down several times.

Someone said, "Gone. That arrow's gone."

They began to feel ashamed for having listened at all and a little chatter started here and there as if the day were over.

"Shut up! Listen!" Someone was shouting, "Listen!"

Well, they did. There was a thin sound, distant, distant, growing.

*Do you hear that?*

*Yes, yes, I do. What is it?*

Soon it became a shriek, a high-pitched disastrous scream descending at an impossible speed.

And here was the fourth surprise of the day, the reason the story was so long remembered:

Directly over them the people saw the figure of an eagle, his wings laid back, his beak thrust earthward, coming. The feather-tips vibrated so madly that they made a shrieking sound. As in a holy manner every Lakota saw the yellow eye of this eagle clearly, acutely, and they saw that it was seeing them, one by one, blinkless and accusing.

The backs of their necks tingled. People dropped to the ground and covered their heads.

But just before it hit the earth, that eagle spread his wings and caught the air and landed lightly on one claw just in front of the boy. Look! In the other claw was an arrow.

And look! The eagle, fully as big as the hunter he faced, held the arrow out until the boy reached and took it—then he opened his beak and shattered daylight with a most terrible cry, then he leaped into the wind again and on huge flaps rose to heaven and vanished.

No one cheered after this shot.

Fire Thunder uttered a low curse and stalked away. People stood up and sought some little dignity after such an open display of fear. It had just been a contest. A game. Why did it have to turn so serious?

The day had ended poorly after all. No, they were not happy with this child. It was not in admiration that they told the story later that year. It was because the boy was strange and this had been their first evidence. It was because the boy would finally have very much to answer for.

"Who is this *hokshila*?" they said. "To whom does the boy belong?"

"His name is Moves Walking."

"He comes from Slow Buffalo's band."

"He doesn't belong to anyone."

"Ah, yes. *Atkuku wanice*. Yes. Yes."

A queer child indeed. Even after receiving the attentions of a spotted eagle, when someone else might have swaggered through camp in public pride, this boy was heard to sob, to weep and to whisper: "O Mother, I'm sorry, I'm sorry. I was not worthy of the eagle's life."

# 28

# An Accusation

"Why Fire Thunder?"

"No one is better to lead us than he."

"Why?"

"He is known."

"What does that mean?"

"He is known to us. The men of this band. We will surely follow him. But he is also known to the world which quakes in fear at his name."

"Why do you speak of quaking and fear? Is there a reason why the world should quake and be afraid?"

"Well . . . well, yes. Of course."

It was night. Fire lighted the interior of the *tiyokihe,* the double-long tipi, but only those standing nearest the flames could be seen clearly. The rest of the men receded into shadow.

The six members of the Chief Society sat in a row with their backs to the west wall, facing the door. They were old men, the weight of many years in their faces, the weight of age in their stomachs: the Big-Bellies. They were in the process of choosing someone for Slow Buffalo's position but they would not ignore the wishes of the people of that band and therefore they were questioning them in a public and appropriate manner.

Near the door stood the one whom every man of the band referred to, that black slash across his left eye, his right eye an ice, himself a cave of silence. He listened to the proceedings as one might listen to the chirping of children, heedlessly.

"Why should the world quake and be afraid?"

"Chiefs, the glory of this warrior already covers the earth. As far west as the mountains whence come the thunderbeings, north to the house of Waziah the Giant, east to the morning star, and south to the source of our life, this warrior is known. If he leads us all Lakota will be glorified the quaking and the fear of our enemies will make a way for our strength and glory."

Those within the tipi spoke loudly so that those without could hear. Therefore a huge roaring now rose up outside in order to show how many warriors desired this man's elevation. Thousands. The excitement for him and the hunger for war had spread through seven bands. Tens of thousands.

The chiefs said, "He is thirty-one years old."

Seldom was an *itancan* younger than forty.

"With respect," said a shrewd young man, "what old man is able to unify so many hot-blooded fighters the way he has? Listen to the men outside. Fire Thunder has a genius. He owns the loyalty of the strongest among us—"

"Count his ponies," one hot-blood shouted.

"If he kept a coup stick," cried another, "you could *not* count the notches!"

Someone began to describe his icy manner in battle, how he shot arrows more swiftly than other men breathe, how he never lost a shaft: whenever he shot he killed.

"And I have seen Fire Thunder's arrows dodge trees to hit the hidden enemy! If he kills the soaring goose six at a time what will he do to the creeping Crow? Ha!"

"Well, and *I* have seen how he walks through a rain of enemy arrows untouched!"

Someone shouted, "I believe he covers his eye in kindness to us because it is a crystal sphere with fire in the center. His look is lightning and kills."

"No," cried a short man with much sweat on his forehead. "No, he hides his eye to save us from fear. An eagle's beak grows in that socket, hooked and wicked and lethal. His look is a screaming."

But the Big-Bellies said, "Why this one and not another? Why do you speak of quakings and fear? Why is this important?"

Well, and then one man after the other repeated the plan that had seized the soul of so many warriors:

"He will lead us in a war that shall not cease until our enemies do. The Lakota can rule and shall rule west and north and east and south—greater than all other peoples together, Shoshone, Flathead, Blackfoot, Cree, Cheyenne, Arapaho, Pawnee—"

These warriors could not lower their voices when they spoke. Their eyes flashed in the firelight. Their words rushed out like a floodwater. Moreover a loud persistent roaring of support sounded outside the *tiyokihe*, countless men with one single desire in mind.

Only one man was silent, his jaw a stone and his confidence as solid as stone.

The Big-Bellies of the Chief Society now leaned together murmuring, listening, nodding—solemn and slow and stern. They were in no haste. Their age had extended the time it took to make a wise decision.

In the days and months that followed—in the *years* that followed—it was reported over and over as if it made all the difference that the chiefs indeed had finished deciding, that they had chosen Slow Buffalo's successor.

"We know they were done. Didn't they call for the Criers of seven bands? Isn't that a sign that there was a word for the people?"

But it was exactly then, even before the first Crier could come in, that a voice yelled, "No!" A voice different from all the others outside began to shout in a shrill tone, "No!" This was a boy's voice, both piercing and anguished, "No! No, no, no, no! This man cannot become *itancan*," it screamed. "He is sinful! He will taint the nation! No! No—"

Silence descended upon the warriors both inside and outside the double-tipi. Absolutely no one had anticipated any obstruction to their choice for chief. Who could possibly cry *No* to Fire Thunder?

The short warrior threw back the flap of the council tipi and there stood a boy. *That* boy! The one whose hair hung nearly to his knees.

His face was twisted with feeling now, his black eyes boiling with passion. But it was *that* boy. The men of Slow Buffalo's band grinned and shuffled and shook their heads: *witko*. The crazy child. Moves Walking. Him. There is nothing to worry about from him.

The short warrior hit Moves Walking in the chest. "Get back. Go away. This is no place for you."

But one of the chiefs said, "Wait. Isn't this the one to whom *Wanbli Galeshka* returned an arrow yesterday?"

"Well, yes, but—"

"That is not worth nothing. Let him speak." And to the boy the Big-Belly said, "Come in, *hokshila*."

So Moves Walking entered the close warm air of the council tipi and stood among the staring men, the suspicious and scornful men, no man here his friend. He moved past Fire Thunder without so much as a glance and he approached the row of chiefs.

"You have said something very strong," one said. "Repeat it please."

The boy's voice trembled. It came with difficulty now. Moves Walking had to swallow to set it free. Nevertheless he said, "Someone should not be *itancan*."

"Who should not?" said the chief.

The boy turned and pointed. "He should not." His own face seemed aflame but he kept his body erect and his chin tilted upward. Proud Lakota boy. "Fire Thunder. Him."

A growl ran through the tipi but the child turned his huge eyes to the chiefs and then did not look left or right.

The chief said, "You oppose him?"

"Yes."

"Do you know that you alone oppose him?"

"Yes."

"What is your name?"

"*Waskn Mani.* Moves Walking."

"Moves Walking, tell the truth and do not lie. For what reason do you oppose Fire Thunder's elevation to the Chief Society?"

The boy's right leg began to shake at the knee. His face, burning still, was fixed like a mask of wood. He said, "Fire Thunder killed my mother, Rattling Hail Woman. He slaughtered an entire *oyate*, the people of a mountain, all of them."

"*What? What?*"

"Moves Walking," the chief said, ignoring the noises of the hotbloods, "tell the truth and do not lie: did you yourself witness this?"

"No."

"Then how do you know it?"

"*Shunkmanitu Tanka* told me. She was there. He killed her children and ate their livers and she was there. She does not lie."

"Why do you believe this *Shunkmanitu Tanka?* Why should we?"

"Because," whispered the boy, "I have proof that he is able to do what she says he did."

"*Witko! Witko!*" cried the warriors.

"Silence!" said the chiefs.

But the noises kept increasing. Men were furious that any attention at all was given this boy. Some kept glancing at Fire Thunder, seeking some direction. Others frowned in earnest thought: *No one ever knew what happened to Rattling Hail Woman—*

"Moves Walking," said the chief, "what do you mean, 'He is able'? How do you know? And what will persuade us?"

"He is able," whispered the boy again. "He did it to me. Look."

Trembling violently in his right leg, but solemn still and straight and proud, Moves Walking pulled the hair back from the left side of his head. Behind the cheekbone was a livid, spiral scar, a lump of pink flesh and a waxen hole. "Fire Thunder did this," the boy whispered. "He cut off my ear when I was very young."

Suddenly a hissing arose by the door of the tipi. Fire Thunder had gone taut and white. In a ghostly voice he said, "Someone should mention that this fellow is *atkuku wanice*, a bastard. There is no one to affirm his word, no one to support him, no relatives at all. He has no standing in this place nor in this proceeding. His accusation is *tachesli*. Worthless."

Fire Thunder had come to life. It silenced the tipi.

Gravely the chiefs considered this information.

"Moves Walking," they said, "you bring a serious charge against this man and he is right. We cannot credit your report without the good repute and warrant of a family. Where is your father?"

For the first time the boy dropped his eyes. The trembling spread through all his limbs. "I don't know."

"*Who* is your father?"

"I don't know."

"Ah, what then? Moves Walking, if you have no relatives what can we do? You alone oppose him and you *are* alone. You alone—"

All at once the child howled in a high voice like a wolf: "I am not alone! I am not alone! I have relatives! They will testify—Fire Thunder killed my mother!"

A long silence followed his cry.

The *Tezi Tanka* glanced at one another to see whether they might be in agreement. The night had progressed with more tension and trouble than any had expected—and it had not come to conclusion. The fires in the tipi were dying, neglected. The boy bowed his head and stood still. The trembling had stopped in him.

Finally the chiefs said, "Go get them. Bring your relatives here. Have them on the riverbank by dawn and we will hear the accusation one more time after which we will appoint the next *itancan*, not before. Be ruled by us."

Silently the boy departed.

Fire Thunder had composed his features again, drooping the lid of his right eye and fixing his mouth in a straight line.

He too stepped into the night and as if to no one in particular said: "The boy can do no harm. He has no relative but one old woman. I know this as a fact. All will go well tomorrow."

# 29
# Mitakuye Oyasin!

As soon as the meeting of the six chiefs was over seven Criers were dispatched through the Lakota nation to make official declarations of three pieces of news: the name of the single candidate for Slow Buffalo's place on the Chief Society; the accusation lodged against the candidate; and the name of his accuser, who was also of Slow Buffalo's band.

"It is Moves Walking who makes the complaint?"

"Yes."

"A *boy?*"

"Yes."

"He must be a very bold boy to speak against Fire Thunder."

"Well, perhaps. But he seems soft-spoken. Solitary. He has little standing in his own band."

"Ah, but he's the boy who met an eagle face to face in the *hoco-ka.*"

"That boy? The *atkuku wanice?*"

"Yes. That one. Him."

In the name of the Chief Society the Criers described the judgement to be rendered in the morning: "Either the charge is true and Fire Thunder shall be removed from candidacy or else the child's a liar and shall be rejected."

So the Criers invited all who would be witnesses for Fire Thunder to gather on the eastern shore of the river at the bend near the dance circle.

"And those who can support Moves Walking, affirming the goodness of his spirit and the truth of his word, let them gather on the western shore of the river. Water will be the wall between good and evil. *Hetchetu welo!*"

So a murmuring arose in that great village and continued through the night. "Murdered? The boy said murdered?"

Lakota were talking, inside their tipis and through the walls of their tipis with their neighbors.

"Yes, murdered. He said that Fire Thunder killed his mother whose name was Rattling Hail Woman."

"Ah. Perhaps she scorned him."

"No, no. Who would deny such a man? Such a marriage? No."

That night the darkness grew deeper and deeper until its black was absolute. Clouds came and closed the sky. Neither the moon nor the stars gave any light.

One could not see his hand in front of his own face.

The wind ceased blowing. The air lay down so heavy upon the earth that fires guttered and lent no light.

The people grew uncomfortable. Only the children slept.

"What is wrong?"

There was the sense of a soundless motion, the movement of things invisible.

Some remembered that they had dropped the Sacred Cottonwood Tree. The Lakota sighed and stared against the moist and stony darkness and saw nothing.

Nevertheless as the dawn drew near warriors began to assemble on the east side of the river, more and more valiant men, an army of

Fire Thunder's supporters. They kept crowding together, bumping and nudging each other in the gloom, glad to be touching, glad to be so many. Hundreds. Thousands. They filled the great embrace of the river's bend.

The farther shore made the sound of a whispering susurrus like the washing of small waves along the bank, but the voices of Fire Thunder's men like night insects covered all sound except their own.

"He's just a boy. His story is outrageous," they said, filling one another with the assurance that this morning's business was an irritating interruption, nothing more. Fire Thunder would be chief. "Why, this hunter hunts buffalo not women, ha ha ha!"

"And Moves Walking is an orphan. *Wablenica.* No relatives since his mother ran away, none."

"Ha ha!"

If men smiled making laughter other men could not know it. The darkness laid so black a blanket over the earth that they could touch and talk but could not see.

Families that crept from their tipis held hands to keep together.

"Listen!"

"What?"

"*Listen!* The other side of the river. Do you hear it?"

A hush fell over the Lakota—first the farther families who came creeping toward the center stopped and strained their ears. The women, the children, then even the warriors: yes. Yes! There was a rustling across the water, a sound like the sweeping of shadows aground. Motion! The most delicate sort of progress, as if spirits were walking with scarcely a footfall.

And when people peered westward they seemed to see darkness within the darkness, one deeper than the other.

"Something's moving. I see movement."

It looked against the pit-black sky as if mountain ranges were rising up, a harder horizon above the horizon. A groping enormity, the back of a kneeling giant.

Someone wailed, "Forgive us! We dropped the tree!"

"Silence!"

*That's Fire Thunder's voice. Fire Thunder is here!*

All at once, directly over the valley of the Lakota, the sky divided and two bright stars appeared so low and so huge they seemed the size of moons, shedding a pale light and—so it seemed to the people—singing. They sang a low note, one star's voice like the wooden flute and one's a muffled drum.

Suddenly the Lakota could see each other—ghastly white flesh in the starlight. Everyone saw the strain in every other face. Why were the stars coming so close to the earth?

"Look! Look! Oh, look there!"

The people turned and stared as though they were themselves a valley of stones.

Across the river the starlight shined bright silver and soft on a gathering there—for there *was* a gathering after all, a multitude more numerous than the nation on this side of the river.

And from the very center of that gathering Moves Walking, the black-haired boy, cried out at the top of his lungs, "*Mitakuye oyasin!* Here are my people. Here are all my relatives!"

At his feet in riverwater, up and down the western shore, floated a garden of water lilies, white, luxurious, rich, and shining as if they carried starlight in their hearts: *Mitakuye oyasin.*

Left and right of the boy ran rabbits like a silver snow. And porcupines pressed themselves against his ankles. And tiny mice and tinier voles covered the land. Moves Walking spread out his arms to an endless host of animals: coyote stalking the ground behind him, wolverines of indisputable courage, the canny fox come this once into the company of others, the nervous antelope on legs of willow. "*Mitakuye oyasin!*" he cried. "All my relatives!"

And like mountains massed above him stood deer and elk and moose and *Mato* the bear. Still descending the far valley wall were mountain goats on quick toes, mountain lions, meat-eaters, warriors. Squirrels and martens and prairie dogs were there. Swallows swooped the river, magpies chattered, ravens talked in seven languages, the dragonfly was a tiny ghost of perfect beauty—

And standing beside the boy, her head high, her slant eye regarding the nation that stared back at her, her brow as broad as *waga chun*, herself all silver in the starlight, *Shunkmanitu Tanka* the wolf.

The boy put his hand upon the wolf's neck and wound his fingers into her fur.

"These are my kin," he cried. "These are the virtue of my word. They know me and they witness the truth of what I say. Where are the chiefs?"

No one answered. That vast company of fur-creatures, each with a white eye looking back at the people on this side of the water, not a single animal growling, all brutality standing in peace together—the relatives of Moves Walking struck fear even in the hearts of the warriors. No one knew how to answer.

It was at this moment that the song of the two stars stopped and absolute silence gaped in the night. Still the Lakota were stone. And it seemed to them as if the stars bestowed a brighter light on the boy alone, for he shined in the midst of his milling congregation as smooth and white as a wolf's tooth.

He lifted up his voice and cried out: "Fire Thunder murdered my mother. Fire Thunder killed as well the mothers of these children here. There was no reason for the slaughter. He did not ask. In the evil of his heart he slew them! He shot them with arrows and those he could not shoot he burned. No, Lakota! No, no, this man must not be an *itancan* of my people—or else the nation shall become sick with his sin."

At the mention of their mothers the animals grew restless. A tiny chittering began, some single creature expressing her grief. Then a groaning arose, other beasts recalling the sorrow. Then barking and baying and bellowing, each in his own language: howling, bleating, grieving, remembering—

And that sound, all the tribes in all their tongues, was more than the people could take. Some Lakota threw their arms over their heads and some dropped to the ground in fear.

The boy called to them, "Don't be afraid! *We are all relatives together—*"

But his plea was lost.

"Get up! Get up!" thundered another voice from behind the warriors. It shook the earth. "Get up! Attack! Attack him!"

Out of the eastern darkness came Fire Thunder riding a wild pony directly toward the river. He was armed.

The force of his speed, the shaking of the earth beneath his galloping wrath, the fierce conviction in the man—all these drove warriors out of his way and to their feet and forward. They didn't think. They drew arrows and shot. Straightway rabbits died. A deer went down to her knees with a shaft in the center of her forehead.

Fire Thunder rode through a running tumult of young men, causing in them the fear that fights in order not to die. A thoughtless desperate self-defense: arrows spanned the waters. Porcupines and coyotes and antelopes perished.

The boy was running forward screaming, "These are your brothers and sisters—"

But no one was listening. Chaos had come to both sides, one side scrambling and stampeding to escape death, the other rushing to battle and to kill.

As his pony approached the river Fire Thunder bent forward and whipped it the harder so that it soared from the bank, plunged deep beneath the water and came up swimming, the man still astride its back, shooting arrows with a twitching speed. His arrows fanned the whole shore of animals but his eye was fixed on the boy. Fire Thunder killed many creatures by means of the long-distance bow. That boy he would strike by hand. His face below the black slash seemed passionless and calm now.

But he had not reckoned on the wolf.

When his pony mounted ground again, pouring water, pounding its hooves among the small animals, Fire Thunder was suddenly confronted by the low yellow eye and the tooth of *Shunkmanitu Tanka*. Moves Walking screamed, "No! No! Run away—" But the wolf only lowered her head till the snout puffed dust. She uttered a gutteral threat so horrible that the pony reared and drew backward, rolling its eye.

Immediately she launched herself at its throat, ripping the arteries by the bite and slash of her fangs. The pony came down on its right shoulder and pondered surprise for a moment, then lay its head upon the earth and died.

In that same moment Fire Thunder had sprung to his feet with a knife in one hand, a spear in the other, and had started toward Moving Walking. The wolf spun round from the pony, barked a warning behind the man and charged. In a smooth feint he sank sideways to one knee, turned, and just as she flew over him he thrust his knife up into her belly. Her weight pitched her into a somersault. Her intestines spilled out. The boy began to wail. The one-eyed warrior rose to his feet and continued toward him.

By the extremest will *Shunkmanitu Tanka* interposed herself between the warrior and the boy, dragging the intestines like ropes and mincing in order not to step on them. Poor Moves Walking knelt down for sorrow.

She said, Run, *Waskn Mani*. The wolf said, Run. I cannot. I give you my life. Run.

The boy wailed, "I did not ask for it!"

The wolf said, You don't have to. The choice is not yours to make. Listen, little brother, I have taught you well. You will honor me hereafter. I love you—

So saying, *Shunkmanitu Tanka* leaped for the neck of Fire Thunder.

Quickly he leveled his spear so that she flew into it, piercing herself at the base of her throat. But she was more courageous than he had reckoned. She grabbed earth with her powerful claws and dragged herself forward. She caught the warrior unaware: she was using his body as a fixed wedge for the spear which she was thrusting through her body. By tough lunges the wolf came to the man and seized his wrist in her jaws and she did not release him. It was a grinding grip. She did not let go.

Run, little brother, she said. Remember my sons as I have remembered your mother. Go. Go.

Sobbing, the boy turned and ran with the rest of the four-leggeds from this field of slaughter. Twice he glanced back, then he leaped into the river and curled himself small and let the current carry him away.

The image remained:

Under the dead-white light of the stars two figures were locked in a contest, each attending to the other as if there were no other beings in the world, a man standing massively among water lilies, his left arm raised above his head, a wolf hanging from that arm by an unbreakable bite—but the man with his right hand was stabbing her, stabbing her, reaching for her heart with the point of his knife and stabbing her. She did not let go. The only way this warrior could loose himself from the will of the wolf would be to cut off her head. Thus had she chosen. Thus it would be. Because she had come to love the boy *Waskn Mani*, his enormous black eyes, his enormous heart.

There was one more song that sorry night, a lamentation deep and terrible. Some said the animals sang it. That is certainly possible. Others, however, said the singing came from the sky, that the stars themselves were mourning.

*Waskn Mani's* grandmother said, "No. It is the earth. *Maka* is weeping for her children."

# 30

# They Did Not Dance

It is no small thing to record that the Lakota did not dance in the Mystery Circle that year.

They dropped the Sacred Cottonwood. It touched unconsecrated ground. This was a desecration but it was not irredeemable.

Nevertheless the newly chosen *itancan* canceled the dance.

The Holy Men of every band disputed his decision. They said there were several ways to cleanse the fault of a fallen tree. Was there ever a year when the people had not danced? Never. For how could a nation prosper if it had not honored *Wakan Tanka* or humbled itself before him in prayer and sacrifice? Well, it could not. But this chief was impenetrable. He exerted such an influence over the nation that his will alone prevailed. He set his single eye against them and the Lakota did not dance.

Rather, they went on the warpath. Fire Thunder's hordes went forth like fire over the plains. And lo, they triumphed wherever they went.

What spirit did this *itancan* worship?

None.

Whose rules did he obey?

His own.

# Part Four

# 31
# The Black Road

The same night when *Shunkmanitu Tanka* perished *Waskn Mani* traveled away from his people. He went crying and cutting his hair until none was left except in patches on his head. His old grandmother followed that trail of long hair on her sorrel pony. She found the boy in a little cave where she held him and rocked him and wept and sang old songs. Thereafter they lived in solitude together—and except that they survived, what happened to them for the next two years is not a story.

What happened among the Lakota during that same time, however, is a story one must tell in sorrow with two titles, for the people called the first year Bloody and Beautiful, the second Bloody and Bare.

In the Moon of Making Fat (June), the young men, the hot-blooded warriors painted their faces black. They painted the jagged lines of lightning down their legs and tied up their ponies' tails, and taking each three mounts (one for traveling, two for fighting) in war parties as huge as storm clouds they rode forth conquering and to conquer.

There was a Crow woman named Magpie Outside who received a

very bad burn when her little boy knocked over the tripod which held a buffalo paunch of boiling water. This was the first of a series of small accidents.

Magpie Outside had been forking hot stones from the fire in front of her tipi and dropping them into the paunch of fresh water in order to make a soup. She had just stood up and turned away for some onions when her child rushed by swinging a stick. Well, his stick hit one leg of the tripod and the heavy paunch tipped forward and gushed its load of scalding water over the moccasins of Magpie Outside. She let out a small yelp—enough to stop her son who then stood still and watched with large eyes while his mother sat down and bit her lip in order not to scream. She groaned quietly then she whispered, "Little Nest, go inside and get me a knife." The child, seeing her pain, had begun to let some tears roll down his cheeks. But neither did he make a noise. It had been rumored in the village—rumored, in fact, through the whole Crow nation—that the Lakota intended to start a war of unimaginable proportions. They had appointed a chief whose only reputation was for the skill of killing, nothing more, one who had begun to earn that reputation in cold cunning among the Crow themselves more than thirteen years ago—even in such villages as this one. When she was much younger Magpie Outside had seen the results of his ghostly slaughters, though she had never seen the man himself. Almost no living Crow had seen Fire Thunder.

She whispered, "Bring me your father's sharp knife."

The child ran inside and came out again with a knife of chipped flint. Magpie Outside said, "Thank you," then bent forward and cut through the tops of her moccasins. When she peeled the wet leather from her feet the skin split and came off too, like a boiled plum skin. This was a bad injury. The boy sobbed for what he had done. So his mother comforted him by giving him a job to do. "This is very important, Little Nest," she said. "Run to my sister and tell her we need good, clean buffalo grease. Tell her that I will not be able to walk for a while."

In fact, the Lakota had not yet attacked anyone. Only the news of them had come running across the plains, not the warriors themselves. Maybe they were coming. Maybe not. This Crow band could not spend time worrying about that now.

There was another more pressing problem which had caused the village to break camp and travel three or four times now. It was a sudden, curious absence of game. Lately no buffalo had been sighted, no elk or antelope either—none of the creatures that lived on the plains. Not even the gopher, which is a meat the Crow will eat when it is well roasted. So the band was moving by stages toward the mountains, another sort of land where other kinds of animals might be found.

For many nights after she burned her feet Magpie Outside could not sleep. She lay awake listening to the sounds of her child and her husband, soft snorings, moist breathings.

On the fourth night her husband made a grunt and slapped himself. He did this twice. With the second slap he woke up and his snoring stopped.

Magpie Outside said, "Cold Wind, what is the matter?"

"Lice," he said, and that was the second little accident.

Magpie Outside said, "I'm sorry. I know what we need, but I can't get it for you. I can't walk."

Her husband was by nature a kind man. In darkness she heard him rustle his buffalo bedding and then she felt the touch of his hand upon her cheek. "There is no reason for you to get it," Cold Wind said. "I will go."

"But it's woman's work," she said.

"Oh? And where is the woman to work it? Tonight you are a fish. You can't walk. Tomorrow I will be the woman. It is done."

In the morning, then, Cold Wind went off into the foothills alone. Actually he was going for two reasons: since lice disliked the smell of mountain-mahogany leaves but people enjoyed the spicy scent, he planned to pluck some leaves to spread around their buffalo skins at night. That was the women's work. But the other reason he went was to see whether he might find meat in a certain mountain valley. Magpie Outside knew the path he planned to take, a difficult one, winding, narrow and steep. It was kindness that kept him from mentioning the more dangerous purpose of his journey and it was kindness that kept her from asking—but she knew.

That he was gone was the third accident. It should have been herself. Often in the time that followed she said that it should have been a woman gone to get the mountain-mahogany leaves, not Cold Wind, not her husband.

Even seven nights after she burned her feet Magpie Outside still could not sleep well. She woke very early that morning, just as grey light showed in the smoke hole of the tipi, thinking she'd heard a footfall outside. "Cold Wind?" she called softly. "Cold Wind, is that you?"

There was no answer. Instead it seemed as if silence had turned into a fierce concentration.

Suddenly Magpie Outside realized that she could not hear the breathing of her son.

"Little Nest?" she whispered.

She reached toward his bedding and found the skins warm but empty.

"Little Nest?"

Now she was sure she heard someone outside. The hairs down her back began to tingle. Something was wrong. On her hands and knees Magpie Outside crawled to the doorflap and pulled it aside and crawled out. Dim light. The dim dawn light made it seem as if the morning was foggy and still. But then a small foot scuffled behind her and she turned and there, black as shadow, stood a man of tremendous size, tremendously close to her, holding her son with a hand across the boy's mouth.

*"Little Nest!"*

The woman could stand if she had a stick to lean on, but there was no stick nearby. Her feet had formed scabs as hard as shells. When she put her weight on them the blood pounded and swelled as if to burst the skin. But there was no stick to lean on here! So Magpie Outside reached for the man himself. She clutched his legs and pulled herself upward.

The giant did not move. With all her might she was yanking the arm that held her son but neither did it move. It was stone, she was helpless, and the poor boy was staring at her from eyes white with terror. Magpie Outside swung at the man's chest—but his right arm shot out and grabbed both her wrists and lifted her from the ground like a captive in ropes.

In absolute silence this man had stolen her child from the tipi while she slept. In the same cold silence he had seized her too, an arm for each of them. *Who is this mountain cat? This ghost, who is he?* For the first time the woman looked straight into his face and saw in the dawn light a great black scar descending sideways from the right temple to the left cheek—a deep cleft, it seemed to her, as if an ax had cracked his skull in two. He had but one eye, cold and small, and it stared steadfastly into her soul.

Now he spoke in a voice as soft as an owl's flight. He used the tongue of her people but his accent was foreign: "Here is the shield of the head of this lodge," he said. He was referring to the shield that stood on a tripod in front of every Crow tipi to identify its inhabitant, Cold Wind's shield. "It has a black sun painted in the center," he said. "Does the man who lives here also have a black sun tattooed to the center of his forehead?"

Magpie Outside stiffened. She said nothing. She drained her face of all expression but she could not help the stiffness. Yes, Cold Wind had a black sun in the center of his forehead.

The giant gazed at her a moment. He had read her reaction rightly. Yes, yes, the man of this lodge wore a black sun on his brow.

"Your husband?" the one-eyed man said quietly. His manner seemed almost friendly. "I know him. I want to meet him face to face. Go get him. I will wait. I am patient. The child will wait with me. Go. Get the man of the black sun."

The tall warrior released Magpie Outside. Truly, she wished to be brave for the sake of her boy, but when her feet hit the ground they exploded and she fell down screaming. She couldn't help it. She screamed and several men looked out of their tipis. They saw the giant striding away with the boy beneath his arm, so they turned back for their weapons but when they came rushing out into the dirty dawn light each man groaned and fell down dead.

For every Crow warrior who ran naked from his tipi there came a small whine like a bee, then the sound of a slap—but when that warrior hit the ground an arrow was buried in his chest. Seven good men died. Ten. Fifteen. Magpie Outside could not stop screaming but her eyes were calm and clear, and now in the morning light she saw the silhouettes of warriors surrounding the whole village, many warriors, hundreds and thousands of warriors like a great fence of death, some standing in silence, some mounted on ponies, warriors faceless in the dawn awaiting the return of the giant who had flown like an owl into the village, into Cold Wind's lodge, and had stolen his son.

Finally that giant stepped out onto a high promontory and cried down to the village: "Bring me the man that wears a black sun on his forehead. I have something for him. I wish to return the gift he first gave me. I am Fire Thunder, Chief of the Lakota!"

And so it was that a Crow woman went forth on wounded feet in search of her husband, moaning as she went.

All the world was a disaster now. Never had anyone seen so many warriors massed in one place. Her village was under siege. No one was sleeping. Nor could any man lift his face since every man had been humiliated by the surprise invasion of ten thousand Lakota. How did the Crow scouts miss such a vast passage? The woman's son was a captive. Her people had no food, neither game to hunt nor supplies in their parfleche bags. And she herself was crippled, leaving a trail of blood upon the mountains.

She groaned. She stumbled and bled. She grabbed at the branches of bushes. Thorns tore her flesh. It was easy to follow her.

On the tenth day since she had burned her feet, Magpie Outside looked up and saw her husband standing on a mountain cliff near the head of the creek that ran down to the place of their present encampment. "Oh, Cold Wind," she breathed, "it's you!" Many emotions rushed through her breast. She wanted to cry out, *Hide! Run and hide!* She wanted to sit down and weep because the mere sight of her husband was a comfort when everything else was so horrible. She wanted to scream, *They have taken Little Nest!* But Cold Wind was too far away. He would not hear her.

She saw that he was raising his arms. It looked as if he might be praying—but then she realized that he was plucking leaves from the bushes above him. Mountain-mahogany leaves. Ah, she had forgotten about the lice. She had forgotten that little accident and now she began to weep truly. Great sobs shook in her chest because lice had been such an easy problem. She began to walk again, weeping for the ordinary things—and for Cold Wind who was plucking leaves for their tipi. He did not know that nothing was ordinary any more. She was coming with bad news.

All at once she saw another man on the mountain, someone standing on an eminence above her husband.

"Cold Wind!" she shrieked. She was running forward on bloody feet. "Cold Wind, look out!"

He heard her. He turned and peered down from the cliff and saw her. Immediately the good man grinned and began to wave: "Magpie Outside, what are you—"

But in that instant the figure above her husband leaped and dropped and struck him from behind. Cold Wind fell to the edge of the cliff. In a twinkling the giant grabbed him and pulled him back. Then both men turned to face each other, but the other was bigger and had the advantage.

Bigger? A man of such tremendous stature—

*Aiyeee!* It was that Lakota chief. It was Fire Thunder!

Magpie Outside ran and ran, crashing forward through briars and broken rock. It looked as if the two men were talking. Perhaps they were acquaintances. It was a crazy thought but she started praying that it might be true, that they might be friends. She was begging God for mercy. She had ceased to feel her feet at all. She felt nothing. Her heart was on the cliff above her.

The Lakota wore nothing but a loincloth. He carried no bow, no weapon, neither a spear nor a knife. But in his right hand he held a single arrow. It had Crow markings, not Lakota.

Now grasping that arrow in his fist he turned it around and aimed the flint at his own eye. His left eye. Which, the woman saw, was covered by a flat strip of leather. The Lakota warrior was talking, lowly, slowly. Her husband was not talking. She kept running forward. Maybe she could say something helpful. Maybe she could stop—

Suddenly the Lakota drove the arrow into his own head. He may have been her enemy, nevertheless that gesture made the woman cringe for him. He himself showed no pain. No expression whatsoever. Slowly he pulled the arrow out again, bloodless. He spoke three more soft words to her husband—and then, with a cry like the scream of an eagle, savage, thrilled by some secret hilarity, the Lakota chief sprang toward Cold Wind. He flew! He seemed to *fly* at him, that single arrow extended like a beak, that arrow stabbing, stabbing, piercing in swift succession the left eye and the right eye of Cold Wind, his left eye, his right eye, and then the center of his forehead: one and one and one, all in the time it took the raptor Lakota to fly past her poor astonished husband. And then it seemed to Magpie Outside that this chief of the Lakota spread his arms and soared upward like a great bird, that he swept toward the sun and vanished in its bright light. Anything was possible now. She kept moving forward on her numb bloody feet. She did not stop. The only difference was that she was no longer running. She walked. There was no hurry. Cold Wind was lying on the cliff with an arrow deep in the center of his forehead. He was not going anywhere. He would wait.

This, then, is how the territorial war began: Fire Thunder insisted that all his warriors—all of them and none left out—should surprise a particular Crow village, one he himself had chosen. He commanded them to surround it and do nothing until he gave the word to rub it out.

His decision was somewhat surprising since he had chosen a small band. There would be no glory in the victory. Yet no one questioned the chief's choice. They surrounded the village. They guarded it. None of its people could escape. Then one day Fire Thunder was gone and the next day he was back and on that day the whole village was slaughtered, warriors, old men, young men, women, children, animals, all. All, said Fire Thunder, save one woman whom he left as a witness to carry the news of this horror everywhere across the plains. What woman? The warriors had been thorough. They had taken a wild, bloody delight in utterly rubbing out this first village. What woman?

"She," said Fire Thunder, "that married a midnight sun."

And so the war began.

The great gathering of warriors was divided. War parties rode west and north and south across the land. The hot-bloods went howling in excitement and pride, fighting harder with every attack, feeding on fear, laughing at the terror of their enemies and traveling faster than rumor can fly, for when a scout came crying, "Lakota!" it was already too late. Another camp was scorching heaven with its smoke. Another band had been utterly destroyed with but one person left alive to bear witness to the extremes of these warriors' horrors.

Thus all the talk turned into action. All the winter planning became a summer's slaughter. Fire Thunder's young men scarcely slept. They grew thin with fighting. Their eyes glowed a new light and they showed their front teeth like wolves as they rode. They moved in a tense delirium, inexorable, killing without discussion, killing immediately and completely. It was as if their fingernails were flints, their arms two spears, their faces the flat of a hammer.

Ah, this was monstrous! Whoever had heard of so many men rising up in so perfect a union, one mind and one purpose—to murder others? *All* others?

"Why are you doing this?"

A Cheyenne advisor was walking from his village, boldly presenting himself as a target on the chance that this war party might negotiate. They sat on their ponies in a wide line waiting the approach of the old man. They grinned as he came, showing their teeth. Apparently they did not intend to speak of treaty.

"Why are you doing this?" the advisor shouted, trying any means to forestall the murders about to fall upon his people. But he also truly wanted to know. Everywhere people were trying to understand this foreign thing, this unearthly business.

"Why?"

The young warriors looked back and forth at each other. Then one fellow shrugged and said, "Because we can."

That was as good an answer as any. The warriors whipped up their ponies and soon that Cheyenne village was making a glorious orange fire. It was a beautiful day. There was a high blue sky and the chill of a new season in the air, the red paintbrush of autumn upon the leaves, the grasses gone dry beneath ponies' hooves, and praise embracing every warrior at his heart. For lo: sitting at a distance on his mount, watching the long smoke blow across the plains from Cheyenne tipis, watching all with his single obsidian eye, was Fire Thunder, expressionless.

Fire Thunder! Chief, spectre, he whose *wochangi* was air in the lungs of the young men, the source of the wars, a man like sunlight, ubiquitous: Ahhhh! Fire! Thunder!

Here near the Cheyenne, there against the Cree, everywhere north and south and west was Fire Thunder. His appearing was silent and sudden, his disappearing the same. But his presence was ever a lash to the hesitant warrior, a sting for cowardice, a focus for ten thousand hearts.

He did not shout. Everyone else cried, "Hoka! Hey!" But Fire Thunder fought forever in a liquid silence, the first of every charge, his massive back like a red storm going before his warriors.

Sometimes he would ride directly into a cloud of arrows so thick it seemed a swarm of grasshoppers. The warriors' spirits went crazy at the sight. They drove their ponies the harder and followed their chief with a giddy laughter, fearlessly doing more than even they knew they could do: "Hoka! Hey!"

Who could withstand a people for whom there was no thrill but in killing, no goodness but to kill completely? Who could speak with such a people? No one. Neither *Wakan Tanka* nor human reason persuaded them. Neither mercy nor weariness slowed their bloody arms.

"Please! Why are you doing this?"

"In order to take the earth for ourselves."

"What? What does that *mean*?"

"That it is ours. That we shall possess it."

"I don't understand. I can't understand what you are saying. What do you mean, *possess*?"

It was an impossible concept. The nations abroad could no more comprehend this possession of land than they could conceive of carving the blue sky into blocks to keep in a tipi. The very absurdity of the war diminished their ability to fight these hot-bloods. Mental confusion caused a sort of battle confusion. The cold madness of this enemy horrified strong men. It broke the brave men down and whole villages therefore fell before the hordes of Fire Thunder with scarcely any resistance, and when any village fell it fell absolutely. Always everyone died save one, one heart, one tongue, one woman to declare the evil she had witnessed.

*What rules do these warriors obey?*

None.

*What do they honor?*

Nothing.

*But who controls them? Who can govern so insane a force?*

Fire Thunder. Him.

*Ah, then what does he obey? Whom does that one worship?*

Soon every nation under heaven had begun to realize this nearly ineffable truth: no one. No one. Himself. So far as they could see, Fire Thunder obeyed nothing but his own desiring.

"Then," the people whispered one to another, horrified by the word, "then he is *wakan shica*, that evil which is equal to *Wakan Tanka*, wickedness in proportion to God!"

The war that began in the Moon of Fatness continued all year long. In *ptanyetu*, autumn, the smoke of destruction went up and in *waniyetu*, winter, cries were still going up from dying lips to heaven. In the north and the south, east and west, a fire covered the land, a furious fire swallowed the people.

Yet in the end there was no glory gained in all that war.

No glory! Destruction and sorrow only—and for all.

For there was another enemy walking the earth wherever Fire Thunder's warriors went. She was always one step ahead of them, a presence more stealthy than Fire Thunder himself, a foe more powerful than all his forces put together, more silent, invisible and deadly and utterly pitiless. In their wild delight the hot-bloods never saw her. And those whom they put to the torch could not be sure of her existence, for she always arrived a few days before Fire Thunder's hordes came to kill.

In the end she attacked the attackers. She surrounded them that had surrounded the earth—and she it was who finally turned Fire Thunder's triumph into failure.

She was, in fact, a nothing. An absence. An emptiness. Silence. Hollowness. Craving.

She was this: that all the four-leggeds fled from the young hot-blooded unholy warriors who came in the name of Fire Thunder.

Everywhere his war was waged, the animals ran away. All the creatures whom *Wakan Tanka* loved, they vanished.

This enemy—greater than all the warriors, all the peoples of all the nations, all their arms and all their hearts both good and bad—had two names.

Her first name was loneliness.

Her last name was famine.

# The Lakota Tell This Story:

In the beginning all the world was only water. There was nothing but water everywhere. But *Wakan Tanka* needed some mud for making an earth. So who could he send to get it for him? Who could swim so long and strong that he might go even to the bottom of the sea and bring up a little mud?

Well, Turtle could.

We know this because we have seen what a strong heart Turtle has. Even when you take the heart out of his body it keeps on beating and it does not stop beating for several days. Turtle has great endurance. Yes, Turtle could swim to the bottom of the first sea.

So Turtle swam down beneath the waves. He was gone for seven lifetimes. He may not be fast but Turtle is very faithful and finally he poked his head out of the water right in front of *Wakan Tanka*. Where was the mud? Well, Turtle has strong jaws. If he bites you he might never open his mouth again, not even if you kill him. You have to cut that bite apart. But Turtle loved *Wakan Tanka*. He was glad to obey the Creator. So he opened his mouth and there inside was a perfect ball of beautiful mud.

So *Wakan Tanka* made the earth, lovely and sweet and green.

Then he thought about all the peoples who were going to live on this earth, the four-leggeds, the two-leggeds, and those with wings, and he loved them. He loved them very much. He did not want his creatures to suffer. But what if the waters tried to cover this new earth as once they covered everything else? So *Wakan Tanka* needed someone to guard the earth from the water. Who could stand at the farthest shore and protect all the peoples who breathe air?

Well, *Tatanka* could! Buffalo, mightier than most and more honorable even than those who are stronger than he. Buffalo could.

So *Wakan Tanka* commanded one great Buffalo to stand watch between the infinite water and *Maka*, the beautiful earth that he had made.

Buffalo is still there even down to this very day.

But we know of Time and toil and tiredness. We know what Time does to all things. We have seen wrinkles in old faces and gulleys in old soil and canyons in the ancient mountains. And we have felt weariness in our own bones. And we know, too—yes, we know very well—the destructions some people commit and other people suffer.

Therefore, this is a truth we do not ignore:

That the story of Buffalo Guarding the Earth has an end. For every year that he has stood at the edge of the everlasting sea,

*Tatanka* has lost one hair. And for every age that has passed since he began, he has lost one leg. There are four legs for every buffalo born. There are four ages granted unto this world. Four.

When finally *Tatanka* is bald and his fourth leg breaks, then shall come the end in flood. The rolling blue waters shall return to cover again this mouthful of mud, the earth.

So when times are very bad we have a saying among ourselves and all our relatives understand what we mean when we say it. We shake our heads. We lower our faces and shake our heads and whisper: "He is on his last leg," and then they also bow their heads in sadness.

"Yes," they say, "it is obvious. He is on his last leg now."

# 32
# Onshika, Onshika: The Pity

The women saw it first. The men were busy. They forgot the duties of more normal times because the war filled up their days and their remembering, their talk and all their imagination. Besides, whenever they came back to camp they brought the meat of the people they had defeated, so there was always food enough.

But women must mend the tears in their tipis with that sinew which travels down the spine of a buffalo. It is a tough important cord. It sews and secures so many things that a woman soon uses her last one and needs another. She notices when the men don't bring her new sinew. Or new skins. Women must, especially in preparation for winter, make new clothes, moccasins, leggings, a robe with a pretty ruff, a dress. Moreover, she truly wants to put her hands to work. If she can't work she suffers boredom and frustration. She knows when there are no skins to tan, no meat to dry for the hungry times, no quills with which to weave a good design, no horns for a new spoon or bones for tools or teeth for adornment. She knows and she worries.

By the end of the summer, therefore, the women were wondering where the buffalo had gone.

They had not seen buffalo.

They asked the men whether they had noticed any herds on the plains but the men—frenetic with their bloodier business—said they had not been looking for buffalo. They would see *Tatanka* when they wished. As for now, they did not wish.

Privately the women said that so much warfare might have scared the buffalo into another region.

Yes, but it was not just the buffalo they missed. Elk were gone. Wolves and coyote. Rabbits! When they put their minds to it the women realized that they had seen no four-leggeds at all since the spring. None! Absolutely no animals large or small. Whole villages of prairie dogs were silent. These little people did not stand up by their doors or shoot down a tunnel any more. But neither had owls or snakes taken up residence in an abandoned hole. No animals? Ah, that caused the women to lie awake at night. No supplies for the winter. No work tomorrow.

No company in the world.

Things felt still and dirty, as if a nation had not washed for a very long time, as if they were sleeping in their own old sweat.

Where had the animals gone?

In the fall, then, when the men returned with that crazy look in their eyes—no longer smiling for all their triumph but seeming scared that even victory might contain some sort of defeat and therefore preparing immediately to go forth again, to go farther and farther abroad—the women did not meet them with the tremolo of support and joy. They scarcely glanced at the returning warriors. So the men frowned. They made fierce faces. "What?" they said. "Aren't you proud of us now? Have you begun to look down upon us now?"

The women only sighed, neither proud nor afraid. They said, "Did you see any game near the mountains?"

"We weren't looking. We had more important things to do."

"Did you see any four-leggeds anywhere?"

"What? What are you talking about?"

"Have you seen even a little mouse? Have you seen an antelope? Have you seen a raccoon or a beaver or a mountain lion or a wolf? What about a silly swimming otter? Have you seen the river otter? Or a rabbit?"

"Make me some supper. I go out tomorrow."

"Yes, I will make supper when you bring me fresh buffalo meat."

"I brought you bear meat from the Cree."

"That was very old meat. I said fresh buffalo meat."

"I'm hungry. Make me some supper!"

"No. No, no. No, I am tired. No."

So the women grew sad and lethargic. And when the men were gone again they gathered near one another and did a little work. They ground what little corn the men brought west from eastern nations. They took their digging sticks and went looking for turnips. Then they stared into the sky. They felt very sad and lonely. They shrugged and one by one they said, "Yes, he is on his leg. *Tatanka* is on his last leg, surely."

This mood made the men mad. For all the wonders they were accomplishing, they thought the women should praise them. But these did not smile when their men came home. Smile? Why, they didn't even obey them. They did not look at them. They did not work for them. They did not love them. They did not care. Before the end of the autumn the women had begun to look like ghosts. *Wanagi*. They had grown as pale as one's breath upon the frozen air.

So the men would get angry and shout but it did no good. The women neither submitted nor fought back. They sat down and closed their eyes. So the men yelled louder and began to break things. No matter. The women didn't object. So the men began to beat the women and even then they didn't do anything but cry quietly. They didn't even blame the men.

This was frightening.

Well, and worse: the women were right. Even the men had to confess that the world was different, that the animals were gone.

       ❊ ❊ ❊

In the Moon of Frost on the Tipi (January), just as his war party went riding toward a river village to attack it, a man named Poor abruptly brought his pony to a dead stop. He sat staring at the backs of the other warriors for a moment, then he turned around and slowly rode all the way back to his own village.

His wife was standing in front of the tipi when he arrived. Her arms were folded across her bosom. It was very cold. She didn't move. She gazed at him. "*Wachpanne*," she said, "why have you come home?"

"I am done fighting," he said.

Then he took a long-handled war club and struck his pony so hard below the forelock that it sank to the ground and died. Next he squatted beside the beast, drove his knife into the lowest region of the belly and cut upward to the throat. He butchered his pony. The snow in front of his tipi turned scarlet with blood. The blood froze into large crumbling chunks. Immediately the dogs of the village came to eat these cakes of blood. Poor didn't worry about the blood but he had to protect his meat from the dogs. Threats were not enough. He had to kick them very hard in their snouts while he took the stringy muscle meat and the softer meat of kidney and liver and brain into his tipi. All the while his wife watched with her arms folded, not moving, not very interested. Finally Poor handed her the pony's tongue.

"What shall I do with this, *Wachpanne*?" she said.

"Cook it," he said. "I am hungry. I want to eat."

So they ate. Strangely, it did not make them happy. It made them feel even sadder. They sat inside the tipi eating with their heads bowed down.

Poor said to his wife, "I miss *mastekola*, that little friend who used to rise up early in the morning and go flying straight to the sun. I miss the meadowlark."

His wife looked at him. For the first time in many months there was some love for him in her eyes. She said, "I miss him too. I even miss the noisy magpie."

Poor nodded in agreement. He said, "*Tatanka* is on his last leg now, I think." And he sighed.

Just then a hot-blooded young warrior began to yell outside of the tipi. "Where is Poor?" he shouted. "What happened to *Wachpanne?* Fire Thunder wonders why he went away? Is he a coward?"

Clearly this young man was very angry.

Poor got up and went outside.

He said, "My pony is dead. I am tired. I am done fighting."

Well, that young hot-blood was so angry that he didn't even wait to talk. He took a long cord of braided rawhide and began to whip the man named Poor. But Poor did not fight back. He must have been as tired as dying. He bowed his head and covered it and that was his only defense. He did not cry out or groan. He went down on his knees. Soon the flesh around his neck and shoulders was broken and bleeding and now the dogs were back, waiting to eat some more blood, and still the young man in a mad rage kept whipping Poor. He swung the cord over and over until he, too, went down on his knees. Then suddenly that young man was crying. He was sobbing as loud as children do. "Hownh, hownh," he wailed rocking back and forth. "Hownh, hownh, hownh." He could not stop. The man named Poor did not come over to comfort him. He was himself much troubled with his pain. He crawled back into the tipi. His wife, too, was crying, but quietly. She began to wash his wounds. The young man outside got up and walked away, crying and crying like a child. The dogs fell on the fresh blood and fought each other for it.

This is the way the war ended.

The warriors just came home.

This was the start of the year of terrible hunger and loneliness. And maybe the loneliness was worse than the hunger. It is hard to believe that company can be more important to a people than food, but it is true. The Lakota missed the sounds and the smell and the presence of the animals. All human people began to feel solitary in the universe. Strangers. No wolf packs howled in the black winter's night. No one barked. No one sang the first birdsong. Crickets were gone. The little tree frogs did not call to one another. The evening did not talk. The night did not peep or chirp or rasp the insect's melody in ancient rhythm. Silence lay like a mountain on the hearts of the Lakota and no man was war-like any more.

It must be said on Fire Thunder's behalf that he went forth alone that winter in order to find food for the people. He was the seventh *itancan*. He did not ask anyone else to go. When every warrior had ceased his fighting, when all their spirits had sunk in sorrow, Fire Thunder rode west. He went to the mountains. He went over the mountains and yet farther, farther, applying every skill he ever had, skinning his eye, tuning his ears, seeking the least sign of animal life, traveling even as far as the endless sea but in all that journey finding nothing. The animals were gone. He rode north into the giant *Waziah's* land. He walked on the dead white tundra in a cold so hard that his spit was ice before it hit the ground. Nothing. Not the white bear. Nothing. He rode east and found there only famine, people with large eyes who showed no fear and offered no fight. Fire Thunder was not great in the sight of a starving people. Fire Thunder was not even very interesting. He rode south into desert lands and saw not so much as a lizard, no, not a snake nor a spider nor even the creatures whom God formed to withstand extremes of weather and hunger. Nothing. No one. The people were alone. Fire Thunder himself had seen and could bear witness: the people were alone in the world.

It was late in the spring when he returned.

The wind on the plains made a vast rattling sound as if dry grasses were fingers scratching the flaps of the earth.

Soon the countless ponies that had been taken in last years' victorious wars—all the ponies were gone. The people had eaten them. They had eaten the dogs too. Now they ate what grew, prairie apples, turnips, bitterroot, berries, leaves.

The Lakota did not gather the Seven Council Fires together. Survival had become the more immediate necessity.

And all the nations everywhere had now become the same. Both the warriors and their victims, the aggressors and those who had escaped their aggressions—there were no differences between them any more. Hunger leveled everyone.

"Oiyaaaa! That Buffalo is on his last leg surely. This cannot go on. Soon it will all be over."

Through the hungry summer they boiled the skins of their drum-heads. They cut swatches of hide from their tipis and boiled them too in order to make a thin soup. Their bellies began to swell.

They said, "*Wakan Tanka* has turned away from us."

They said, "Who sinned? Who is not confessing his sin?"

They said, "Where did *Tatanka* go? Why does he hate us now? Why did he leave us to die?"

It was an empty land. A dead land. The sky was high and dry, a brilliant faraway blue. The hot wind did not cease blowing. The grass rattled like small bones. The air smelled of serpents' skins. The earth cracked. The earth herself was dying.

So the people came and stood outside of Fire Thunder's tipi. They could see him sitting inside. The hides were rolled up from the bottom in order to let the wind blow through, therefore they could see his crossed legs, his naked back, the spine-bones thrusting through his skin. They saw his left forearm, the skin gouged deep with scarring. But his face was hidden.

By autumn the desolation had grown so great that one woman no longer held her opinion a secret, but she spoke the feelings of all the people. Outside his tipi and yet within the hearing of the *itancan* she said, "What good are you now, Fire Thunder?" It did not matter to her what sort of reaction this might cause in the great warrior. Nothing mattered any more. Therefore she said, "Fire Thunder, what good are you now?"

"*Onshika, onshika!*" the people whispered among themselves. "It is all so pitiful!"

And they said, "That Buffalo is bald by now. Yes, he is on his last leg, surely."

# 33
# Red Day Woman

Here is a sign of how bad things had become: Red Day Woman stopped smiling. She had smiled all her life till then. She had smiled no matter who was near her or even if no one was there at all. She had smiled no matter how good or bad the weather, no matter the time of day or night, in darkness and in sunlight. The simple-minded, kind and slant-eyed child whom the people called Red Day Woman stopped smiling.

Well, according to her age she couldn't be called a child any more. By now she had been with the band maybe fourteen or fifteen years and she had already been walking when she first appeared, so she must be in adulthood. But no one knew the mind of Red Day Woman. And she had remained short. She still seemed a child, drooling, sucking the two middle fingers of her right hand, watching the people pass, content in the silence of her own mind.

But something must have changed for her. Something must have happened in that mind. Red Day Woman stopped smiling. The flat happiness of her face sank into a thoughtful sorrow.

Of course, no one was smiling in those days.

No one had stroked her whispy hair in a very long time. All luck was gone. There was no luck in this strange child either. They scarcely saw her. She was like one of the dogs that used to creep behind the camp when it moved. People didn't see her any more—except to notice that while they were all wasting to bone in the famine, Red Day Woman was growing fatter. Bloated, really. Her thighs were as large as another woman's waist, though she herself stood but half the normal height. She looked like a ball filled with buffalo hair. She huffed and puffed and sweated through the summer, swelling especially in her hands and feet.

Red Day Woman was eating grass.

She had begun to chew the roots and the leaves of bushes.

She drank water at every stream, at every opportunity.

She began to groan at night.

And then, late in the Moon of the Falling Leaves (October), Red Day Woman opened up her mouth and started to scream. Not loud. She did not scream loud enough to draw people to the old tipi where she'd been sleeping since its people died. No one came, then.

Red Day Woman screamed all night long, but no one came because many people were dying from starvation in those days and people died in different ways, some in silence, some in screaming. Every family was looking out for itself.

By morning Red Day Woman stopped screaming. For a little while, then, just as dawn light streaked the eastern sky, the camp of Fire Thunder's band was absolutely still.

# 34

# Calling the Buffalo Back

Early one morning Standing Hollow Horn thought he heard birds outside. It made him feel so happy that he got up immediately and went out in nothing but his loincloth. The skinny old man was not thinking. He had a dim smile on his face. He was just reacting to the sound of birds.

The morning air was cold and still, able to carry a soft sound very far. No one else was stirring. People did not rise early any more.

Standing Hollow Horn had not heard the voice of any sort of animal in over a year. A long time. Well, so if he truly found birds he would have some good news for the world today.

The old man looked sick. As gaunt in the neck as a buzzard. The flesh of his breast hung down in flat folds. His buttocks were two strings of gristle. His fingertips were huge and blue. So were his lips blue. His cheeks had sunk between the jawbones. Nevertheless, that old man's eyes glittered like sunlight on the water—and he was not coughing. This was a good sign. Besides, old ears can sometimes become so sensitive that they magnify small sounds. Standing Hollow Horn was convinced that the footsteps of an ant had lately been hurting his ears and forcing him to cover them with his hands. Maybe that ant was trying to tell him something.

But he was not thinking about the ant right now.

It seemed to him that the birds' voices were coming from one poor patched tipi at the edge of the village. Yes, yes, he was sure of it. It sounded like soft talking.

When he stood in front of this tipi he tipped his head left and right in order to prove that the voice was real. Yes: he still heard those birds distinctly inside this tipi, yes. Or perhaps just one bird cooing. And now that he had come close he was convinced that the bird was *wakinyela*, the mourning dove. She made a sound like, Mm-*MMM*-mm, mmm, mmm. Not happy.

This was the tipi where Red Day Woman slept, squat and square and dumb but goodhearted. Yes, he knew Red Day Woman. And of course! Who else would a wild creature choose to visit but the smiling mindless Red Day Woman? Her spirit lived halfway between the beasts and *Wakan Tanka*, a stranger among human people.

Well, to Standing Hollow Horn it all seemed to fit. With a joyful heart he pulled back the flap and went inside.

There he saw someone wrapped up in a blanket. Even her head was covered. But the song of the mourning dove was coming from that blanket.

"Red Day Woman?" he croaked. "What do you have in there?" He spoke as kindly as he could but he was an old stick of a man. He knew his voice was harsh.

She did not answer. She didn't even move. But the sweet music continued without pause: Mm-*MMM*-mm. Mmm. Mmm.

"Is it a bird, then? Are you talking with a bird, Red Day Woman?"

Standing Hollow Horn thought he saw some movement inside the bedding, so he knelt down and gently rolled the blanket back, first a little way, then all the way. There lay Red Day Woman, just as he expected, but she was altogether naked. And behold: there was a tiny baby sucking at her breast. This was the sound that he had been hearing, not *wakinyela* but the sigh and the gurgle of a nursing baby!

For just an instant the old man felt like scolding Red Day Woman for bringing a child into this terrible world, but then he reached out and touched her cheek with the tender pads of his fingers and discovered by the coldness that she was dead.

"Oh, no," he croaked. "No! Oh, no!"

Standing Hollow Horn leaned back and began to stare around the tipi as if he were looking for something. Oh, no, no! Red Day Woman was dead. Her slant eyes were closed. Now he saw a place in the tipi where the dirt had been scooped out like a bowl. It was black with much blood. But the little baby was clean. Sucking its mother's breast. But its mother was dead. Oh, who could do such a thing? Who made this smiling girl–woman pregnant? So, so, this is how we walk the black road! Everyone for himself, each one with little rules of his own! So! So!

The old man's eyes began to sting him. He could scarcely see. But he slipped his bony hands beneath the infant, whispering, "I am sorry, *hokshi cala*. This is the last milk you will get from your mother."

Slowly he pulled the baby away from the breast. A tiny girl. When she lost the nipple she gasped and started to cry.

As soon as he heard her grief—the inarticulate woe of the newborn caught between two worlds, and the second world no better than death—Standing Hollow Horn knew exactly what he wanted to do.

He carried the baby of Red Day Woman out of her tipi and through the village. He was shaking with fury, his face twisted in ghastly shapes of wrath. Hatred and age—they had set him free from fear.

It occurred to him that he should thank *Wakan Tanka* for taking his cough away because he had a speech to make.

He did not pause to scratch on the flap of Fire Thunder's tipi. He put the crying baby in the crook of his left arm and with his right he threw back the flap and went in.

"Fire Thunder!"

The giant lay on his bedding, the slash across his left eye, his right eye open and cold as if he slept that way. He began to sit up.

But the old man was already screaming. "This is what comes of all your sinning, you Glutton! *Iya!* Eater of people! You son of Rock and Thunder! Here is a baby! Look at this baby! Do you hear this baby crying? She is crying because of you! She is all sorrows come to life in a tiny body! She is our hunger in the flesh! Look at her! Look at her! No, you *look* at the child, mighty chief! A naked baby born to cry and then to die. Everything else has been stolen from her. You have stolen it all. And the only thing left for this child is crying. Damn you! Oh, God damn—"

By now the baby was shrieking, her poor tongue quivering, her face gone red and puffy with the effort.

Standing Hollow Horn could no longer contain his anger in words alone. He put the baby down and jumped at Fire Thunder and began to kick him in the face, yelling, "Kill me! Go ahead and kill me like you kill everything else. Kill the baby too. You killed her mother. Red Day Woman is already dead—"

Without expression Fire Thunder accepted the barefoot kicks of a sick old man. He sat with his head bowed, his great arms folded over his knees, the left arm ravaged with red scars.

But when Standing Hollow Horn yelled the name of Red Day Woman, Fire Thunder looked up with a wild look in his eye. Then he stood up and seized him by his throat, his right hand surrounding the whole neck of the old man, and he lifted him off the ground.

Standing Hollow Horn said, "Awk." He expected now to die.

But Fire Thunder did not close his hand on the windpipe or else break the old man's neck in a pinch. Instead he gazed at him a moment, his eye unreadable, then in perfect silence he carried the Crier outside the tipi and set him on his feet and returned inside and pulled the flap closed.

Right away Standing Hollow Horn was running back to his own tipi. He was coughing: *hoc! Hoc, hoc!* The coughs shook his poor skinny body as powerfully as if someone were punching him in the chest. Water came out of his eyes, perhaps because of the coughing. But he didn't stop. He was in a great hurry.

The old man knew a trick, a dangerous sacred magic. If it went wrong it was strong enough to tear open the tipi of the sky. But if it went right it could so magnify the voice of one man that the mountains themselves would hear the roaring and the lost buffalo might be called back home again.

Well, and if someone was going to die soon anyway let him die trying a violence to save the people. No matter. He didn't care what happened to him. Except he must hurry or the cough would kill him first.

So he took an elk antler and carved it in the shape of a rattlesnake, a flat head at one end and rattle-rings all down its back. That is, he notched the length of the antler with deep grooves. Then he stretched a piece of rawhide over a hoop of wood. At the same time he was chewing the leaves of *hehaka tapejuta*, a certain horse mint that grew in dry hills. It was a very powerful herb. Now he spat this mash on the elk-horn rattlesnake and, pressing its head against the rawhide, he ran the shinbone of an antelope up and down the grooves. The rawhide took that living vibration and turned it into a sound that matched the old man's mood. It thundered forth his rage and his yearning and his sorrow and the love that he had never in all his life been able to turn into words. *Zooop! Zooop! Zooop!* Here was a sound that roared the truth, the nation's sad condition, a begging of the buffalo to come back again and save them. *Zooop! Zooop!*—a steady bellowing so loud that the leaves in the forest shivered and fell.

That day the Lakota bowed their heads and ceased to argue. They felt in their spirits a dreadful condemnation. These bursts of choked thunder were like the roar of the bull at the edge of the world, the breaking of his fourth leg: *Ohhh! Ohhh, no!*

By afternoon the sky turned white. If anyone stared at it long enough he could see that it was trembling like a drumskin. It was as if a stick as tremendous as seven trees was beating it from above. It could break. The stick could break through, and what then?

Standing Hollow Horn had removed himself to a bare knob of rock outside the village. It was there he caused a sound like the clapping of *wakinyan* wings, the collision of the sun and the moon together, the anguish of humanity, a hunger as huge as heaven. He was coughing constantly now. He had closed his eyes. His chest and throat were ripped with his coughing. His mouth tasted of a foaming blood. He could not sing. He let the bone and the antler of departed beasts sing for him.

Then, beneath the roaring of his magic, he heard the snap of a small twig. He began to smile. He thought it was Fire Thunder come to kill him and he smiled because under such a sound as he was making, great Fire Thunder was diminished to something like a deerfly.

But when he opened his eyes Standing Hollow Horn saw a sight so unexpected that he dropped his shinbone and the air was still. The hill and whole day were still.

He saw a young man ascending the stone hill not from the village but from the wilderness, a tall and ruddy young man solemn and strong—steadfast eyes, enormous eyes, his huge eyes streaming tears, a wild black unbraided hair exploding over his head, a scar where his left ear should have been.

Oh, no! Oh, no, this was more than the old man's heart could stand! This was not a young man, but a boy: Moves Walking!

*Waskn Mani, you have come home again!*

As he approached, the boy cried, "Grandfather, is it you? Are you the one who sends forth so terrible a voice? Oh, grandfather, let me bear the sorrow! *Hehlokecha Najin*, let me be your tears!"

Standing Hollow Horn could stare but he could not speak. Coughing had driven the air out of his lungs. Coughing continued still to constrict his poor chest even when there was no breath left to come out of it. Maybe instead of air the eyes would pop out of his head. That was a funny thought. So then the old man was laughing as well as coughing, but both were one long soundless squeak.

*Waskn Mani* came and knelt down next to him and embraced his old bony breast and so, by pressing hard around his ribs, took the pain out of his silent coughing.

The old man gazed at this marvelous apparition, the thing that his magic brought. He wanted to say, *Oh, Moves Walking I am glad I did not die until I saw you again.*

He wanted to say, *You idiot, where have you been? Contrary boy! Wrong-headed boy, why did you leave me alone?*

With all his might the ancient crier returned *Waskn Mani's* embrace. A wobbly sort of hugging it was. One wonders whether the boy could even feel it.

The old man wanted desperately to say, *I am your grandfather, Waskn Mani, now and always. And you are my grandson—*

But he could not say anything. He could not breathe.

So he worked his face around and kissed the boy on his young chest just below the collarbone. He saw that he left a little blood there. But he didn't have time to wipe it off again.

# 35

# Washigla: He Is in Mourning

*Waskn Mani* heard a baby crying. There was a baby crying down in the village. This was the second sound that day which had caused him suddenly to grunt in pain.

There are sounds which can hurt a dog's ears so much that the beast whines and runs away or else runs straight toward the sound in order to fight it or maybe to understand it. But for *Waskn Mani* the pain lodged in his breast like an arrow.

A baby was crying, a tiny misery no larger than the palm of his hand.

He was gazing down at Standing Hollow Horn, skinny old man, mostly bones upon which hung flat sacks of skin, exhausted old man who had just kissed him and closed his tired eyes and died. *Waskn Mani* had been holding him up off the ground, hugging him and begging him not to cry, asking that he be not so violently sad. *Waskn Mani* himself was sobbing for the old man's sadness.

In fact, the urgent thunder of the rattlesnake antler had been the

first sound that day to wound the boy. Such an anguished roaring!—
it had awoken him with a start. It had pierced him high in his chest
so that he drew his breath in pain. It had hooked him and pulled him
from his *Unchi* and from the tipi out over a wide dry distance to this
lonely knoll, calling him, calling him as the grumbling grandfather
clouds call *Wakinyan–Tanka*, that thunderbeing who lives at the top
of a mountain where the sun goes down. The bellowing air had called
this boy as surely as the spring clouds call thunder to come and
cleanse the earth. *Waskn Mani* had come running. And sobbing. And
then he was astonished to find that the source of such impacted roaring was but a busy, hunched, and bony old man. But then he was
overcome with joy: that old man was *Hehlokecha Najin*, his grandfather, whom he had not seen in seven seasons!

*Oh, Tunkashila, is that you?*

The boy had dropped to his knees. So then he could see that
Standing Hollow Horn was leaking water at his eyes. He was looking
straight at *Waskn Mani* and weeping at the same time. *Let me bear
the sorrow, Hehlokecha Najin! Let me be your tears.*

But his grandfather had answered not a word. His mouth was wide
open. His yellow teeth were long and useless. He was striving to
breathe but no air went in. No sound came out. So the boy gathered
the old man's bones into his arms and hugged him very hard, trying
to help the air go in or out. And Standing Hollow Horn had known
who was with him. Yes, he knew that it was *Waskn Mani*. Yes,
because look: He kissed him. That old man had kissed his grandson.
And then he had closed his tired eyes. And then he had died.

And *Waskn Mani* would have sat a long, long time with his grandfather in his arms—all night and maybe the next night too—except
that far away a baby began to cry. That tiny misery shot into the boy's
chest just below the collarbone, as sharp as a dart, causing him to
grunt with the sudden flash of pain.

He had to go.

He said, *I'm sorry, Hehlokecha Najin.*

So he composed the corpse just where it lay. This high stone hill was as good a burial scaffold as any. And then he turned his attention downhill toward the village, toward the baby that was crying there.

It had been seven seasons since *Waskn Mani* had approached the village of his people. In all that time he had assumed that he and his grandmother had lived in a deeper sorrow than they because the two of them had lived alone. Well, he had been wrong. What he saw now was much worse.

As he entered the village he began to think that the baby's wail was a lamentation for them all—the true voice of the people. For these people were helpless altogether and sad and hungry and perishing. There were white bones and the splinters of white bones in the road. How many times had they been boiled? No one threw them out or buried them.

Tipis were torn. They sagged on their poles like old ponies. Their color was grey. No man painted his tipi any more. No stories there, no boasting, no identity, no remembering—and for some lodges no inhabitants at all. Empty. Soon the poles would be stolen. Soon the hides would be cut into a stiff clothing.

And the people! His people! No one greeted him as he walked through the village. No one looked at him. No one noticed. Their eyes seemed to see nothing. Their eyes were glassy and sunken, a sort of yellow rheum thickening in the corners.

It was a cold day, almost the evening. But the people wore bald robes, all the fur worn off. No moccasins. Barefoot. Their hair was clotted with forgotten mud. Tired, tired people.

Perhaps they were past shame by now.

Or perhaps it was shame that kept their faces ever downward.

The children walked slowly, pushing huge bellies before them, mild and thoughtless faces. Watchfulness was in no one's face, no, nor interest nor openness either. Lethargy. A slack sadness.

They were losing teeth. Their fingers and toes had gone crooked. Some people's skin was covered with scabs and ruptures. No one spoke.

But a baby was crying. It was an infant voice so tiny that it sound-ed like the long croak of a frog, each wail wringing the last air from some little lung, *ooooh! Ooooooh!*

One child came up to *Waskn Mani* and put out a hand as if to receive something. But *Waskn Mani* had nothing to give. He shrugged and shook his head. It was impossible to tell whether the young one was a boy or a girl. No matter. It picked up a stone and threw it at *Waskn Mani*. The stone hit his forehead and caused a lit-tle blood to trickle down one side of his nose. But the child showed neither fear nor remorse. It didn't even run away. "*Wasna!*" it demanded over and over: "*Wasna! Wasna!*"

This small child kept repeating the word even when *Waskn Mani* had turned and walked away.

"*Wasnaaaaah!*"

So then water was coming out of the boy's eyes and mingling with his blood.

A baby was crying.

In the middle of this ragged encampment a baby breathed and wailed, breathed and wailed.

And suddenly *Waskn Mani* saw the infant lying naked on a leather apron in front of an open tipi. Fire Thunder's tipi. This living infant was scarcely bigger than a man's moccasin. It waved its fists like threat in the air, trembling arms, trembling little legs, a face squashed with sorrow, a pitiful little voice. Nevertheless, that voice was like a shaft in the breast of the boy who heard it—much more painful than any stone that broke his skin.

*Waskn Mani* sobbed, surprising himself. The air was cold! Why wasn't the baby covered? Where was the mother to care for it? He bent down and picked it up and stroked its little back. It was a girl. Immediately she curled herself against the boy's warm neck under-neath his chin. She made sucking sounds. She wanted to suck. *Waskn Mani* put his finger in the baby's mouth and felt a very strong and eager tongue. But where was the mother to nurse her?

He bent down a second time and looked into Fire Thunder's tipi and there, to his astonishment, he saw the huge warrior sitting with his back to the door. His heart jumped. He had not expected to find a living person in there. Always he had been able to feel the presence of mighty Fire Thunder even without seeing him—but this time there seemed to be no presence at all. Emptiness.

The boy spoke. He said, "Do you know the mother of this baby?" He was speaking through a door to the back of the *itancan*. He could not see a face. But he assumed that it wore no expression because that is how he remembered Fire Thunder and the man did not move.

*Waskn Mani* said, "Is this your baby?"

Nothing. Stillness. The day was passing into evening. The interior of the tipi was filling up with shadows.

"Do you remember me?" the boy asked. "I wish you would turn around and remember me. I am fifteen years old now. I have been a member of this band. I am acquainted with its people. Please tell me who will take care of this baby so that I can carry it to her. My name is Moves Walking. Don't you remember me?"

That massive back was as still as rock, two braids reaching down, the line of a loincloth across the hips. Fire Thunder did not move.

"My name is Moves Walking," the boy said. "My mother's name was Rattling Hail Woman. Surely you—"

Fire Thunder dropped his head from sight. Only the braids showed. *Waskn Mani* took that for a sign and entered the tipi. Still holding the infant against his neck, he moved one step sideways and saw a sight so grave that he himself became immobile. He scarcely breathed.

The water kept running from his eyes.

Lying on a backrest directly in front of Fire Thunder was a small woman clothed in a beautiful white doeskin dress. Her throat was adorned with necklaces of elk's teeth. There were bracelets of sage on both wrists, anklets on both ankles and beautiful paint on her cheeks.

She was dead. She had been prepared for burial. There were three tiny pairs of moccasins lined up on the ground beside her, the size of children's feet. *Waskn Mani* recognized the girl of slant eyes and smiling. This was Red Day Woman. Someone had brushed her hair. Someone had woven her wispy hair into two braids as thin as mice tails which now stuck out on either side of her head. And someone had cut a lock of hair from her forehead—

Someone? Why, Fire Thunder! Him!

For *Waskn Mani* watched in wonder while the warrior now dipped his finger in a rouge of ochre and reached across the round face to the part in the middle of Red Day Woman's hair and studiously drew a red line down her white scalp, a lovely scarlet line.

*Waskn Mani* stood behind Fire Thunder on his left. He could not see that giant's expression, only the headband that covered the eye and divided the head in two. But there was in the tipi a small note of woe: *Eeeeee*. It could not have been the baby in his arms. She was sleeping now. But it sounded not much different from the cry an infant makes, a sad, abandoned weeping, *Eeeeee*.

Who—?

Softly but very distinctly *Waskn Mani* said to Fire Thunder, "Well, this is the way things are now. I am taking the baby with me." He could not stay. This new sound went into his chest like an awl. It caused enough pain to make the boy grit teeth and gasp.

"Yes," he whispered, "this is the way things are now."

The warrior never looked around. He did not acknowledge the boy's coming or his going either.

*Waskn Mani* left the lodge of the *itancan*. He left the village of his people. He walked at first, but then he began to run. It was a cold evening. The Moon of the Falling Leaves. Autumn. And he hurt. He suffered a strange internal burning and it frightened him. Even his breathing rubbed the wounded place.

But when the baby cried, that turned the hurting into a streak of purest fire.

# 36
# A Moving Flint

*"Unchi!"*

It was midnight when *Waskn Mani* saw his tipi again. There was a bright white moon. The baby in his arms had awoken and was crying, drawing pitiful gulps of air and causing a sinew of pain in the boy's shoulder. He kept rolling the shoulder and dropping it in order to find some ease. No good. It merely disturbed the infant the more and she croaked such small woe that her face was swollen.

*"Unchi! Unchi!"*

His grandmother was standing when he entered. She had heard him coming.

"A baby!" she whispered.

"Take her, take her, please—she is hurting me!"

The old woman gave her grandson a single shrewd glance then gathered the tiny life into her arms. "Feed the fire," she said.

He did. It became a good red flame and the tipi grew warmer.

*"Unchi,"* he said, "the village is so sad. There is such sadness in the

people. Each person moves like a *wanagi*. Every face belongs to a floating ghost. *Hehlokecha Najin* died today. Here is a baby that I found in front of Fire Thunder's tipi. And do you remember Red Day Woman? She is dead too. Fire Thunder gave her three pairs of moccasins for the ghost road. Fire Thunder did that. I don't understand us any more. It is very bad. It is the black road—

"Oiyaaa!"

The boy had been kneeling beside the fire. Now suddenly he fell backward to the ground and arched his chest and stomach and hips: "*Unchi, Unchi,* why do I hurt like this?"

The baby had been quiet a while. But now she was cutting the air with a new wail and her voice had thrown the boy backward as though a bear's paw had swiped at him.

His grandmother knelt down and peered at him with her bright eyes. "*Waskn Mani,* tell me the truth. What are you feeling?"

He shook his head, staring at her. Sweat made his face shiny.

She said, "The baby's crying hurts you?"

He nodded.

She said, "The roaring we heard this morning? And the voices of all the Lakota—they hurt you?"

*Waskn Mani* touched the upper part of his chest, just below the collarbone, his eyes beseeching her.

The wrinkled old woman put her crooked fingers in that place. "Here?"

He nodded and her face seemed to collapse like an empty bag.

In all his years the boy had seen his grandmother cry but once, when the *itancan* Slow Buffalo, her old friend, died. Not even when his mother had disappeared. Well, if she had cried then it was in secret or else he had forgotten. But now, gazing steadfastly at her grandson, she let tears run into the thousand gulleys of her cheeks. Tears washed the lines of long sunlight and old sorrow. But she did not say anything.

The woman arose to her crippled feet and took the baby and washed her, then tucked the tiny one inside her robe against her ancient breasts to warm her. Two sisters, young and old, both of them wrinkled, one hungry but the other having no milk.

So then *Waskn Mani's* grandmother poured the liquid of *wojapi*, some fruit soup, into a bladder which she pricked with a sharp bone. She put the small holes into the baby's mouth and the baby stopped crying. The baby sighed and sucked and cried no more. So *Waskn Mani* was able to relax and let his poor body lie softly on the ground.

Next his grandmother took a very old bundle down from the place where it had hung as long as the boy remembered. She brought it near to him and sat down and untied it. Among a few other things there was a pipe in there with a finger-worn stem of wood and a stone bowl as red as blood and an eagle feather where the wood and stone were joined together.

"*Waskn Mani*," she said, "are you still awake?"

He said, "Yes."

"I want to give you a gift," she said. "It belonged to your grandfather and my husband, Black Elk. It is time that you should own it. It is time for you to use it now."

Suddenly she leaned over and slapped his face. "*Wachin ksapa yo!*" she said. Her bright eyes were very fierce, like the spotted eagle's eyes. "Be attentive, my grandson. Listen to me. I know why there is a pain in you. I have felt the same pain, but I was foolish and selfish and did not know what to do with it. Well, concerning the *cangleshka wakan*, the sacred hoop of the whole world, it is important that you know what to do with it."

# Waskn Mani's Grandmother Tells This Story:

My story starts long before you, my *takoja*, were born.

I lived with Black Elk as my husband for ten years. Ten good years. People envied me. I liked to be envied. I was not a shy woman when I was young. No, but I stood up straight and proud and most especially proud of that man, my husband, Black Elk.

Well, he had a virtue which made all the Lakota love him. Not wisdom, although he was wise; but a wise man is revered, not loved. Nor skill in killing buffalos, though Black Elk could do that too; but the hunter is admired, not loved.

Listen, *Waskn Mani:* your grandfather knew how to laugh. *Hau!* Black Elk laughed a good booming laugh. He could not help it. And whenever his big laugh went out over the plains, everyone who heard it laughed along with him. Then everyone felt good and healthy and happy too.

In those days people did not think of Slow Buffalo as the next *itan-can.* It was expected that Black Elk would take over that position. But we were all young then. We were all friends and we were happy together. Slow Buffalo would mumble some joke and Black Elk would throw back his huge head and laugh like the thunder—not in scorn, no, never in scorn, always in delight because he was truly at peace with all things and he loved to laugh. His laughter banished fear.

So then that was his gift to the people, noisy friendship and loud confidence.

We had ten good years together. And then he died.

This is what happened.

One night Black Elk suddenly sat up on his pallet. No light. No sound. He was like a shadow but the motion woke me.

"What?" I whispered.

"Crows," he said. "They're stealing the ponies."

Right away he got up and slipped outside naked. I followed. He was right. Two Crow warriors were creeping inside the corral, unhobbling our ponies and getting ready to stampede them all at once. The guard lay bleeding by the gate, unconscious.

Black Elk glanced once around himself and then he made a decision. He jumped up and started to wave his hands, yelling "Hoka! Hey!" as if he had weapons and was planning to attack. But he had no weapons!

I was so afraid for him, but I made the tremelo of encouragement.

The two Crows whirled around and each one leaped on a pony bareback and started to ride straight for Black Elk, the first one with a war club, the second one pulling an arrow from his quiver.

He didn't run away. He kept yelling "Hoka! Hey!" and I kept making the tremolo as loud as I could, but I was afraid. I thought I was already looking at his death.

Well, but just as the first rider charged him Black Elk sprang straight up in the air and threw his body crossways against the Crow's chest and they both came down behind the galloping pony—Black Elk on top! I felt so happy! Black Elk had his forearm over that man's throat, choking him.

But as soon as the second rider passed them by he wheeled his pony round and notched an arrow and drew it back to his ear and then shot Black Elk in the back. That arrow went in very deep. I saw it go in slowly, as if in a dream. Black Elk was bending forward. The arrow pierced his lower back and thrust upward inside his ribs until just the feathers were sticking out, low and evil.

Black Elk stood up and stumbled sidewards.

I started to scream.

The Crow warrior that Black Elk had been choking—he got up now. He went for his war club. But I was so mad that I ran for it too and I got there first. I picked it up. When the Crow jumped at me I swung my club with all my might. He put his arm up. I broke it. The bones popped out. I was screaming. I swung again and hit the warrior between his eyes. He went down. But I was so mad for what they did to Black Elk that I kept hitting him and hitting him. Soon he was bloody all over. He was not moving any more, but I could not stop hitting him. I was crazy, screaming at the top of my lungs, hitting a dead man.

Then someone grabbed me from behind and wrapped his arms around my whole body and lifted me from the ground. Well, there was only one person who could have stopped me. I smelled the smell of Black Elk. It was Black Elk, whispering in my ear, "Hush, hush, hush," over and over again. He wasn't dead after all.

I turned around and held him, and of course he was laughing low and softly. His laughing made me cry. I could not say how glad I was then. So he laughed and I cried.

But the arrow was still inside of him.

I lit an oil lamp in the tipi. He lay on the bedding on his stomach and I sat on the back of his legs to pull the arrow out, but I couldn't.

It would not come backwards.

Black Elk said to push it through, but that would not work either because the point had stuck in a bone below his left shoulder. It went up inside of him like a second backbone.

He told me to twist it, then, and pull at the same time.

I did. There was a loud *Crack!* sound and then the arrow slid out easily. But when I looked I saw that at the end of the shaft were loose rawhide strips. No flint. The flint had stayed in him. It was still stuck in the bone beneath his shoulder.

Black Elk saw this too. We both saw it and were silent. I bandaged the low wound by sticking a little sage to the blood. He put some *kinnickinnick* in his pipe and smoked for a while and then turned over and went to sleep. That night I did not sleep. I wondered about the flint inside of him: what did that mean?

In the morning he woke and said, *"Hihani washtay"* to me. He said, "Good morning" as if nothing had happened last night. I kept quiet, but I was still wondering about the flint.

Well, but those were good years. Ten good years. They were the red and blue days for me.

We had a baby together. A girl.

She was so beautiful! Black Elk boomed with laughter every time he looked at her and all the people rejoiced because of the sound of his wonderful laughing. His daughter was just like him. Even when she was tiny she would grin and giggle with no teeth. She would giggle fast and hard as if she were trying to catch up to her father for laughter, as if it were a contest. Well, so he named her according to the little sound of her giggling. He said she sounded like the tiny tinkling of ice on a frozen lake: *Wsu Sna Win*, then. He called her Rattling Hail Woman.

It was in these days that the people of our band began to say that Black Elk should be the next *itancan*. Even Slow Buffalo said the same. And I truly believe that if it had come to pass there would have been no jealousy in anyone just because there was no guile in Black Elk. Only kindness. And love. And great laughter in that huge chest of his.

Then one day he went out and caught a certain wild pony that he had been trying to catch for a long time. He was a beautiful black stallion with white dapples and a mane like dark fire. Perhaps if it had been some other pony Black Elk would have stopped trying to break him after three throws. But he did not stop. Four times that stallion threw Black Elk down to the ground. Five times. Six.

In the end the pony was broken.

So was the man.

All night long I heard something like cracking twigs in Black Elk's breathing. In the morning I saw that blood had come up. It was crusty brown around his lips. It was red between his teeth.

He looked over at me and cleared his throat several times and spat to the side. Then he lifted his hand and laid a finger against his chest on the high left side. He tapped that place, saying nothing. He didn't have to say anything. I knew already: the flint had broken free. The flint was moving inside of him, cutting something when it moved. The crackling sound in his breathing was blood.

No, he didn't have to say anything. I knew of his pain because I, too, *Waskn Mani*—I felt exactly the same pain in my chest in exactly the same place. Exactly! In him it was a flint which the enemy had put there. In me it was love. The love in me was as sharp as that Crow flint and just as real. *Wachin ksapa yo!*

Well, Black Elk had to be very careful now. He could not ride the stallion he had just broken—not hard, and hard was the only way that stallion could run. So, not at all! He gave the pony away.

And though Black Elk was a good hunter, he should not hunt buffalos any more either. That motion drove the flint and made it travel through the soft parts of his lungs, sending up new blood. He should not fight. He should not run, no races, no games, no dancing, no sudden moving of his body.

And most especially, Black Elk should not laugh. No, no, the laughing shook his lungs and the flint cut deeper. No. If he laughed in the night, well, the next morning he would tap his chest and I would see that the tapping had always come a little closer to his heart—but I knew that already because the pain in me was also closer to my heart, a sharp pain, a piercing pain in my chest, though the only stone in me was love. But love can kill, *Waskn Mani*, and that is what I am telling you.

One morning after he had laughed, when his mouth again was rounded by new blood, I said, "Now you must promise that you will not laugh any more. It is killing you, Black Elk. It is killing me with you. But we have a child now. For her sake you must never laugh again."

I argued very hard that morning. I would not let him go. Finally he said, "I promise."

I said, "I am a witness. I will remember."

He said, "*Hau*. Yes. I know."

And so he was a solemn man after that and I was sorry for it but I was not wrong and I did not apologize.

He did not bleed again in that whole year.

Neither did I hurt. We were alive together.

But then it was your mother, *Waskn Mani*. It was *Wsu Sna Win*. And she never knew. This is the part of the story that I never told her, but I am telling you.

No one could ever convince the girl that she was not a warrior, the best fighter among the Lakota. At five years old she had made weapons for herself. At five she thought she was a hunter.

So one day I saw her creeping through the underbrush crouched forward, tip-toe, tip-toe. She had painted the jagged yellow lines down her legs and a fierce red color on her face. She carried a little bow with arrows, a little buffalo-horn knife, and a whole dead mouse was hanging beside her ear.

Tiptoe, tiptoe: right behind her came a dog, his ears twisting, trying to understand what the girl was doing. She didn't know he was there. She took a step, he took a step. She stopped, he stopped.

Then all at once that dog got happy as if he understood the game and he grinned and pushed his nose in the girl's butt.

*Boom!*

The child exploded in fright. She jumped straight up. The bow and the knife went flying. The whole dead mouse flew backward at the dog. The dog yelped and ran one way; the girl screamed and ran the other way; and then I heard Black Elk laughing.

Black Elk had been watching too!

He couldn't help it. After a year he was laughing again and he was not stopping. "Girl, you are Lakota!" he roared. "You look for the enemy in front. He comes behind and you run. But he's only a dog! Ah, ha ha ha ha!"

I shouted, "Stop it!" But he didn't hear me.

He grabbed his stomach and boomed with laughter. He thundered laughter.

"Stop it!" I screamed. "Black Elk stop it! You promised! Stop it!"

The tears ran from his eyes. He went down on his knees. He was not even trying to stop! I was so mad that I ran at him. I began to beat him. I hit him with my two fists. He was shaking with laughter. Didn't he know what he was doing to us? What was the matter with him? I hit him and hit him. I could feel the flint cutting me—*cutting through me because I loved him!* I didn't want either one of us to die! I was screaming, "Stop! Stop! You stubborn selfish man, stop laughing!"

And then for one moment I thought he was obeying me.

He drew a deep breath and fell silent. He put his hand up to my arm and pulled me down. I stopped hitting him. I bent over him. He was looking up into my eyes and reaching with his right hand across his breast—and suddenly something like a spasm grabbed his body and the blood burst from his mouth in a stream, but he didn't look surprised. He was gazing at me and tapping his chest.

I took his head against my breast. I was not mad any more. I was so scared. I was sorry that I had been mad. I rocked his head against myself. I rocked him back and forth. But the blood was running out of his mouth now and there was no way to stop it. He took my hand and put it on his heart. That's where the flint was. I knew. I knew. I knew where the flint was. It was in my heart too. It was killing me too.

I leaned down and kissed his bloody lips. I kissed the blood that came from his heart and my heart too. I kissed Black Elk and he crinkled his eyes and his stomach moved as if he were laughing low and slow, but only pink bubbles came up and foamed at his mouth and then his face went slack and his eyes closed and he died.

We died.

We both died, *Waskn Mani*. This is the truth. The flint in him, the love in me, cut my heart the same as his and we died together but my death did him no good.

*Wachin ksapa yo!*

*Waskn Mani*, listen to me: my death did not do any good for anyone. No one took benefit from my dying because I did not give it away! I fought it! I fought dying all the way to the end, and then I was only merely dead.

Our daughter, your mother, *Wsu Sna Win*—she laughed alone after that. I never laughed with her. She was happy and the people loved her just as they had loved Black Elk but I could not share in happiness. I was dead. She was lonely, truly. No one took the benefit, do you hear me?

And Slow Buffalo, my dear friend, waited a decent period of time and then offered to marry me. He asked me to marry him because he loved me. But I was dead. I loved no one. We stayed friends even unto the end, but neither did he ever marry. No one took the benefit of my dying. It was not a sacrifice. I did not give it away. Do you understand?

*Waskn Mani*, the wrinkles in my face began on that very day. I am a badlands on account of dying with Black Elk. I did not know that there might have been a choice. So I fought dying, his dying and my dying. I only hated it.

But you have a choice, boy. *Waskn Mani,* you are the same as I was before my dying. The pain in you is your love for the people. It is like the flint in Black Elk. In them it is starvation, a craving for company and food, all the four-leggeds and life again. Oiyaaa, it is a killing ache. In you it is love. It is a killing love.

But you, *Waskn Mani,* if you choose the death that is at the end of the loving before it kills the people, if you choose a willing sacrifice, if one person should die in the place of the people—well, then they all might have the benefit. The people might live.

Love always suffers the same as the beloved. It is not a question, *koshkalaka,* whether true love suffers. To the extent that it is true, it truly suffers. The only question is whether it might do a little good before both of them die. One might make a gift of his life for them he loves.

Pray, grandson.

*Waskn Mani,* pray.

Take the pipe of your grandfather, Black Elk. Go to a sacred place and pray to *Wakan Tanka* for a vision that can save the people. If someone does not heal the hoop of the world, everyone will die. Go, *hokshicantkiye.* Go, boy of my heart. Go and do what your selfish *Unchi* did not do. Pray.

# 37
# Chanunpa:
# The Pipe

Dawn streaks the sky now, a grey light coming, a grey sky. But the plains have gone white in the night. It is a ghostly earth. Frost has come down on everything. The air is cold and still.

There are pools the wind did not trouble during the night. These pools now wear a thin ice.

Growing things will soften and blacken before this day is done. The sun will sicken them. But right now the grasses and the bushes and the trees are beautiful. Tiny hands have drawn white lines upon their faces. Their limbs are dressed in white designs. The whole earth, our *ina* and the *ina* of every living thing, seems clothed in a fine white buckskin as far as the eye can see, west and north and east and south. That is the way we turn when we pray, first to the west and finally to the south, then down, then up. This morning the sky is grey. *Tunkashila* is frowning.

What does it signify that the earth is clothed so completely in white? Something very happy. Something very sad. In a sacred manner it may be both.

There is one tipi in the middle of a white plain. Smoke goes straight up from it. Not far away there is a small sweat lodge built of willow branches and very old buffalo skins. A hot fire was burning in front of it on the east side, but now that fireplace is black. There is a path between the sweat lodge and the fireplace. No one is walking on that path.

Suddenly a voice goes up in the silent white world, singing a frightened song: *Don't leave me alone! Don't leave me alone!* This is the cry of an infant. It comes from the tipi.

Now we see why the baby is crying.

An old woman is coming out of the tipi. A young man is following her. He is much taller than she is. When they turn to face each other in the greylight her eyes are at the level of his chest.

The young man removes his shirt. He has a long body, good muscles. His arms are long and smooth. He gives the shirt to the old woman. He gives her his leggings and his moccasins too. There is no robe. He is naked now except for the loincloth. His joints and his face look relaxed. He wastes no motion. His breath goes out in white streams from his nostrils. We say *waniyetu* when we see that breath. We are thinking of the winter.

This young man may be a boy, so beautiful is his face. He has high cheekbones and eyes as huge as smoking suns. His eyes are the smudges in which we save fire from camp to camp. His hair is a black rain upon his shoulders. He does not have the braids of a man. There are no marks of the hunter upon him. None of the warrior.

Well, but it is as a man that he smiles down upon the old woman in front of him. It is evident that they have love each for the other and that hers is filled with fear and admiration.

The woman is cradling a bloodred pipe in her two hands. She lifts it now as if to give it to the man–boy and he puts out his own hands as if to take it—but suddenly she withdraws the pipe. See, he drops his hands and lowers his face because of that. He is disappointed. Perhaps he is not worthy.

She offers the pipe a second time and a second time refuses to give it to him. Twice! It increases his disappointment.

Old woman, old woman, you are so bent and wrinkled. Your fingers clutch like a hawk's claws. You do not let go of the pipe stem. Even a third time you raise it as if to give it away. You raise it as high as your eyes. You gaze at the boy and wait until he reaches out yet again the third time. He is so uncertain now. But just when he reaches out you take it back again. Old woman, your hair is like the hoarfrost. Why do you humiliate the boy in this manner?

Well, but the woman must be strong in her persuasion. Yet again a fourth time she offers the pipe and though she must now wait long and long she neither leans nor trembles and finally the boy obeys her patient gaze. He brings up his own hands the fourth time and holds them beneath the pipe stem. She nods. She lowers her arms and allows his hands to become the pipe's cradle now. She steps backward and sighs and a cloud goes out from her mouth and now she does not look at him any more. They part.

The boy turns and with a long stride begins to walk westward. Soon he is running. He has the wolf's lope and the wolf's endurance. His hair streams backward through the air. Black hair dancing in a white world. Clearly, he can run the day-long and not grow tired.

Wherever his foot strikes ground the boy–man cancels frost. Each footfall leaves the black track of a human. A narrow trail goes westward, far, far away.

The old woman has not been watching.

She has returned to the tipi and now bends down to tug its pegs from the ground, one after the other. When the last peg is pulled its whole covering sucks inward. She unpins the buffalo skin covering up its front. She must climb a pole–ladder to get at the higher pins. It is obvious that the ladder hurts her feet. But when the covering slips down the tipi's skeleton of poles, there is that tiny baby, wailing in the blind air of the morning: *Don't leave me, don't leave me!*

Now the crooked hawk's fingers have tied the tipi poles together in the pointed shape of a pony-drag. And the thin arms have folded the tipi covering into a seat between the poles. And the old face leans down to comfort the baby. She places the infant among a few possessions on the pony-drag.

There is no pony, of course.

So the woman pulls the long crossed poles over her head and rests them on her own shoulders and she bows and she begins to walk eastward.

The walking is painful to her feet. She goes slow, like Turtle.

So the icy plain is left with the sweat lodge only and a circle where the tipi was and a trail of human feet to the west and the black scrape of a pony-drag eastward.

Listen: all the world is white and quiet now.

The cry of the baby is gone.

# 38
# Hanblechia: The Crying for a Vision

The day upon which he woke to the buffalo roaring and pain high in his chest—the day he helped Standing Hollow Horn die and then returned with an infant in his arms—that was the first day. And the first night was the night his *Unchi* told her story. He neither ate food nor drank water from one morning to the next.

Then all the second day he ran westward. He carried the pipe in his left arm, the stem pointing forward upon his palm, the bowl tucked tightly by his body. He did not eat or drink.

There still was the remembered ache in his chest.

And though the day was cold he did not feel it.

Late in the second day he looked up and thought he saw something familiar ahead of him. It caused his heart to thump with joy. He could not be sure because the sun was in his eyes, but he thought he saw a four-legged. Hi ho! Were they coming back? He ran faster. No, but this poor beast looked like a skeleton standing up. Long-legged and bony, its body a grey lump. *Waskn Mani* squinted but could not see a face or eyes.

Then he saw five more creatures exactly the same, skinny and seeming to graze on a hillside.

No! There were more than five. Many! A great herd of four-leggeds all over the western hills!

Oh, the boy wanted to be happy. It did not seem to be a dream. But these animals were so gaunt. They were all the color of earth. They stood so still. And this, too, was strange: that every beast stood alone, no groups, no families together, none lying down. It caused a queer feeling in *Waskn Mani's* stomach. What was the matter? Could a whole herd die standing up? Oh, but that is a foolish thought.

Foolish, foolish, so foolish!

As he drew nearer the boy began to know his error and he slowed down.

He stopped running. He walked very slowly with his head down.

These were not the four-leggeds. They were the scaffolds of a thousand Lakota dead. Four long poles and a platform of sticks and on every platform a body. His people. Some but recently left here, their robes unweathered. Some left long ago—but there were no birds nor beasts to claim the corpses. There was only the wind and the cold and the sun. And the seasons. Time. The bodies could only wither and shrink and grin.

How many bands had come by here leaving their dead behind?

*Waskn Mani* walked for miles among the people of his nation, down a hill and up another. The scaffolds were taller than he. The dead were in all sizes, children and elderly, mothers and fathers and warriors dead without glory.

*O Wakan Tanka,* the boy said while water began to run from his eyes. *Wakan Tanka, the Icke Wichasha. The people!*

Here a beautiful black braid hung down between the sticks. Everywhere little bundles were tied to the scaffold. In some places the poles had broken and dumped grandparents to the ground. And all was absolutely silent. The nation lay uncomplaining and utterly still. Only *Waskn Mani* moved. His step caused a crunching sound.

*But we were like the buffalo once, laughing among the tipis.*

He drew a breath of air in order to speak aloud, but the cold evening and this stinking congregation caused a sudden stab of pain in his chest below the collarbone. *Oiyaaa!*

By the middle of the second night the boy was running again, as tireless as the wolf. He had the wolf's deep heart and her memory and her knowledge of the night. He knew by instinct the land ahead of him. And he knew precisely the place where he would pray.

*If the hoop is not repaired, she said, everyone dies. This is the end of the world. But the sacred hoop may be repaired when someone gives his life for the sin—either in punishment or else in sacrifice.*

*The boy with the black eyes said, "But who died, Shunkmanitu Tanka? How?"*

Here was a little lake. *Waskn Mani* paused and rested but he did not drink. There were stars in the sky now, making a solid darkness of everything earthbound. The lake reflected this dusting of stars. There were no leaves on the water to cover their reflection. No lilies.

And there in the south, a black immensity blotting out the light of any star, stood the mountain.

Invisible was the figure on the face of it, that woman whose braids flew wild around her head, whose arms were raised in supplication, whose grief was mute and intolerable. She was a black burn. The mountain was but black shadow. The night was blackness itself.

*Waskn Mani* now ran at full speed flat out as if he had not yet run at all. There would not be another pause. There would be no more rest for him.

By sunrise of the third day he was throwing the bones behind him, the white bones, the dry bleached bones of the mothers of his relatives. His crying had found its sound: "Hownh," the boy cried aloud. "Hownh, hownh," for all the dead and the dying too, for his *ina* and his *unchi* and his *tunkashilas*, both Standing Hollow Horn and the Black Elk whom he had never met, and all the band among whom he had loved, for Red Day Woman also dead and for the man who sat cross-legged in front of her preparing the body for burial, for him too, for the one-eyed *itancan*, him. Him. Fire Thunder.

"Hownh, hownh, hownh."

At midday *Waskn Mani* was climbing the high escarpments of the mountain, his face against the rock, his fingers split, and his legs bloody.

Finally, at sunset of the third day, he was running barefoot over the old snow of the summit of *Scorched Mountain Woman*, stumbling for the great weariness of his quest and for hunger and thirst, but not resting. Upon the extreme peak of the mountain he knelt down and scooped a hole in the snow, then he stood up and faced the place where a red sun waited upon the rim of the earth. *Waskn Mani* lifted his voice. He bellowed, "*Unshe ma la ye!*"—raising the pipe in his left hand, pointing its stem directly toward the bloodred sun. "*Unshe ma la ye!*" he bellowed and immediately a wind began to blow from that place and the boy walked straight into that wind ten paces, beating the snow down with his feet and making a path. "*Wakan Tanka, unshe ma la ye!* O God, be merciful to me!" he yelled.

But he was crying too. Ever since the scaffolds and the great hills of bones on the mountain, he had not stopped crying.

Now he returned to the hole in snow in the center of the mountain in the center of the earth and then turned north and strode ten paces toward the bitter coldness of that region, pointing the pipe before him. With a flash of red light the sun jumped off the edge of the earth and it was the night. But the mighty wind continued, tearing the boy's hair eastward.

"*Wakan Tanka, unshe ma la ye,*" he wailed, "*oyate wani wachin cha!*"

Suddenly—just as he cried *oyate*—he dropped to his knees. He bowed low and with his right hand grabbed at his breast, crying, "Ow! Ow!" There must have been an exquisite pain in that place, but yet there was no pausing. He stood up again and turned back to the hole in snow and then walked eastward ten paces and made a path in that direction too and in that place cried out, "*Wakan Tanka, unshe ma la ye oyate wani wachin cha*! Oh, God be merciful to me that my people may live!"

Once more back to the hole in snow he stumbled and this time he turned south and walked ten paces. He prayed to the south, pointing the pipe there. He prayed the same agonized prayer, the wind still tearing it from his lips so that one wondered whether he had been heard at all.

And then he faced down to the ground and prayed, and then up toward heaven he prayed, and these six directions he repeated over and over again, ever beating his four paths deeper in the snow, weeping, weeping while the terrible wind kept blowing from the west where the sun had jumped off the side of the earth.

By midnight nothing had happened.

In the hours that followed, though the boy wept and prayed with all his might, nothing happened. The stars walked no slower, no faster toward morning. The stars did not pause or stop. Time did not honor the prayer of the boy. He was running out of time.

Finally he collapsed in the center hole and could not get up again. He started to scold himself. He made a fist of his right hand and hit his chest as hard as he could. "*Witko!*" he said. "*Waskn Mani, witko! Witko!* You are crazy to think that you are good enough to pray for the people. What good are you? Hownh, hownh. *Atkuku wanice,* fatherless bastard. It is only pride that makes you think that you are worthy, hownh—" The boy struck himself with the knuckle of his thumb. Not lightly! No, the beating seemed hard enough to break bones. "Why should *Wankan Tanka* send you a vision for the people? What good did you do for your *unchi?*" he said. "What good did you do for your grandfather? He called you contrary. He was right—"

All at once there was a terrific clap of thunder in the west. The thunder said: *WACHIN KSAPA YO!* The boy was stunned to silence. All his bones went cold. *BE ATTENTIVE,* the thunder commanded.

*Waskn Mani* looked and saw a cloud coming up over the western rim of the earth, a cloud the size of his hand. He started to get up.

But: *Crack–BOOM!*—the thunder spoke a second time and knocked him down. When he scrambled to stand again he saw that the cloud was growing and sailing straight for his mountain. The wind was like a hammer against his forehead. The boy bent into it. He was trembling so badly he thought he would fall again.

The thunder had said, *I AM HERE TO TEACH YOU.*

The boy cried out, "What do you want me to do?"

And the thunder said, *SHOW ME THE PIPE THAT HOLDS THE WHOLE WORLD IN IT.*

"The pipe!" It was gone. The poor boy looked here and there and then he saw it lying in his hole. He picked it up and aimed the stem to the west—and now he saw that the cloud was not a cloud at all but a buffalo, a mighty buffalo, a white buffalo cow stampeding across the sky in his direction, her brow broader than the moonlight, her shaggy coat a curtain of light, her horns two forks of lightning, her wide eyes darts of a silver lightning. And her voice was the thunder that he heard.

Small *Waskn Mani* shook so hard that he could not aim the pipe. It danced and jiggled before his sight. Its wooden end scribbled the sky.

The white buffalo was galloping closer and closer.

She was looking directly into the boy's face. It was not an unkind looking. But suddenly she glanced at the pipe in front of him and fire flew out of her eyes. A needle of fire pierced the air between them and touched the bowl of his stone pipe and left it burning bright red.

*KOSHKALAKA*, the thundering buffalo said, *BREATHE ALL THINGS IN ONE THING. DRAW THEM INTO YOU. SMOKE THE PIPE.*

Quickly, before the buffalo had come close enough to trample him, *Waskn Mani* obeyed.

He put the stem between his lips and inhaled and immediately he was stabbed with the pain of it. Oiyaaa, this smoke was flame in his left lung. The pipesmoke like flint cut downward toward his heart—but this, he saw in a sudden calm, was as it should be. All was right. All was good: that the people might live.

So *Waskn Mani* exhaled a huge plume of white smoke—as if the mountain itself were blowing smoke—and willingly he drew another breath through the burning pipe and again his throat was scorched and his chest felt like a fireplace filled with coals. But he was no longer afraid. He felt ready for anything. He blew out a whole cloud of white smoke. The buffalo galloping toward the mountain—she was galloping in his smoke now!

*Waskn Mani* smoked the pipe a third time.

But when he drew smoke and exhaled for the fourth time he saw that his breath was no longer white. It was red—and the boy began to giggle: his breath was like the red dust the buffalo cow blows when she is calving. It went up from his mouth like a sunrise red; he was making a blood-colored cloud in the firmament. Perhaps he was making the morning!

Now the white buffalo cow jumped down from the sky and landed on the mountain. The boy thought the earth would be shocked by her great weight. He thought the ground would tremble beneath her feet, but it didn't. Instead she walked with a soft step. She was walking toward him and she was speaking in a gentle voice. *Waskn Mani, Waskn Mani,* she was saying, *I have come to praise you for the strong son that you have become.*

The boy gaped at her. Suddenly he felt so weak that he sank to his knees, but his ears and his eyes were very clear.

As she came, the white buffalo cow lay down in the snow and rolled over, and when she stood up again she was a woman of grace and beauty. She kept walking toward the boy. *Well-bred, Waskn Mani,* she said. *Well-bred, my son. Yes, you have brought honor to me all the days of your life. Hetchetu welo. It is very good.*

He could do nothing but kneel in his snow-hole and stare at her. She wore a white buckskin dress so supple he saw the body beneath. There was no other adornment. Dark woman. Tall, grave, smooth and beautiful. Familiar! He had seen this woman before. No moccasins. Her ankles and her arms were bare and her black braids lay upon her breast.

*Hush,* she said. *You needn't cry any more. I have loved you since I bore you. I will love you forever.*

Yes, it was true: he was crying. He had forgotten that he was crying.

"*Ina?*" he whispered. "Is that you?"

*Ohan*, she said moving closer, lifting her long-fingered hands.

"Have I found you? Have you come to me?" the poor boy whispered, transfixed, unable to move, kneeling and gazing upward into her black eyes. "This is you and not somebody else? Rattling Hail Woman? Mother? Mother?"

*Yes*, the beautiful woman murmured, reaching down with both hands to touch the boy both upon his forehead and upon his breast. *Yes. Yes. Yes.*

# 39

# Wanagi Yuhapi: The Keeping of Her Spirit

Here comes an old woman doing the work of a pony, doing the work the dogs did before there were ponies. Here comes a small woman, crouched and weary and old, pulling a pony-drag. This is a sad picture. It should not have been, no, not in anyone's lifetime. Look: the long staves come up over her shoulders and then they cross before her face and go on ahead of her as far forward as she is tall. They are long poles. In another life they were long enough to frame her tipi. Behind her at the spread of the poles a little bed is made. Upon that bed there is a baby bound tightly in order that she shall not fall off. She is looking around. The ends of these poles have been worn sharp by the dragging. It is clear that the old woman, caught in such a traveling drag, cannot go backward. The poles would stab the ground and stop her.

It is the middle of the day.

The old woman takes three steps then rests, three steps and then another rest, always just three steps.

She has entered a dreary village.

There is a man sitting in front of his tipi watching her. As she pass-
es by—three steps, resting, looking groundward as if her mind were
elsewhere—this man calls out: "*Wakanka*, how long have you been
traveling?"

*Wakanka*, he said. That is a particular sort of old woman. One who
lives alone outside the camp circle. One who might bring fortune or
misfortune with a glance. A witch.

But the man does not speak in reverence nor in fear nor in supplication. Therefore his word *Wakanka* is a mockery. Without mirth
he is laughing at the woman.

The reason for her pausing every third step is that her feet are
crooked and filled with hurting. There is a small dabble of blood
under each right foot print behind her because the dry flesh cracked
some time ago. Watch closely: when she pauses she lifts the right foot
slightly from the ground and lets the left take her weight. The broken sole must hurt.

"*Wakanka!* Where do you come from? How long have you been
traveling?"

"I am *Hihan kara*, back from the ghost road," the woman says, still
facing the earth because of her burden, "where I choose to send men
like you over the edge."

The man makes a pale smile and nods. He gives her a grudging
admiration: a joke for a joke.

"I have been walking since yesterday noon," sighs the woman. She
is no longer joking. "Since yesterday. A day, a night, another day."

The man nods again. But he does not get up. He does not offer to
help her. Soon his attention wanes and by the time the woman has
moved away the man is in the stupor of the starving, staring nowhere.

It is like this throughout the whole village.

There is an *itancan* here, to be sure—one of the most glorious
chiefs that anyone can recall. But it doesn't matter. No one much
obeys the *itancan* any more. No one fears him. The authority has
passed out of his word because hungry people do not care about
threats or about praise either. Desolated people are free of the power
of leaders when that power cannot find food or else inspire hope.

Dying people do not distinguish what sort of death they die, whether by starvation or by a big man's arrow. Well, and maybe the arrow is the better way. So, shoot us, Big Man. Or feed us. And if you cannot do either, then what good are you?

This is the band of Fire Thunder, for ten years a band of prominence and, until last year, a band of unimagined power and triumph. But throughout the summer and now in autumn there has grown up a saying to signal the desolation of the people. Women muttered it first, then the older men, then everyone. And just yesterday a woman said it directly to the chief himself because she does not care about anything any more: "What good are you now, Fire Thunder?" she said as a measure of her deep indifference.

This is the wife of a man named *Wachpanne*, a man of some repute whom the people called Poor. She happened to be passing the tipi of the *itancan* and she saw him sitting inside, so she said, "Fire Thunder, what good are you now?" then turned and walked on, not so much as looking back. It is the truth of her heart. But her heart is empty of all feeling and she does not care what the chief might do to her for her insolence. Yesterday *Wachpanne* finally died of wounds which he had received almost a year ago, wounds that continued to fester for ten months, refusing to heal no matter how often his wife washed them. She could clean them from the outside but not from within. Nothing could clean his wounds from within.

*Mighty Chief, you terrible itancan, what good are you now?*

Once the one-eyed warrior was legendary for his casual killings, for fearlessness in a shower of arrows. But now death is everybody's yesterday or else his tomorrow. So what? Now the stories regarding Fire Thunder's glory have lost the ability to interest anyone. Hunger causes equality. Famine reveals the human flesh—that none is not dependent, none is not helpless on his own. None.

So shoot us or feed us, Big Man. We are very tired. Feed us or kill us quickly—or else what good are you?

The old woman pulls her pony-drag through a dreary village, three steps and stops, three more steps, three, three.

Whenever the infant behind her begins to cry the woman lays the crossed staves down and searches through her few possessions for a thin soup in a bladder, then she sits and suckles the child. The listless people watch. But no one offers to help her. Perhaps no one recognizes her. Much has changed in the two years since last she lived among these people—and even then she was separated from them by her great age. All the people of her generation have died. All save herself. Perhaps she should be dead as well.

Three steps and a rest. Three steps on ruined feet whose lumps show through the moccasin.

"*Wakanka*, how far from here to the ghost road and back again? How far?"

And now it is late in the day. And here she is in front of the chief's tipi. The baby starts to cry. The old woman takes the crossed poles from her shoulders and lays them down. But this time she does not go back to comfort the infant. She goes instead to the closed flap of Fire Thunder's tipi. She hesitates a moment, as if deciding whether to scratch and ask permission to go in. No. No, she reaches and with her hawk's claw of a hand she snatches the flap away. Her little body is so bent that now she enters without bowing down.

The baby outside squalls louder for being alone.

Inside there is only a little light. No fire. But Fire Thunder is here.

Immediately the woman sees that giant standing full height, twice her height, facing the door, facing her, gazing at her with a single dark eye. He seems to be frozen in the middle of an act. With his left hand he is holding the right hand high before his face, its forefinger is extended as if broken or wounded or terribly tender.

Fire Thunder whispers in a strangled voice, "Can you pray for the dead?"

The woman's face wreathes with deep wrinkles and a curious frown. "Pray?" she says. "*Pray*, Fire Thunder?"

"No holy man has come," he whispers. It is a ghastly voice. "Do you know how to pray for the spirit of the dead?"

He still has not released his right wrist. Perhaps he wants to show the woman his finger.

She says, "Do you know who I am?"

The infant outside has not ceased crying. Her wailing is a thin string trembling between grief and grief, between loneliness and hunger.

The woman says, "I am the grandmother of Moves Walking. Two days ago he took a crying *hokshi cala* away from your tipi. I have brought her back again."

"Yes, I know you," whispers Fire Thunder, his black eye steadfast upon the tiny woman's face. "No, I do not want that baby in here. No," he whispers, "but I want you to pray for the spirit of a dead woman before she must walk the *wanagi tacanku* alone."

His right eye is a rod of iron. The black slash across the left eye troubles the old woman's looking. But the deep scars on his left arm cause a tiny pity in her, and now he carries his forefinger closer to her vision and she sees something like a ring around it. No, not a ring at all but human hair, a lock of human hair, a most thin and wispy lock of hair.

"Who is that?" the woman asks, lowering her own voice now. It is almost inaudible. *Who is that?*

A muscle works at the back of the big man's jaw, pulsing, pulsing when he is not speaking—as though the thinking in him were made visible at that place.

Very quietly the old woman says, "Is this Red Day Woman?"

The man, Fire Thunder, nods: *Yes.*

"Is it the spirit of Red Day Woman that wants prayer?"

He nods again: *Yes.*

"Then she has died."

*Yes.*

"And you have lifted her to her burial scaffold?"

*Yes.*

Now there enters the tipi a long, terrible silence. Both people stand still, looking at each other while the light for seeing grows dimmer and dimmer.

Finally, softly, scarcely moving her pursed and wrinkled lips, the woman breathes, "And the child crying outside, that baby was born to her."

*Yes. Yes.*

Suddenly the old woman steps forward, reaches up, and slaps Fire Thunder across his face.

He does not move. He does not react.

She slaps him again. And again.

"Red Day Woman died in childbirth, didn't she?"

*Yes.*

"She burst and died in a bloody childbirth!"

*Yes.*

The old woman's voice has risen to a hectic shrieking. "*Wakan shica!*" she shrieks. "Evil! Evil! Wicked, the thing that you have done to her!"

No, slaps are not enough for this one. The woman sees a war club in the tipi. She grabs the war club and rushes at Fire Thunder and beats him on his arms and shoulders. She beats his neck. With stone she beats the back of his skull. She cannot stop. Neither does he try to stop her.

And all the while she is shrieking, "What did you do to Red Day Woman? You got her with child! You raped her, you killed her, and now you want to pray for her? Oh, Fire Thunder I am *Hihan kara*, yes! That is who I am." She is so mad that she swings the club with two hands, full swings of the arms.

The man has closed his eyes and bowed his head but he does not try to protect himself.

"Yes, I am the woman who damns the wicked," she shrieks. "Yes, I drive their spirits over the cliff at the end of the ghost road! Oh, yes, watch out for me, Fire Thunder, because first I will kill you and then I will send your evil spirit back to roam the earth forever! You murdered Red Day Woman! You tore her! You tore her twice! And now you deny your daughter a place in your tipi? I am *Hihan kara!* I am that witch to the wicked! I am—huh! Huh!" The old woman is so tired, so tired. She sinks to her knees. "I am—huh. Huh."

And now there are two voices making a painful lament in the evening, the baby outside and the ancient woman inside, crumpled down like a load of broken sticks. "Huh. Huh. It is all so sad—huh, huh, huh."

Finally Fire Thunder moves. Slowly he lowers himself to sit beside the old woman and there he waits with his head bowed, stroking his cheek with that pitiful wisp of human hair.

Yes, he is bleeding from various hard parts of his body. Yes, the old woman had the force and the fury to split his skin to the white bone. Nevertheless, it is the lock of hair that has his attention now and he waits.

Finally the old woman is simply too tired to weep. Even the infant outside subsides and silence returns to the entire village.

It is night.

"This," says Fire Thunder in a voice as soft as a flute, "this is the thing I could not do. And because I could not do this thing, every other thing is dust. Old woman, you are right. I have done no good thing in my life."

"What? What is the matter with you? Do you think you are already dead?" she whispers, weary and filled with scorn. "Do one good thing *now*, great Fire Thunder. Take your baby back."

"No. It is not my baby," he says, his voice sliding higher and higher until he himself is whining like a baby. "No. No, I did not hurt Red Day Woman. Never in her life. But neither did I save her. I came to keep her safe but I could not and that is the thing I could not do. That. I was not there when someone raped her. Who did such a thing to her? I would kill him too, but I don't know who he is. And I did not know she was with child. I did not even know that she had died until Standing Hollow Horn came to tell me so. Old woman, you must pray for the spirit of Red Day Woman. You must. Here is a lock of her hair. I myself have cut it. Pray for her!"

"Why?" whispers the old woman, weary of the weight of her body, weary of the world and all its mysteries, weary and wishing to die and wondering why *Wakan Tanka* should have preserved her life so long. "Why? What is Red Day Woman to you?"

"She is my sister," says Fire Thunder. "Red Day Woman is my little sister."

Now he closes his mouth. His jaw grows hard, *inyan*, that muscle pulsing at the back of it.

Suddenly Fire Thunder reaches behind himself and brings forward a small bundle. He unties it. One by one he takes out articles of some seeming meaning: a brush made from the rough side of a dried buffalo's tongue, a tiny buckskin doll with hair from the curly mane of a colt, a bag of soft doeskin.

"When she was born," the warrior whispers, "our mother tried to give her away because she was strange. This baby had a tongue so thick she would choke on it. Her fingers were as short as toes. Her eyelids were fat and slanted. *Mihun*, my mother and her mother, tried to give the baby away. But no one would take her. So I watched out for her. When she learned to walk she went wherever she wanted. So I followed. I fed my sister. I washed her. Other people laughed at her or ran away from her. She scared them. They did not feed her or wash her. I did."

"Give me that little bag," the old woman says all at once. "That doeskin bag, give it to me. Give me the lock of Red Day Woman's hair. I need some sinew and a needle–bone. Get them."

The giant arises and obeys.

When he brings them the woman snatches the bone and sinew from his huge hands. "I do not love you," she says. "But this woman should not suffer any more for your sins."

Fire Thunder folds his arms and bows his head.

"Springtime," he says. "Sixteen, seventeen years ago—"

Listen: this voice can be as sweet as the sad song of *wakinyela*. Only now does the woman realize the beauty of this warrior's music. *Why does it take us so long? Ah, Wakan Tanka, I am so tired.*

"Seventeen years ago during the gathering of the Seven Council Fires," says Fire Thunder, "my sister wandered over to your band. I watched in secret. I saw a woman give her some berries to eat. I saw the *itancan* hand her a piece of *wasna*. The *wasna* made her stay because it took so long to eat that she fell asleep outside the chief's

tipi and then she never went back to our band again. I followed. I hid
for a while. But finally I came to live with Slow Buffalo's band in
order to keep my sister safe. Who else would? No one in the world.
Red Day Woman was stupid and strange. She could not talk.
Children laughed at her, adults rubbed her head in ways she did not
understand, everyone told her to go away. No one else would watch
out for her. I did. I did. I . . ."

Finally the man falls silent and says no more.

The old woman is poking in the ashes of his fireplace. "Watch,"
she says. "This is how you pray for the spirit of the dead." She has
found some dried sweet grass in the tipi. When she uncovers one
bright coal she places a pinch of this grass upon it and leans forward
and blows till a little smoke begins to curl upward.

"*Wachanga*," she whispers, "to purify the place of her spirit here
on earth."

Wrinkled, watchful, stern and weary, the old woman now takes the
precious whisp of hair and holds it within the smoke. "You who could
not keep your sister safe, here is how you shall keep her spirit near a
while.

"I do not love you, *Wichasha*," the woman whispers sharply. "No,
I do not trust you. With all my heart I hate what you have done to us.
And I am not sorry for the beating that I gave you. But even you, Fire
Thunder, if you do this rightly and well—even you can keep the
goodness of Red Day Woman in the world! Do you hear me? But you
cannot lie and do this thing."

So saying, still holding the lock of Red Day Woman's hair in the
smoke of the sweet grass, the old woman prays: *Wakan Tanka, this
smoke comes to you and goes throughout the whole world. Let every
living thing smell the goodness. Let everyone know by this sweetness
that we must all be relatives together.*

And then the woman tucks the wispy hair into the soft doeskin
bag. That bag, the buffalo-tongue brush, and the doll she rolls into a
bundle and then sews the bundle shut with sinew and the needle
made of bone.

Again she speaks: *O soul, wherever your bundle rests, it shall here-*

*after be a sacred place. Everyone who comes here, children and grandchildren—the people of Fire Thunder's band—let them learn to walk with pure hearts and firm steps the straight red path of holiness.*

"Now you are keeping your sister," says the old woman as she stands up and aims her finger at Fire Thunder. "This is the *Wanagi yuhapi*, the keeping of her spirit. *Hetchetu welo*: it is good. And I am done. And I am very, very tired. But I go to take care of a baby now— because who else will care for her if I don't? Who else will watch out for her? No one. Certainly not great Fire Thunder, brother of Red Day Woman."

The woman is old and bent. She does not have to bow down in order to leave the tipi.

And when the baby starts to cry again she feeds her and rocks her back to sleep, this offspring of a strange woman and no father any- where in sight, this orphan. This *atkuku wanice*. This bastard.

# 40

# Hetchetu Welo

In the middle of the night, even while she held an infant within the scoop of her stomach and slept outside Fire Thunder's tipi, *Waskn Mani's* grandmother dreamed a dream.

In her dream she saw Rattling Hail Woman walking in a blue valley where every good fruit and every sacred herb grew. *Wsu Sna Win* moved slowly, with her head bowed. Seeing her daughter, the mother felt such tremendous loneliness that it was as if there were a lake of water inside of her. She tried to call out, but she was not in the valley where her daughter was walking.

So she burst into tears. The sadness ached in her throat. She sobbed and sobbed because she missed her daughter. Ah, but it was a relief to be crying so hard. The heavy lake was pouring out of her. Perhaps if she had permitted herself to cry more often in her lifetime—

Then she heard the voice of her grandson.

*"Unchi? Unchi?"* he said.

She looked and suddenly it was a dream inside a dream, for here was her grandson standing in front of Fire Thunder's tipi and gazing down upon her sleeping self—that wrinkled old woman who was protecting a baby from the cold night air. The boy had love in his black eyes. Look at him! Wasn't he a handsome *koshkalaka* after all?—his high cheekbones exactly like his mother's? Yes, it thrilled her to see him again. She wanted to say, *Waskn Mani, do you see how easily I can cry now? Stay with me, and I will be better. I will cry more often. I will laugh*—

But then she noticed that her sleeping self was continuing to sleep. The bony old woman had not opened her eyes at all.

Well, then where was *she*? Where was the one dreaming this?

"*Unchi?*" the boy said. He knelt down by the face of his sleeping grandmother, who sighed and did not know that he was there.

"*Unchi*, I have found my mother," he said. "She is happy," he whispered. "She has a message for you and I have one for Fire Thunder. My mother says that her mother did very well in raising a grandson. My mother is proud of the work her mother did with that boy, for it has brought honor, she says, to two women. Two women, she says. And both women must now rejoice and give thanks to *Wakan Tanka*. It is good, *Unchi*. It is very good."

Oh, how *Waskn Mani's* grandmother did cry then! Hot tears. Wonderful tears. Proud tears.

Yet all her crying made no sound. Her grandson did not notice the good crying that she was doing—because she wasn't in this dream either.

So her tears were also lonely tears still.

Because look: *Waskn Mani* was taking one of the sleeping woman's braids in his hands. Such a lovely gesture!—but the sleeper did not wake up. She could not know what was happening. The boy was lifting the grey braid to his nose and snuffling it for the scent exactly as a buffalo snuffles the grass before he clumps and eats it. "I love you, *Unchi*," he whispered, and that fortunate, foolish old sleeper did not even hear it!

*Can't I be in this dream too?* said the dreamer, sobbing. *Won't you look also at me?*

Then the boy began to stand, saying, "Here is my message for Fire Thunder." Oiya! Now his voice was terrible. And he never finished standing up! It was as if he kept unfolding, going higher and higher until his shoulders were holding the poles of the sky and his hair was a cloud and his eye was black moonlight.

"Tell Fire Thunder," he commanded, "to make an ax from the whole trunk of a cottonwood tree, a very big ax with the head of a boulder. Such a boulder has already been prepared for him. If he looks he will find it. Tell him, *Unchi*. Wake up and tell him right away. There is very little time left."

Immediately the woman awoke. She opened her eyes to the nighttime. The infant at her stomach was fast asleep. Nothing was stirring, not the wind, not the lonely cricket. Her grandson was nowhere in sight. Her poor old bones ached from the cold ground. Her feet hurt because of the great strain she had given them for the last two days.

And her eyes were as dry as firestones.

# 41
# *O*hunkankan:
# The Ancestors
# Tell This Story

In the night of a dead moon, in *ptanyetu*, autumn, the season of changes, just before the appearing of the Moon of the Popping Trees, we heard wood-chopping deep in the northern forest. *Chun! Chun! Chun!*—someone was cutting a tree down. The sound made us afraid. We all heard it. All the people woke up and listened: *Chun! Chun!*

Well, but you must understand that the forest was far away. No one had camped in the north land that year. We were scattered because of the great famine and because all the four-leggeds were gone and there was nothing to hunt, there was no one to keep us company in all the world. We were a people alone. Yet every man and every woman, no matter where they had set their tipi, could hear that faraway chopping: *Chun! Chun! Chun!*

Today we say that we were meant to hear it. *Lela wakan*, we say: something very sacred. But on that night the sound made us afraid and we lay inside our tipis waiting to see what would happen next.

Listen, now, and we will tell you the story of that night. We will leave nothing out, no matter how difficult. But you must listen as if it happened also to you.

First there came the chopping sound that woke us.

Then we heard the cry of a falling tree and we knew that he had been a brave tree. There was the power of wooden things in his voice.

Next came the smaller biting sounds of someone trimming his branches and peeling the bark away.

Then the sky began to move. The whole night sky. All of the stars as far as the horizon. Everything.

Oh, children, how can we tell you the great fear this caused in us? We crawled outside and looked up and grew so dizzy that we could not stand. We kept falling down. It felt as if the earth were turning over.

The sky was moving! Not clouds. Not moonlight. There was no moonlight. The sky. *Wanagi tacanku*, the ghost road. All the stars. All of them, faster and faster like a river rushing westward. It was as if the waves of a great flood were rolling over the earth, but this flood was not made of water; it was the congregation of all stars now flowing toward the place where the sun falls off the earth.

We could not speak, so scared were we. Neither did we cry out or wail. We just gaped upward because it seemed that even heaven had decided to run away from us.

What would we do if heaven were gone too? What would be left?

So we started running. All of us: *tiwahe, tiyoshpaye, oyate, tunwan*. Every family and band and people and nation, the children of earth went chasing the stars of heaven, determined to go wherever they led us. Even to the place where the sun falls off. Even as far as the sea.

Well, the earth had been so terribly lonely without the four-leggeds and the wingeds that we would rather die than live beneath a lonely sky as well.

So we ran very hard and very far from many different directions on earth—and in a sacred manner none of us grew tired. *Lela wakan!* Neither did it matter where we started from: soon all the people were arriving at the same place at the same time.

For everyone had seen where the stars were falling down. No, it was not the edge of the world. The stars had started to turn in heaven. They were sweeping round in a great circle as in a dance, the whole universe dancing, ten thousand times ten thousand stars, and thousands of thousands—and we saw that the center of their circle was like a whirlpool spinning down from heaven to earth: *there! Look! Heaven is touching earth. The stars are counting coup on a mountaintop!* That is the place we ran to, all of us coming to one spot, a mountain. And we knew by the signs which mountain she was: *Scorched Mountain Woman.*

Oh, we were many, many people. We filled the valleys around the mountain. We covered her foothills like sand and climbed her sides like a moving swarm of grasshoppers.

And then when the star-dance was done and it seemed as if pure darkness should next descend upon us, someone in heaven began to sing a song:

*Hee-ay-hay-ee-ee!*

We looked and saw that two great lights were coming. Two stars were sailing the night sky so gravely, so gloriously, and so close to the ground that they seemed like moons to us. One was carrying a quiver and bow, the other was singing a song of greeting:

*Hee-ay-hay-ee-ee!*

As she sang her greeting a drum began to answer her. We felt the slow beats deep in the bosom of the earth. But we did not sing. We did not answer. We did not even move. We held still.

These two stars paused above *Scorched Mountain Woman.* And then the one who was not singing took an arrow from his quiver and notched it and began to aim it at the earth. The flint burst into flame. He drew the arrow back and shot, and it tore down from heaven in a terrible blaze, while the other star sang louder and louder:

*Hee-ay-hay-ee-ee!*

That fiery arrow hit the side of *Scorched Mountain Woman*. It hit that picture of a praying woman and exploded. It caused an earth-boom that threw us down to the ground and showered us with sparks. We covered our heads.

When we looked up again we saw that the highest slope of the mountain had ignited and now was burning with a strange white fire. It was a field of flowing light. And lo: that field had taken shape! We saw the huge figure of a human, the arms upraised as if in prayer, the braids all wild around its white face, its blank face. This was a face without features.

*Hee-ay-hay-ee-ee*!

Slowly, slowly the arms of that luminous figure came down and spread wide as if in welcome and then two eyes opened up in the face and we saw that we had been mistaken: there were no braids in that picture. The hair was all loose. The hair was snow on the mountain. And the eyes! Those black eyes—

Oiyaaa! Here was a boy above us! An enormous boy, a beautiful, burning boy! His flesh was pure light, his body the rock of the mountain, his cheekbones two cliffs too high for climbing. But his eyes—those black caverns of an infinite seeing—his eyes were looking straight at us! At *us*, you see, so that suddenly we were feeling our own presence in that place, our bodies and *our* faces. We were not hidden. Someone knew that we were there.

The earth-drum beat and beat, shaking the ground beneath us.

And then we saw some lightning ripple at the boy's mouth, like a fluttering of hair, like a visible whispering.

Then serious lightning forked from his mouth in a long arc to the stone at the foot of the mountain.

That bolt was a word made manifest.

The word was *Fire*!

And immediately came a crash which was the second word: *Thunder*!

The boy had uttered a name. We heard the name and we knew the man. The mountain had said, *Fire Thunder.*

And there, where the lightning bolt had struck, stood the man himself, the grim *itancan* who had led a world to war. Yes, there he was. It was none but Fire Thunder, his left eye hidden under that black slash of headband. He stood alone in a ring of light which might have been the boy's looking. He stood holding in his hands a tool so massive no three men could lift it. Four men must. But Fire Thunder held it alone, its handle the size of a tree, its head made out of something like flint as big as a buffalo.

Well, he was a mighty man, Fire Thunder. No one could deny him that. There was strength in his right arm and stone in his jaw and the rolling force of the thunderstorm between his shoulders, beneath his braids. But no one loved him any more. No one honored him now. He stood at the foot of the mountain alone.

And the mountain spoke.

In lightning cracks the burning boy above us said: *Come.* And then, again: *Come up.*

We were watchers now. We were a thousand silent eyes shifting up and down the mountain. We were the breathing, listening life of the earth, *icke wichasha*, plain people.

But even from the beginning Fire Thunder had not been common. He had always hunted as One–Alone. Now therefore, bearing before him that tremendous tool, he began to climb a straight path toward the field of light above. Step by step his foot was firm; the muscle in his thigh clenched and took hold; he mounted cleanly— until he came to the lowest skirts of the light. There, suddenly, the warrior stumbled. Another step and he almost fell. He caused a sound of clattering beneath his feet—and then he was forced to climb on four legs, dragging that enormous club behind him. Bones! The man was climbing over a gorge filled with old bones, very many, very dry, and very difficult to cross.

The black eyes of the boy gazed down upon the warrior's effort with a seeming pity. But the voice of the mountain was no less commanding:

*Come up, Fire Thunder.*

A continual rumbling was calling the warrior.

*Nearer. Nearer.* ·

He obeyed. He climbed the light itself. He mounted glowing stone. He toiled upward on the body of the boy—and he became a blot, a black figure dragging the shadow of a treetrunk.

When the man arrived in the region of his chest, the boy said, *Stop.* And the man did stop. He stood still, waiting.

The splendid boy spoke in a riddle of lightning, flashings and crashings at his mouth. He said, *Have you brought the ax?*

Fire Thunder's voice was much diminished upon the mountain. But we could hear him. As in a sacred manner, we could see him too, everything, everything.

Fire Thunder said, "Yes."

*Are you ready to use it?*

Standing black upon the boy's chest, throwing back his head in order to look into the boy's bright face, the warrior said, "I have made a great ax and I have brought it. But I do not know the use of it. I don't know what to do."

The boy said, *Kill me.*

Fire Thunder closed his mouth and became like stone. A muscle tightened at the corner of his jaw.

As softly, now, as a south wind blows the boy said, *Kill me, Fire Thunder. Strike with all your might. Kill me.*

The man lowered his head and muttered, "Who are you?"

*What?* said the boy. *What?*

"Who are you?"

*BOOM!*—in sheets of a visible wind, in a voice of terrible veracity, the mountain roared, *You know who I am!*

Oh, we shuddered at the splitting sound the mountain made, and the warrior himself dropped down to his knees.

*I am the same as when I moved among you, walking!* cried the shining boy. *I am Waskn Mani still!*

Moves Walking! Him?

*Kill me!* he commanded—and this time there was neither softness nor pity in the boy's black eyes. His brow was the glacier.

Fire Thunder, still kneeling in light, his face bowed down, muttered, "I can't."

*What? Fire Thunder, what?*

"Who knew that Moves Walking could come like this? I can't."

So the lightning broke forth in blue bolts, striking all around the warrior, describing a violent circle—and the mountain drum grew urgent, beating, beating.

*If you do not kill me the people will perish*, declared the lightning. *Once what you chose to do began their dying. Now what you refuse to do will finish it and rub out all the people. All the people!*

Hearing that, we ourselves then began to wail. We couldn't help it. Our voices went up from everywhere in the valleys and over the mountain, a vast lamentation: Ahhhhhh!

So then we saw Fire Thunder stand up. He turned and looked down from his height, squinting against the radiance around him, and he seemed to see us for the first time, a very great multitude, more than anyone could number, all of us crying like children and watching him—all of us.

So then the warrior turned and looked up at the boy's face and sighed and squared himself to do his duty. He lifted the ax in front of himself, hefted the weight of it, spread his legs for leverage and began a deep swing backward—

*Fire Thunder!* cracked the glorious lightning.

"What!"

*You did not ask me!*

"What?"

*Ask, wichasha! Ask if I am ready to die. Ask if I choose. Do not steal my life by slaughter as you slaughtered my relations before me. Honor me! Ask me if I give my life away! Ask me for it, Fire Thunder. Ask!*

When the warrior spoke this time, he made a strange nasal noise, an astonishing sound, a baby's whine!

He said, "But you told me to kill you! You said that I should kill—"

*ASK ME, WICHASHA!*

Poor Fire Thunder! He made a mewing sound in his nose. He bent his head down and one braid fell forward. *"Ohan,"* he murmured so softly—but we heard him. "Yes, yes," he spoke in that infant's puling whine. "Yes, I ask. Moves Walking are you ready to die? Do you give me your life?"

*Yes.*

A dazzling display of flashings high on the mountain whispered, *Yes.*

So the warrior raised the huge ax again in his two hands, though without the old arrogance. He stared down at the bright rock beneath his feet. His nostrils flared for breath. The muscle kept flexing in his jaw. He was thinking.

We who covered the valleys and foothills around the mountain stood still, watching and waiting. All the world was waiting now. The boy himself, as patient as eternity, was also waiting, waiting.

Finally Fire Thunder raised his head and drew a very deep breath. He tightened his shoulders and began to haul the great ax backward, swinging toward the death-cut—

But the boy said: *FIRE THUNDER!*

"What?"

*WAIT!*

"Aieeeeee!"

The man threw down his ax and started to wail in that shrill voice which children use when they are lost. "What do you want from me?" he cried. "Moves Walking, Moves Walking, what are you doing to me?"

And then we saw great Fire Thunder crumple down to the ground and begin to cry. "Hownh, hownh," he wept. And we saw that his shoulders were shaking with the sobs. And we, too, perhaps because we were all so tired, so tired—we were crying too.

The boy said, *Ask in humbleness. Ask in the truth of yourself.*

"What?" the poor man sobbed. He did not understand. We did not understand. Fire Thunder wrapped his arms around himself and rocked back and forth and crying, "What? What? What? What?"

The boy said, *Remove mystery. Take off glory. Be one man only, the plain person. Put your headband away, Fire Thunder, and then ask me for my life.*

The drum within the mountain was beating. It had never ceased.

But now it was as if Fire Thunder heard the earth-drum for the first time. We saw him nod to the beating. Yes, and then he seemed to dance according to its rhythm, for he rose up with a smooth and dreadful beauty, stepping, stepping in one place, lifting his hands palms outward in worship toward the sky and the four directions, stepping, stepping always in one place—and now we saw that he bowed his head and covered his face with both hands, stepping, stepping still in one place, and then he pulled the headband off and dropped it and he raised his face again and turned in all directions, stepping, stepping always in one place—but we saw. We could see. None of the people did not see: that there was no crystal sphere for Fire Thunder's left eye. There was no eagle's beak sprouting there. There was only a hole and tendons writhing in that hole like twigs in a bird's nest. And if we saw anything wonderful there, it was this, that even an empty eyesocket can weep tears, for when he took away the headband—stepping, stepping ever in one place—water came out and gushed down his face.

And the man said softly, "Moves Walking, do you give your life that the people may live?"

And the mountain looked down upon Fire Thunder, and the light grew warmer around him, and the boy said, *Yes, I do. I do.*

So Fire Thunder, standing on the chest of that resplendent boy, took the ax in two hands. He felt the heft of it once, twice—then suddenly threw the heavy ax head backward, backward and upward behind himself, sliding his hands together; he wheeled the great flint high then doubled his body down in order to give his whole strength to the downward stroke, down, down—

A voice called, "I love you, Lakota!"

—and the ax bit light. The ax drove through the bright boy down to rock.

*Crack–BOOM!*

The whole earth felt that impact. It shook and threw us down. The field of light grew dim and the ground itself began to divide. A fissure shot up and down from the ax. A crack went through the rock of the mountain. The crack widened and widened until it became a cave where the chest of the boy had been.

And now the earth-drum was thundering inside that cave louder and louder like a hundred drums.

Well, we jumped up and started to run away, because all those drums sounded like feet to us, like the feet of a great herd of buffalos, like a thousand buffalos stampeding.

Buffalos!

Hi ho! Buffalos were coming!

Yes, and the buffalos did come back that night, and we saw them run out of a cave in *Scorched Mountain Woman*. We saw them go forth and cover the plains in every direction as they do today.

And the reason why we could see them even in the darkness is that they were all white. All of them! Every buffalo that came out of the mountain was as white as the boy had been, and their eyes were like ice, like hailstones—blank, as if they could not see us. But we could see them and we have never forgotten the sight. Listen, children: when those buffalos had scattered out upon the plains, ten thousand times ten thousand buffalos, they looked like a whole sky full of stars below us.

Who can forget such a sight?

By daylight the buffalos were wearing the common brown colors and we were glad. *Tatanka* was back. Our brother was home. The famine was over and we could hunt again. Oh, there was so much work to be done. But first we had to give thanks: *Pila miya, Tunkashila!* We danced in a sacred circle and we sang new songs and we cried in sorrow and we laughed in happiness because *Wakan Tanka* had decided to send us the red and blue days again.

So that is our story. *Hehanyelo oihanke.* That is all. That is the end.

# AFTER THE STORY
# WATECA

Snow is falling. The old woman is very busy. She has taken a small hatchet and chopped to quarter lengths the poles that once had framed her tipi, the same poles she used as a drag for her few possessions and for the baby.

She is lashing the poles together side by side.

Sometimes she takes a quick look across a small lake to the great grey mountain in the south. Snow has whitened the paths that trickle down its sides. When the snowfall is light enough she can see someone descending a path. When the snow thickens even the mountain is hidden.

The lower that traveler comes, the quicker this woman works.

On the north side of the lake stand four young pine trees in a circle, their lower trunks narrow and straight and smooth. Behold: the woman has built her platform of poles to fit within these pines. When she lifts it above her head, each corner touches one trunk. She has allowed lengths of rawhide to hang from the four corners. Now she rolls a log over to the first tree. She climbs that little log in order to reach high and there to tie one corner of the platform to its trunk. The old woman grunts and strains. She is short. Her feet hurt.

The baby begins to cry. It lies bundled in a blanket, only its brown face open to the snow.

"*Wateca, Wateca,*" the old woman calls, "I will be done soon. Can you wait? Shoosh, shoosh, don't cry."

She climbs down and rolls the log to the second tree. She glances up the mountain. Ah, the traveler is too far down to be seen any more. Hurry! Hurry! She reaches to tie the second corner by strips of rawhide to the pine tree.

This is the Moon of the Popping Trees. So cold. The snowflakes land on the old woman's grey hair. They touch the deep wrinkles of her face, the lines that go crisscross everywhere, sewing her lips, cutting her ancient cheeks, etching her eyelids. Her expression is solemn. But her eyes are bright. Her eyes are clear and shining.

The third corner is tied tightly, now, as high as she can reach. Hurry! But the fourth is the easiest. That corner is already up and only needs the knots to keep it there.

"*Hokshi cala*, here I come," she calls. "I am ready now."

She pulls a robe around her shoulders and kneels down by the baby bundle and gathers the infant into her arms. "It is time to go."

The woman must scuff the snow to walk, dragging the right foot along the ground. Who knows how painful her feet have become in these latter days? There has been so much walking. She moves bent. They go through a long stand of ash trees. She keeps looking upward until they emerge from the rattling wood and the mountain comes back into view.

Here she stops. Her breath comes out in small white puffs. Little cloud-trails also rise from the baby's breathing. The old woman stands and waits, watching.

There is a man coming in this direction across the clean gleaming field south of her. He takes broad strides exploding snow. Nothing slows him. His spine and neck are exactly straight despite the burden in his arms. The woman and the man have seen each other. Neither acknowledges the other but both know that they are known.

The woman's sharp eyes search the man and his burden. Her face grows more and more solemn. Even the baby does not wriggle.

All is still. Except for the snow and the man approaching, all is very still.

The load in his arms is a corpse.

Fire Thunder is bringing *Waskn Mani* down the mountain.

The old woman watches from hooded eyes.

Her grandson droops over either arm of the giant. His head drops backward at Fire Thunder's left elbow; his black hair sweeps the snow; his knees bend at the right arm and his feet swing back and forth, back and forth. The boy has beautiful feet. No clothes cover him from the snow.

Ah!—his body is so pale! So lean! It must be no weight at all for Fire Thunder.

And now he is standing in front of her, and now the water comes into the old woman's eyes. She tips her face up in order to keep it from spilling out. Through a glittering water, then, she sees the wound, the gash in her grandson's chest, so clean and deep that it must reach down into his heart. She puts out a free hand and places it flat upon his breast. It is cold. She touches the rim of his cheekbone with her finger. She traces his eye. It is closed. It will not open again. Now the water spills from her eyes.

So then she looks clearly at Fire Thunder. No headband. Sunken left eyelid, the lashes turned inward. His right eye is looking back at her.

Fire Thunder says, "Here is *Waskn Mani.*"

The woman nods briefly, once.

The man, more softly, whispers, *"Unchi."* He whispers, "Grandmother, I am sorry."

For a long time the woman gazes at him, saying nothing. Soon he bows his head, and yet she continues to stare. She is solemn. Her face is canyons and caves and age and a long remembering.

Suddenly the baby kicks and begins to cry.

So the woman turns and begins to walk away.

"Come," she says. "There is a place prepared for him."

So they return the way she came, *Waskn Mani's* grandmother first, Fire Thunder second, each with a human burden. They break snow through the stand of ash trees. They come out on the north side of the small lake and she points toward the four pine trees.

"There," she says.

It is a burial scaffold.

What was high above the woman is now at the level of Fire Thunder's shoulder. He raises *Waskn Mani* and places him on the platform facing up to the boughs of the young pine, facing heaven, catching snowflakes. The boy's black hair falls down between the poles.

"*Onshika*," sighs the woman, so tired. "*Onshika*. Pitiful."

But the baby squirms and doubles its body in the old woman's arm and cries louder still.

"I will make you a trade," she says suddenly. "Give me a lock of my grandson's hair and I will give you a baby girl."

Fire Thunder, his own mouth sober, produces a knife and carefully cuts the hair that grows at *Waskn Mani's* forehead—long hair, absolutely black hair—and hands it to the woman. She in turn gives him a girlchild squalling for food, squalling for comfort and warmth and life and cleanliness.

Fire Thunder looks down into the infant's troubled face. "I have seen this one before," he says.

"Yes," she says. "That *hokshi cala* and I, we need some shelter now. We have given our tipi away to my grandson."

"What shall I call the baby?" Fire Thunder asks.

By the lake beneath *Scorched Mountain Woman* stand four young pine trees and within them a scaffold. Upon that scaffold lies the body of a boy, his arms at his sides, his flesh receiving the snowfall. Snow catches on his eyelashes. It sifts into the line between his lips. It whitens his hair and fills the wound on his breast.

No one sees the shadow above him. No one expects the return of the winged creatures with *Tatanka*. But high in the white air a spotted eagle is circling, sinking down, coming, coming.

*Unchi, Wanbli Galeshka wana ni he o who e.*

Grandmother, the spotted eagle is coming to carry me away.

I know, *Waskn Mani.* Goodbye, *hokshicantkiye.* Goodbye, child of my heart. Goodbye.

Fire Thunder was gazing down on the infant in his arm. With a tremendously huge thumb he brushed snowflakes from her cheek. Immediately she twisted her face around to find that thumb with her mouth, then she sighed and settled to sucking. She looked up at Fire Thunder's eye. She found the good eye and looked into it.

He asked, "What shall I call the baby?"

"*Wateca,*" said the old woman as they walked north, away from a small lake and farther away from the mountain farther south of it. They went at her speed, slowly. The woman had very bad feet and the unusual labors of her old age had not improved them any. They were knobby inside their moccasins. They were crooked and worse than ever.

"This child's name is *Wateca,*" said the woman. "Call her *Wateca.* Leftovers."

# GLOSSARY
## Some Lakota Words and Phrases

**Ate**   Father.

**Akicita okolakicye**   The "soldier society" which kept order and carried out the commands of the Chief Society and their advisors when bands gathered, say, for buffalo hunts or the Sun Dance.

**Anpetu**   Day.

**Atkuku wanice**   Literally, "No father on hand." It signifies a child whose paternity is unknown; one born outside of the marriage commitment.

**Bloketu**   Summer. Literally, it refers to the potato.

**Cangleshka**   Circle, hoop. Together with the word *wakan*, "sacred," it becomes a symbol for Lakota solidarity and a metaphor for the sacred union of people and all things.

**Chan**   Tree or wood. It may also be the prefix for anything made from wood. When it is used with *wakan*, it refers to the sacred pole in the center of the Sun Dance circle—a cottonwood tree.

**Chanshasha**   tobacco made from the dried inner bark of a red willow tree, also called *kinnickinnick*.

**Chante**   The heart. When it is combined with the word for "eye," *ishta*, it means "the eye of the heart" and refers to insightful or spiritual seeing.

**Chanunpa**   The Sacred Pipe.

**Eyapaha**   The crier, one appointed to make announcements to the band or to communicate community commands.

**Hanblechia**   The vision quest, a personal ritual, called "The Crying for a Vision," by which one seeks direction from *Wakan Tanka*, either in one's life or in an immediate crisis.

**Hanhepi**   Night.

**Hante**   Cedar.

**Hanwi**   The moon.

**Hau**   Greetings; yes. A word of welcome, agreement, affirmation.

**Heca**   Buzzard.

**Hehaka tapejuta**   Horse mint. Literally it is a plant called "elk medicine" because it is used by the healer whose power comes from the elk.

**Hehanyelo oihanke**   "That's all, that is the end," spoken at the conclusion of stories told at nighttime, tales called *ohunkankan* which contain mythic truths, or else fables told "just-for-fun."

**Hetchetu welo**   "It is good." This phrase concludes with affirmation conversations, decisions, rituals, and other gestures of human exchange.

**Hihan Kara**   The old woman who sits on the "ghost road," the path which the spirits of the dead walk south—the Milky Way. *Hihan Kara* lets the good pass into the spirit world. The bad must return to earth as ghosts, *Wanagi.*

**Hihani washtay**   "Good morning!"

**Hocoka**   This refers to the camp-circle space inside the perimeter of the outer round of tipis. *Coka* means center, middle, and *ho* refers to the camp. Everything within the *hocoka* should be Lakota and stable; anything outside may be instability, flux, evil, enemies.

**Hokshi cala**   Baby.

**Hokshicantkiye**   Boy beloved, a favored child.

**Hokshila**   Boy.

**Icapshipshi**   A flock of birds at the moment it scatters in fright.

**Icke wichasha**   Common, ordinary man. The people. A phrase the Lakota use to refer to themselves.

**Ina**   Mother.

**Inipi**   The sweat bath. The ritual renews those who observe it, purges them both spiritually and physically. Its formal name is *inikagopi*, referring to the revigoration of breath, life.

**Inyan**   Rock. Stone.

**Ishnati**   Literally, to live alone. It refers to menstruation, when a woman was required to live separated from the tribe, and designates the place where she stays; fully expressed, *ishnatipi.*

**Ishta**   The eye.

**Itancan**   Chief, leader. This one was elected to lead a *wicoti*, "camp," or *tiyoshpaye*, "band," throughout the year and continued to hold office by the consent of the people who followed.

**Itomni**   Very happy. A giddy, dizzy sort of happiness.

**Iya**   A legendary figure who asked *Inktomi*, the Spider-trickster, for plenty of food to eat. His wish was granted, but Inktomi also caused *Iya* never to be satisfied.

**Keya**  Turtle.

**Kola**  Friend.

**Koshkalaka**  Young man.

**Lela**  Very. The word is an intensifier; with *wakan* translated "very sacred, very holy."

**Mahpiya**  Sky, clouds, heaven.

**Maka**  The earth.

**Maka sitomni**  The whole world, the universe.

**Mastekola**  The lark, whose song, as it flies joyfully up to the sky on a spring morning is, *Masteko, masteko!*

**Mato**  The bear.

**Mihun**  My mother. While *Ina* is a common vocative word for "mother," *hun* is the possessive form, and *mi* makes it first person singular. The third person form, "her mother," would be *hunku.*

**Mitakuye oyasin**  All my relations. This ritual phrase, spoken often during Lakota ceremonies, contains many levels of meaning; for example, the speaker humbly acknowledges union with all people and all creation; also, the speaker declares that he or she is now engaged in a ceremony on behalf of all near kin; a third meaning is that the spirit who inspires this particular activity comes *from* the unity of kin and creation.

**Nagi**  Often translated spirit, or soul. It refers to the eternal element of created things and of people in particular.

**Nape**  Hand.

**Ni**  Breath, life, steam. It is an element in the word for "winter," *waniyetu,* the season when one's breath and life are manifest, visible. Likewise, one's "life" is revived in the ritual of the sweat, *inikagapi*; so *ni* is the second element of the word.

**Oceti Shakowin**  The Seven Fireplaces. The phrase designates the whole of a Lakota social structure, all camps (or bands or villages) gathered together. *Ceti* means "to build a fire." *Oceti,* then, is "fireplace" and refers to a single social unit. *Shakowin* is seven—and from time immemorial, the Lakota regarded the fullness of their *tunwan,* the nation, to be in seven parts.

**Ohan**  Yes.

**Ohunkankan**  Stories of myth, legend—tales touching the supernatural, as distinct from stories of the daily domain of people, called *wicooyake.*

**Onshika**  Pitiful. A sigh of profound sadness.

**Otuhan**   A give-away. After a significant event in Lakota life (marriage, birth, death, a hunt, a ceremony of significance) gifts are given. Everyone shares in the success and the plenty.

**Oyate**   A nation, a particular people. This may refer to one's own tribe— or, in ritual language, to an entire breed of creature: so *Tatanka oyate* means the "Buffalo nation."

**Peta**   Fire.

**Pila miya**   Thank you.

**Pshica**   Swallow. It refers to the swallow's jumping motion. The swallow is also called *upijata*, the forked-tail.

**Ptanyetu**   Autumn. Literally, "the time of changing."

**Pte**   The buffalo cow. The bull is called *tatanka*—but in ritual, *pte* becomes the generic term for all buffalos.

**Ptewoyake**   The cricket, the wingless hopper.

**Sapa**   Black.

**Shica**   Bad. When combined with the word for sacred, *wakan shica*, it refers to the evil counterpart of the energy controlled by *Wakan Tanka*.

**Takoja**   Grandchild.

**Tanka**   Great.

**Tatanka**   Buffalo bull.

**Tate**   Wind.

**Tezi**   Belly.

**Tiwahe**   Family. This is the smallest group to which an individual belonged, by which he or she identified himself. In ascending order according to size, a traditional designation of these groups might be:

> Family   **tiwahe**;
>
> Camp   **wicoti**;
>
> Band   **tiyoshpaye**;
>
> Tribe   **oyate**;
>
> Nation   **tunwan**.

**Tiyokihe**   Lengthened tipi. This is made by attaching two tipi coverings together in order to create a greater interior space for counsels; always erected in the center or the camp circle, the door facing east.

**Tiyopa**   Doorway of a tipi.

**Tiyoshpaye**   Band. See the list above at *tiwahe*.

**Tunkashila**   Grandfather. The term is used in personal address to *Wakan Tanka*.

**Tunwan**    Nation. See the identification of various groups in the social structure above at *tiwahe.*

**Unchi**    Grandmother. The word also refers to the sacred earth.

**Unkcekihan**    The magpie. The messenger bird.

**Unshe ma la ye oyate wani wachin cha**    Place the holy title in front of this prayer, and it reads: "O God, have pity on me that my people may live." It is the prayer prayed during the Vision Quest, and indicates how much the sacred ceremonies are performed for the sake of others, for the survival of the people.

**Upijata**    The swallow. Literally, the forked tail.

**Wablenica**    Orphan.

**Wachanga**    Sweet grass. It is used in ceremonies as an incense, its smoke for purifying the people and the instruments of the ceremony.

**Wachin ksapa yo**    Be attentive! This phrase cautions others (children) to watch for the wisdom of *Wakan Tanka* in any manifestation; even the tiny ant may have something true to say, and one must be ready to hear it.

**Waga chun**    The cottonwood tree. The rustling, or whispering, tree.

**Wakan**    Sacred.

> **Wakan Tanka**    God. This is the common, all-embracing refer ence to the Deity, that which is at once holiest and greatest.
>
> **Wichasha Wakan**    A holy man. A shaman. One who has power from *Wakan Tanka* to work healings, ceremonies and wonders for the people. Emphatically, this is not a "medicine man." To desig nate a "doctor," the Lakota would say *pejuta wichasha,* a man who knows herbs.
>
> **Wakan shica**    Evil energy in opposition to *Wakan Tanka.*

**Wakanka**    Old woman. Also a legendary figure who, though grown very old, was cursed by Sky ever to be stronger than a man and never to die. She appears withered and feeble to young men and women, bringing good fortune if they deserve it, and ill fortune if not.

**Wakinyan**    The thunder-beings, powerful manifestations of *Wakan Tanka* who live high in the western mountains. They come forth with power in spring.

**Wakinyela**    The mourning dove.

**Wanagi**    A ghost. The word is composed of *wa,* meaning "one who," and *nagi,* "spirit."

> **Wanagi tacanku**    The ghost road which the spirits of the dead

travel to the spirit land; the Milky Way.

**Wanagi yuhapi**   This is the ritual for keeping the spirit of a relative who has just died near the living for one more year, at the end of which, by another rite, the spirit is released.

**Wanbli Galeshka**   The spotted eagle.

**Wanbli Galeshka, wana ni he o who e**   "The spotted eagle is coming to carry me away," a metaphoric expression for dying.

**Waniyetu**   Winter.

**Waniyetu iyawapi:** Literally, "by means of the winter, they count," referring to the pictographic calendars by which a tribe kept records of the events of years past.

**Waniyetu opta aiyakpa omanipi:** "Those who walk through a winter darkness," a ritual way to refer to those who are very sick.

**Washigla**   The term indicates one in the state of mourning.

**Washtay**   Good.

**Wasna**   Pemmican. A nutritious food made by pounding dried meat together with whole chokecherries and fat. It is naturally preserved and can be kept a year-long without losing its goodness.

**Wetu**   Spring. It refers to blood and sap, which both rise up during this season of the year.

**Wicahcala**   An old man. Also a synonym for father-in-law.

**Wicahpi**   Star.

**Wicakuje**   Sick.

**Wichasha**   A man.

**Wichinchala**   A girl. A pretty girl.

**Wikoshkalaka**   A young woman.

**Winunhcala**   An old woman.

**Winyan**   A woman.

**Witko**   Crazy.

**Wochangi**   Influence. Power. Every created thing has its own characteristic power. When someone is granted a sacred relationship with one of God's creatures, he receives its *wochangi*, its particular power.

**Wohan**   To cook.

**Wojapi**   A fruit soup.

**Wolakota**   Peace.